Power Play: A Saga of the Year 2290

C. L. Roberts

Published by C. L. Roberts, 2024.

While every precaution has been taken in the preparation of this book, the publisher assumes no responsibility for errors or omissions, or for damages resulting from the use of the information contained herein.

POWER PLAY: A SAGA OF THE YEAR 2290

First edition. August 10, 2024.

Copyright © 2024 C. L. Roberts.

ISBN: 979-8227490438

Written by C. L. Roberts.

Table of Contents

Prologue

Kell stood, magnetically sealed to the hull of a derelict vessel partially lodged in an ice comet, his voice crackling slightly through the comms. "Hey, Piper? Did I tell you about being kicked out of this woman's house recently?"

"Did she discover how loud you snore?" Piper responded, static not hiding her amusement.

"Nothing like that. One minute we're making out on the couch, and the next, she's looking at my palm."

"One of those types, huh? Kell, what is your attraction to crazy women?"

"Hey, they find me, okay?" Kell's magnetic boots thudded with each careful step toward the derelict's access hatch. "Anyway, after this woman looks at my palm, she gets up, goes to her front door, and orders me to get out. No explanation or nothing."

"Next time we're planet-side, let me do the picking for you."

"Not a chance. You'll pick someone who can kick my ass. Not sure my ego could take that."

As he reached the hatch, Kell paused, feeling the eerie silence of space and the distant glitter of starlight reflecting off the ice. "But seriously, what do you think she saw?"

"I know exactly what she discovered." Piper paused. "You're a lousy cook, Kell. No woman wants a man that can't cook."

"I don't know why I bother trying to have a serious conversation with you, Piper."

"You like the abuse, amigo."

Bending down, he turned the old-style wheel set in the center of the door and lifted the hatch lid open. He stared into the abyss below, lost in thought. What he hadn't told Piper or anyone else was what the woman had said to him, the very thought of which sent a shiver down his spine.

For the briefest of moments, he was back in her house, standing at that door as she spoke. "A terrible burden you will soon bear, and the death of many will be on your hands," she had said in an almost dream-like voice. There were even tears in her eyes.

What did she see? he wondered.

"Is there a problem, Kell?" a new voice said over his comms. Startled, he recognized the voice of Captain Barnaby.

Clearing his mind, he responded, "No, sir, Barnaby, descending now."

Down he went, one ladder rung at a time. His only source of illumination came from his suit and helmet. When his feet touched down on the metal grating of the interior, he panned around. Directly behind him was a sealed door with a handprint of blood, permanently frozen to the surface, and smears streaking downward.

"Kell, can you look back up?" Captain Barnaby's voice announced through his helmet speaker. "Was that a handprint we just saw?" he asked, his voice sharp and inquisitive.

Kell swiveled his head towards the bloody handprint. "Yes sir, no body though," he said, scanning the dark. "I am near one of the main airlocks, so it is possible that it was dragged away."

"The handprint is on the engine room door, which is locked down and probably frozen in place, judging by the thick layer of ice surrounding the seams. It will take us some time to get inside, so I'm going to scout ahead."

"Tread carefully," Captain Barnaby said. "And Kell? Slow down your movements; we're experiencing a little lag over here in your feeds."

Kell nodded, using his lights to survey the ship's interior. "Understood," he said. "So far, this entire hallway appears to be pods of some type. The interiors are empty, but spacious enough for humans to stand in."

"Just what I thought," Barnaby said, the *New Horizons* is an old Colony ship from Earth."

Kell took a deep breath as more pods came into view. "There is more blood splattering on a couple of the pods ahead," he said.

"Any idea on what the hell happened over there?" Captain Barnaby asked, voice crackling.

"Not sure, captain, but it looks like one hell of a fight took place here," Kell said. "Blood splatter and smears on just about every pod and floor. But still no bodies anywhere," he said, crouching to look inside one of the pods, finding a pool of dried blood. "Captain, so far, there has been no evidence of any type of ballistic weapons fire onboard."

There was a brief moment of static before he heard Barnaby speaking. "Kell, are you suggesting they stabbed or beat each other to death?"

Kell resumed his stride. "I would have an accurate assessment if I could find some bodies."

"I'm sure you'll come across them," Barnaby said. "The dead don't just get up and walk away."

"Oh, I'm well aware," Kell said. "I'm just hoping they are not piled up in a room somewhere." He paused. "There's a faint glow ahead."

"What are you seeing, Kell? The image lag time has gotten worse on this side; we can't make out anything over here," Captain Barnaby's voice crackled, almost fading out.

Kell walked on until he stood in front of a pod with a small glowing green light on the side and a steamed-over viewing window. Using his gloved hand, he swiped away the condensation and discovered the blood-stained face of a young man with a metal pipe clutched tightly in his right hand. And he was breathing. Kell could see the chest rising with the intake of oxygen.

What in the hell had he just discovered? The corridor continued ahead, terminating at another door, but he saw no other unusual lights. Was it possible this young man was the only passenger? And if so, what about the bloody metal pipe? Had he used it to defend himself or for something worse? What should he tell his captain?

Kell stood frozen in thought, weighing his decision. If he told Barnaby that this young man was alive. Then Barnaby would insist on saving him. But on the other hand he could lie. After all he had no idea of what type of person he could be exposing the crew to. It all came down to hard evidence, which he was lacking. Pausing for a moment, he took in a deep breath, before speaking, "I found a survivor." *In a situation like this, truth was always the best policy*, he thought.

There was a long silence before he heard Barnabys response. He was sure that the captain was weighing his decisions as well, but time with the man had taught him. That Barnaby would rescue this young man. Because that was who he was. "Bill and Lilly...on their way to you. What are we...at, Kell?" Barnaby asked.

The response had been very static, almost to the point of incomprehension. "Based on the evidence so far, captain, this young man has a blood-stained pipe in hand. I cannot determine if it was used in defense or if he was the aggressor."

"Young man?" Barnaby asked. "How old are we talking, Kell?"

"Barely old enough to be shaving," Kell said, picturing the young man fighting with that metal pipe. He still couldn't decide which role he played.

"Kell, what's your gut instinct on this young man?"

And there it was, Kell thought. Barnaby wanted to make his decision based on Kell's initial instinct, instead of hard evidence. He could ask for more time to investigate; the bodies had to be somewhere onboard, and he had not fully explored it yet.

"Captain," Kell said. "I think I should investigate more. Let's have Lilly take some DNA samples. I'm sure I will find the bodies. That will help determine what role this young man played."

There was a long period of static in his helmet before he heard Barnaby. "Agreed. Lilly is yours to direct. Still, instinct?"

The captain still wanted his answer, and Kell had to think. Peering back into that pod, staring into the young man's face. He tried to get a sense of who this blood stained, dark brown-haired person was. Physically he looked fit, with some developed chest muscles, but a little on the scrawny side. Taking a moment he mentally checked himself. What had been his first gut instinct?

Closing his eyes, he let his mind play out a fight scene between this young man and several no face assailants. And there it was, his first instinct was that this person was a survivor and something very tragic had happened here. And he told Captain Barnaby as much, with the words of the woman still echoing in his ears.

"Are you my burden?" he asked in a low voice.

Chapter 1

Personal log entry of Jason Alexander Xavis

10, 16, 2290

Struggling to regain any memories from before my rescue, I've taken Captain Barnaby's advice to heart, jotting down even the faintest flashes that flicker through my mind. I didn't think any of the other crew could understand the difficulties I'm enduring, so journaling has become my outlet to express myself and my troubled thoughts.

I wake up every day only to stare at the face of a stranger looking at me in the mirror. Hell, I don't even know how old I am. Lilly Paxton, who did my medical exam, tells me that my biological age is around sixteen, but because they found me alone and frozen aboard a very old colony ship, they have estimated my age to be several hundreds of years old.

Not a very comforting fact, if you ask me. I wish we could go back and examine the ship more, but apparently a pirate faction has claimed that territory as their own, and Captain Barnaby will not engage them at any cost. From my observations of the man so far, he is solely dedicated to his crew. Every decision made has been for the welfare of the Orion's Belt, *Barnaby's ship.*

Granted, I admit this is a very dedicated and tight-knit bunch, so I can see why the captain watches over them like they are family. In a way, I was lucky they were the ones to find me. They have sheltered me and taken me in as one of their own. If it had been the pirates, I would have probably found myself shackled to the hull of a ship or something far worse.

I owe this imagery of me to Keller, who during one of our combat lessons together, often scolds me about my lack of discipline and respect. This, of course, is coming from the mouth of a discharged Earth Defense League Marine. I had to search the ship's database about what a Marine was, along with thousands of other questions that popped into my head. As I try to fill the void that is my mind at the moment, I must have logged a thousand hours on that terminal in the span of a week, but none of the crew bothered me. I guess it's probably because I'm just as much of a mystery to them as I am to myself.

The main useful things I have learned from Kell so far have been how to shoot the T-15 rifle and the T-12 sidearm. Both are what he has called recoilless rail guns. I am pleased with this training, but the most insightful thing from my past is what he calls an unusual fighting style. In his words, he has never seen anything like it in the EDL. This often prompts him to bring up the unusual object found in my cryo pod.

Apparently, I was found with a blood-stained metal pipe still clutched tightly in my hand. Which has led many of the crew to speculate that I used to defend myself with, but so far there has been no explanation of why. The blood stains revealed nothing about who they had belonged to or anything about myself. And when Kell asked me to show him something with the metal pipe, all I could do was to stare at it and wonder what I could do with it, other than bash someone's head in, of course.

But remembering the state of the old colony ship I was found in, I didn't even want to think about the possibility of swinging the metal pipe, to injure or kill someone. It just felt wrong, and the very thought of taking someone else's life made me sick to the stomach, as if I wanted to vomit.

Instead of berating me, though, Kell procured a cut broom stick and began attacking me with it. It was at this moment my body remembered what it should do. I blocked and countered, even managing to snake his broomstick away from him before he stepped away from the fight. It was at this moment that I had my very first glimpse into who I was, and I felt cold and numb at the implications.

Kell, on the other hand, realized that I had been trained in some form of Filipino martial arts and was excited that he now knew how to lead with his research about me.

So, the first insight into my past revealed that I was a skilled fighter of some sort, and I had injured or killed many people aboard that colony ship. Lilly had let loose the secret that there were ten distinct DNA strands they had found before being forced to evacuate the colony ship. So who am I? Am I a killer? Or is it what the others want to think, that I'm some young teenager, who was fighting for his life? They don't want to venture down the path that I may be something far worse, and at this moment, I have my own doubts about myself, because when that metal pipe was in my hand, it felt good. Even comforting to me. Was this a dark omen, which preceded the next significant event since waking up.

One morning while taking a hot shower, the steam that had formed in the cramped communal bathroom felt crowded to me, and at one point, I was forced to look around. I saw a man with his face and head cloaked in a deep crimson mask of blood staring at me. There was a look of deep hatred in his eyes, as if the look alone could murder someone. When I blinked, the man was gone, but the crowded feeling was still there. As if there had been hundreds of people around me.

I have not had this vision again, thankfully, but I do fear what sort of things I will start remembering. One of the worst thoughts was, what if I was a killer on the run? Would I kill the people that have taken me in and given me a life? Could I do that?

Thoughts like this plague my every waking moment. I don't want to be a threat to the people I am spending time with. I have already made connections with them, and I'm not going to lie, I like these people. They have given me a place to live, and I cannot be any more grateful.

Once again, this is why I dread my past. I would much rather move forward and create the new me, but as every member of this crew has pointed out; in order to move forward, one must be able to look back. It's the only way, according to them. Even though, technically, I am far older than any of them, they are far wiser than me in this respect. So, another reason why I'm sitting here putting all of this down is because hopefully, one day, I can look back at this and ask myself, Who am I? And I truly hope that I can answer that I was a young man who was forced to defend himself for his life and that I was justified in my actions.

"JAX, GET YOUR ASS TO the bridge, now," Captain Barnaby called out over the ship's intercom system, "You're needed at the helm."

Jax scratched the back of his head as he looked around the room he had been residing in. Had he really been rambling on in his journal long enough to have forgotten that he was supposed to pilot the *Orion's Belt* into port on Septis Three today?

It was no wonder Barnaby sounded pissed at him over the intercom. Jax sighed, grabbing his jacket, before he sprinted down the hallways, passing Kell, who was working out with a kettlebell in the recreation area slash mess hall slash sparring area. The Paxtons, a team of husband and wife who served aboard the *Orion's Belt,* waved at him as he sped by. Before he got to the bridge, he almost ran into Piper, who was coming out of her quarters.

"Really, Jax?" Piper said, folding her arms across her chest and looking at him with exaggerated irritation written all over her face, "Were you taking another long hot shower when the captain called for you? I swear to you, if I have to take a cold one, I'm gonna make sure you have ice cold showers every day."

"Plenty of hot water left, Piper," he retorted, snickering as he passed her by. Piper was one of the crew members of *Orion's Belt,* and they had a push and pull relationship. At first, Jax thought she had a bone to pick with him, but he realized that it was how she communicated. She was short and muscular, with a shaved head and lots of strange tattoos. Piper looked like someone he would not have much interest in but after spending about a week in her presence, Jax realized she had a kind and forgiving personality.

During one of the nights when he could not sleep and decided to take a walk around, he bumped into Piper staring out through the large port parasteel window of the ship. They started to talk, and that was when she opened up and told him how the personality she had now came from years of self-reflection and mindfulness meditation. He thought it was bull shit, personally. From his observations of her for the past couple of weeks, Piper was the meanest fist fighter he had ever seen and the worst drunk when the occasion hit her.

"You had better be right, Jax. Now get your ass to the bridge. We will probably be landing in an hour, and we're already late for delivery," Piper shouted from behind Jax while he waved off her worries with a careless hand.

It wasn't his fault they were late, just because he had been piloting when the jump engines cut out on them.

"At last," Barnaby said from the solo pilot's chair, swiveling to face Jax as he entered the bridge. "Jax, glad you could make it. You did remember that it's your turn to approach Septis Three, right?"

Barnaby's tone was condescending, but in truth, he had expected a far worse scolding from the man, for being late. It was not unusual for the man to berate someone, because they had either left some dishes uncleaned in the sink, or a half drunk cup out on a table. Barnaby ran a tight ship, and he expected everyone to follow his rules. And one of his biggest peeves was tardiness.

"Now clear us," Barnaby said, gesturing to the now empty pilot's chair. "And follow the coordinates to our designated landing site, to the letter."

Jax took the seat which was surrounded by hexagonal-shaped parasteel windows looking out into space. The *Belt* was still some distance from the planet, but from his vantage point, he could see white clouds, blue oceans, and lots of green lands covering the planet. It looked a lot like Earth from the images he had pulled up from the terminal a while back.

I can't wait to breathe the fresh air again, he thought as he put his headset on.

"I've got the helm, captain," he announced over the intercom.

Barnaby placed his large hand on his shoulder. "Looks like a lot of ships trying to make port today," he noted, leaning to look at the navigation screen where lots of red dots were lining up single file to approach the planet.

"Guess they want to get a look at the new power node the Locorrans set up," Jax said. "I heard they have a very artistic style in everything they manufacture."

"It's bad enough that Septis Three has sold out to the Locorrans. I know many people believe that they are our ancestors from the time of colonization, but there is something not quite human about them," Captain Barnaby rambled as he often did. Jax had noticed that it was hard for the man to remain still or silent for very long.

Jax turned for a second to look at his captain's uncertainty. "They look and sound human to me. Wait, have I actually met one before?"

"No, you haven't" Barnaby said with a smirk as if Jax's lack of knowledge was a personal fail of his and not because he had been frozen inside an old ship for however many years. He went on to explain, "On the exterior they look just like us, but every interaction I've had with them has been awkward, not a natural conversation I would have with another person."

"Do you think it's because of their altered history and culture?" Jax asked.

"No," Barnaby shook his head, "Septis Three and Praxis seven were founded over a hundred years ago and had about that much time without contact with Earth." He leaned in closer to Jax, watching over his every move. "Everyone I interact with from those colonies still have similar values and customs as all Earthers do."

Captain Barnaby had become a sort of guide for him if there was anything he needed information wise or just something personal. He had gotten teased about the way he had no clue about the way things worked now, but the teasing gave way to actual learning when Jax expressed his interest. He had nothing else to do anyway other than sparring with Kell.

"Is it because they have an emperor? That makes you feel and think differently about them?" Jax asked, watching Barnaby stroke the unkempt beard on his chin.

"Yes, their complete devotion and obedience to an emperor just isn't acceptable," Barnaby replied, poking his tongue into his cheek as he looked on into space as if his mind was lost somewhere far away.

When Barnaby was in one of his contemplative moods, Jax did not bother him much, but this topic of discussion was too good to let go. "Soon to be an empress in his place, from what I've heard, with the emperor stepping down and a young woman taking the throne," Jax added conversationally. This was something that he had overheard from the wife and husband. It wasn't his fault when they were hitting about 100 decibels per conversation.

"You heard right, Jax. Out of the several children the emperor had, this one young woman is chosen. And so far, no one has protested or spoken out against this. Why? I have no clue." Barnaby shrugged. "All through Earth history, siblings and rivals would go to war with each other for the right of supremacy. It's unnatural, I tell you."

It was curious, but maybe there was more to the story than met the eyes. Take his own story as an example. He had no idea who he was, and yet, this crew had taken him in when they could have just as easily discarded his body and left him on that ship. "Perhaps the Locorrans do a really good job of hiding that sort of stuff from the public eye," Jax said.

Barnaby patted his shoulder, "I hope you're right, Jax. Anyway, pay attention. Here comes the EDL."

The monitor to his left indicated the approach of four Earth Defense League fighters. To his visual sight, they were solid black with dipped down wings, ending in two long-barreled rail cannons.

A voice broke over one of his consoles. "*Orion's Belt*, this is Captain Diane of Talon squadron. Please reduce your speed and prepare for a detailed scan of your vessel," the woman's voice announced. It was strong and commanding, making Jax wonder what she might have looked like.

"Well," Barnaby said, smacking the back of the chair. "Are you going to answer her?"

Pressing the yellow button to his right, he spoke. "Talon squadron, this is Jax of the *Orion's Belt*. We are complying." He pulled back on the lever that controlled the throttle and sat watching as another EDL fighter crossed in front of him. Those ships were fast and very maneuverable from what he had observed of them.

He leaned back in the pilot's chair watching as the fighters swarmed through the parasteel window. Way off in the distance, he could just make out a giant blue ring. He pointed it out to Barnaby, "Is that the Locorran jump gate?"

"It is," Barnaby nodded, "It was put in place by the Locorrans a few months ago. You want to talk about a squabble? Half the Earth colonies said no to the gate. The leaders of Septis Three went ahead and did it anyway."

"That was rather bold of them," Jax said, checking his positioning to make sure he was not getting too close to another ship.

"It was smart," Barnaby said, crossing his arms. "And duplicitous."

Barnaby had stopped speaking, which left him to wonder what his captain was pondering. The word duplicitous had a sinister ring to it, but he was honestly gonna have to look up the meaning for. Needless to say his captain probably thought the Locorrans were behind the decision, and this was just one more example of them beginning to exert their influence.

"*Orion's Belt*," Captain Diane said. "You are clear to approach the planet. Follow behind the freighter ship, *Raven*."

"Roger that," Jax said, checking the screen to his left, looking for the transponder identifying the *Raven*. It was directly to his right, and he sped up the *Belt* to get within a few kilometers behind it.

"So. why do you think they did it?" Jax asked, pulling the throttle back again so that the *Belt* glided right in behind the *Raven*. He hoped that Barnaby would answer him this time; he wanted to know what his captain had been thinking about.

"Technology," Barnaby said. "Despite the strangeness of the Locorrans, they have many technological advancements over us. Take the Jump gate, for instance. It allows a ship to enter, and within a few hours you appear at the other end. Our jump engines have a limited range, cool down time and can take us days to reach our destinations. So, the leaders of Septis Three think that they can hopefully acquire this technology for themselves, thereby making themselves the central hub for trade."

All Jax had heard about Locorrans had come straight out of Barnaby's mouth. Yet, he could pretty much understand that these Earthers were not to be messed with. "I can't see the Locorrans giving up this technology," Jax said, "It gives them such an advantage over us. Not only in trade but militarily as well. Do you think the Locorrans are dangerous?"

Through his peripheral vision, he could see that Barnaby was staring out into space at that question, surely weighing his response to Jax's question, if he even had one.

When several moments passed by and Barnaby did not respond, Jax swiveled to his right and nudged Barnaby's legs with his foot, "Barnaby?"

It felt like Barnaby was shaken awake with his nudge. He blinked several times as he answered in a much quieter tone, "I do. I think they are dangerous and for all the reasons I have already told you."

Another voice broke over his communications speaker. "*Orion's Belt*," a man's voice said, "Land on pad two-two-three."

"Shit," Barnaby ran a hand through his hair, "That puts us several blocks away from our drop off point, and we're already behind schedule as is."

Understanding his worry, Jax offered, "You want me to try to see if we can get a different pad?"

"No, like I told you before, don't question or back talk these people," Barnaby warned with a pointed look thrown at Jax, "Otherwise they'll have you flying around in circles for hours or slap some kind of fee on you. It's best to keep your trap shut and go along with the flow."

"Roger that," Jax said, and angled the *Belt* for descent into the planet's atmosphere. Flipping the switch for the ship intercom, he spoke as loud and as clear as he could, like Barnaby would have, or Piper.

"Crew of the *Belt*, we are entering the atmosphere and will be touching down shortly."

Normally during a descent, most of the crew sat down and strapped in, just in case something went wrong, but the captain had remained standing behind him. With his hand still resting on the back of his chair, the gesture of appreciation was noted, but Jax would have felt better if everyone would have followed protocol.

When the *Belt* hit the atmosphere of Septis Three, he could feel the ship buck and jerk slightly. It wasn't enough to knock anyone off their feet, but they still had a long way to go.

"You're doing fine," Barnaby said. "Just let her ride right into the turbulence. Don't try to jerk her away from it."

The next set of turbulence shook the ship like a land vehicle on rocky terrain. Jax found his hand hurting from gripping the stick so hard and he had to take a couple of deep breaths to relax himself.

"See, nothing to it," Barnaby said, slapping him on the shoulder again with the palm of his hand.

The turbulence eased up as they passed through a thick layer of clouding, and at last, he could see the port city of Eries. There were vast bodies of water on two sides of it and tall gleaming white buildings all around. Long and silver gravity trains could be seen circling around the city, and a few were shooting out into the countryside. From this view, everything looked clean and new. Throngs of people flocked about, nicely dressed and groomed.

Barnaby pointed out the window, "There, that must be the Locorran power node."

It took his eyes a moment to see what the captain was looking at. Standing several stories tall with a white veil draped over it, was a four-story object set up right in the heart of the city. Squinting his eyes, Jax tried hard to look at the details, but his vision was obscured by Barnaby handing him a pair of binoculars.

"This will give you better visibility," Barnaby said with a nod.

"Thanks," Jax said, going back to viewing the node as the rest of the crew prepared to get off the ship. There were hundreds of people milling about the area surrounding the node, probably waiting for the unveiling. This wasn't the first time he was going planet side but each new place he visited, the same hesitance entered his mind for a few moments. He felt like an alien in a strange new world.

But he always shook them away because to integrate into society properly, he had to partake in it.

"Having doubts?" Barnaby asked, shaking him out of the hint of nerves trying to get a hold of him.

Jax shook his head, dispelling the uneasy feeling. He had been prepared for this ever since he had found out the course they were taking. Jax had faith in his ability to go out there and act as part of the crew.

Another voice broke over the communications system. "*Orion's Belt*," the male voice sounded perturbed at them, "You have missed your pad, and you need to circle back immediately."

"Roger," Jax grumbled back, looking back over his consoles to get his bearings.

"Guess I should have had you paying closer attention to the road," Barnaby said. "I won't bother you anymore."

He heard Barnaby's heavy foot falls clang on the metal flooring as they faded away. He was alone now, but there was no time to think about that. He had to concentrate on making a perfect landing. The *Belt* was lined up perfectly with the pad and with the aid of a monitor to his upper left he could see the crosshairs of the pad below. There was a slight jolt as the landing legs touched the ground and with a few audible hisses he knew the ship was safely parked.

"Attention, crew of the *Belt*," he announced, "We are now ready to unload. Ramps are coming down."

Barnaby broke in over the ship's intercom system, "Good job, Jax. That was some impressive flying. Now go and deal with the dock master. Then get your ass back here quickly; we're already behind schedule."

How many times was he going to repeat that mantra? Everyone on board knew they were late. But that was Captain Barnaby, he would never let them hear the end of it in this lifetime.

It's not their fault, Jax thought as he unbuckled himself from the pilot's chair and then darted through the ship, passing Piper and the Paxtons as he tore down the cargo bay ramp and out into the warm sunny sky of Septis Three. The warmth felt awesome to his skin and the freshness of the air made him breathe in deeply. It smelled clean and not tainted like the interior of the *Belt*. He had grown accustomed to it, but nothing beat the great outdoors of being on a planet.

It didn't take him long to find the dock master. He was standing in a central location of several pads with an old-fashioned clipboard in hand. What made the man stand out even more was the fact he was wearing a bright red jumpsuit, with lots of badges on it, and he had no idea of what any of them meant.

"You with the *Orion's Belt*?" the dock master asked in a deep, scratchy voice, looking at him up and down.

"Yes, name's Jax," he introduced himself, short and simple.

The man stared at something on the clipboard for a few seconds before looking up, "Manifest says the captain's name is Giles Barnaby."

Jax nodded, "That is the captain's name."

"So, why are you here and not the captain?" The dock master asked, snark clear in his voice. Jax internally said a couple of colorful words for the dock master then passed him a smile, gritted teeth and all. "The captain told me to come and talk with you," he said.

The man looked at his clipboard again, "I don't have a Jax on the crew manifest."

"Sorry, it will be under Jason Alexander Xavis. I'm so used to everyone calling me Jax," he grinned hoping this would resolve any misunderstandings.

There was no smile back, instead the dock master annoyingly flicked through the papers as he muttered something inaudible to himself. Since Jax had been told to be on best behavior by his captain, he remained standing resolutely.

"You're the most recent addition to the crew?" the dock master asked, throwing him a look that was parts curious and parts suspicious.

Jax sighed, "Yes."

"How long have you been aboard the *Orion's Belt*?" came another question.

Jax shrugged nonchalantly. "Couple of months."

"Place of origin?" the dock master asked again.

"Earth," Jax muttered with another tight-lipped smile.

Another question was immediately thrown his way, "City?"

He was about to say Austin, Texas, but then stopped himself as he remembered that there was no more Austin, Texas. There was a new city on Earth, just called Texas. So that's what he told him.

The man checked off a few things on his clipboard, then pulled out a device from a holster on his side, "Place your palm on this."

When he had observed the others like Piper dealing with dock master's before, none of them had to deal with this much red tape.

Jax thought for a moment whether this would be something that could potentially get him into trouble. When he saw no way out, he told the dock master, "Tell you what? I'm just going to go and get my captain."

The dock master stopped him with a firm hand upon his shoulder, "You will place your hand on the device, Jax."

The man's tone had changed. There was a seriousness in it now, and the unease in his gut increased. What made this feeling even worse was the fact that two men in navy blue jumpsuits were approaching and they both wore pistols. From the appearance of the pistols, they appeared to be 9mm handguns.

"Place your hand on the device," the dock master said again, voice hardening even further.

"Fine, scan away," he said, placing his palm flat on the device.

There was a brief moment of relaxation on both sides, and then the next thing he knew, the two men had their arms out and he was being cuffed. And thrown into the back of a small vehicle.

What the hell had just happened? Everything was fine a few minutes ago. Everything should have checked out fine when they had scanned him. After all, he had been to several other colonies and none of them had accosted him.

"Hey, why are you taking me? What did I do?" he asked, voice strained as he struggled to get free, flinching when the cuffs dug into his wrist because of his thrashing. It was certainly uncomfortable, and he had never been in this kind of position. Everything had happened so quickly that he did not even have the chance to call out for his captain.

He was placed inside the back of a vehicle, where the two men left him to go sit in the front. They didn't even glance back at him. It was as if he didn't exist. The only thing he could do was to sit back and enjoy the ride and hope that the others could resolve whatever had just happened.

The vehicle made its way toward the center of the city with flashing lights and a siren as they navigated closer to the new power node still veiled. Neither man said anything as they exited out and left him by himself.

They had left the vehicle at an outside edge near a set of marble white stairways leading down to an ornate wooden bridge that crossed a small creek. A patch of woods was set to either side of the stairway and a throng of people encircled the node. From his vantage point, he could see that the two security officers had taken positions just a few steps away from the vehicle and did nothing but just help provide a barricade for the people, which looked like they had divided themselves into two camps.

The right-hand side of the node contained people who were protesting. They were shouting and holding up signs, while on the left-hand side, people were shouting to the others about moving forward and accepting the Locorrans. It was quite the chaotic scene that Jax had not been able to make out from the binoculars. The atmosphere was much different than he had imagined. Instead of joy and excitement, there was palpable tension in the air along with passionate chanting.

The boisterous chants grew louder as he saw the veil slide from the side of the node. It was a beautiful gem-like structure, radiating a jade color from within. To the casual observer, it looked nothing more than a fanciful art piece, placed at the heart of the city. In reality, though, he knew it had a function. The Paxtons aboard the *Belt* had told him that this node would replace the needs of the hydroelectric dam that was powering the city. Especially as the population had grown in the last decade, the city was reaching the dam's power output.

The jade's light grew brighter, completely lighting the interior of the vehicle in a green hue. It also felt like the air around him had warmed slightly, and the first bead of sweat broke over his forehead. This change in luminosity seemed to have brought out the vocalness of the crowd gathered around as the screams and shouts increased in volume, which made him wish he could use his hands to muffle his ears from the noise.

Closing his eyes for a second, Jax tried to clear his head of the noise. Just when he thought he could not take it any longer, everything was eclipsed by a piercing boom noise, followed by the impact of some force that tumbled his world and sent him into darkness.

For a moment, he was disoriented, not knowing where he was and what was going on around him. It took several seconds for the world to come into focus again. When he was able to open his eyes again, his ears were ringing, and he had no sense of time or space. It felt like the world had tilted off its axis and he could not breathe as his restrained hands lay awkwardly behind his back, and his legs stuck at an awkward angle.

He struggled against the cuffs as his arms started to ache after struggling in the awkward position. He realized he was hanging upside down since his face was pressed up against the hard surface of the ground. The vehicle had been flipped up on its side, and all of the windows had been shattered out.

Instinct had taken over at this point. Jax wormed his way out the back window, feeling the shattered glass digging into his skin with every inch he moved. The pain of the cuts was numbed by the ringing and thrumming in his head. He wished he could make it go away, but he couldn't think of any way to make that happen now. His thoughts were still murky about where he was and what had just happened. That is until he got outside the vehicle far enough to see the devastation around him.

There were dead and bleeding bodies all around. The vehicle he had been in was on fire, and there was light high up in the sky, growing brighter by every passing second. His eyes fell upon the once beautiful node at the center of this destruction. The center portion of it had blown open, and he had a horrific realization that whatever forces had been contained within caused this devastation.

Were they all dead, though? If that was the case, then how had he survived?

So many questions were running through his head as he looked around, taking in the carnage around him. Suddenly, there was movement to his right—a glimpse of someone staggering about. Unsure what to do, Jax continued glancing around until his gaze fell upon one of the dead security men crumpled up against the vehicle.

The upper portion of the man's body was on fire. There was a small set of keys dangling from the man's belt. At the sight of the keys, his next course of action was decided. Worming his way to the body, he backed his hands to the belt and fumbled with the keys, trying to find the right one for the cuffs. His fingers ached and hurt from the manual dexterity exercise he was putting them through. A burning sensation in his shoulders threatened to bring his efforts to a halt.

To make matters worse, the light he had glimpsed earlier in the sky was becoming very luminous now, and he was positioned well enough that he could see a craft of some kind land on the far side of the node. Somehow, he doubted that whoever was in that craft was here to aid him. He wasn't sure where this thought had originated from, but that feeling of getting away from something hyper-drove his body into action.

One of the keys slid into place, and a second later, one of the cuffs came free. The pain that had been building up in his fingers and shoulders instantly relaxed to some degree as he brought them from behind his back. The ringing in his ears had eased enough for him to hear the crack of a gunshot rip through the stillness.

"Shit," he said to himself, fumbling with the keys for the last cuff. That flight instinct and adrenaline was making his body twitch. His heart was pounding against the walls of his chest like a battering ram against a reinforced castle door. Once completely free of the restraints, he got to his hands and knees in an instant. There were two more gunshots, louder and closer than before.

Jax hid against the car and crawled to and fro to see where the gunshots were coming from. He could spy two figures moving amongst the prone people. They were nowhere near, but he knew that they would reach the car in the next couple of minutes, which was why he had to move.

"Time to go," he muttered to himself. He was looking over the security man's body—he knew what he was looking for, and he found it. The 9mm pistol was still secure in the holster. Taking it out, the weight of it felt comforting in his hand. Two more gunshots pierced the night, and this time he could hear pleas for help.

Is this an execution squad sent to clean up any survivors? Jax thought to himself, *But why?*

There was a crunching noise from behind the vehicle, and without thought, he twisted around the burning wreckage and aimed to kill, with his finger already half pulling back the trigger.

His first impulse at seeing the armed female was to pull the trigger, but the look in her panicked green eyes, the scratch marks on her face from debris and frozen posture with the pistol aimed at him told him that she was a victim of this event just as he had been.

Lowering the weapon, he spoke to her, hoping she could hear him, despite the flow of blood still trickling from her ears, "Sorry, I thought you were going to kill me."

Her eyes never left his as she nodded her head in acknowledgment and lowered the pistol.

"Name is Jax," he added and was going to say more, but the next gun crack was a few feet away. The executioners were close by now. He crouched down closer to her. With a lowered voice, he spoke again, "We take those steps down, nice and slow. The vehicle will keep us hidden, got it?"

She nodded her head and gripped the 9mm pistol closer to her chest. She must have gotten it off one of the security men as well. He led the way, still crouched down and walking down the marble stairway. Several bodies had been blown back this way, and they either lay flat out on their back or were curled up on their sides.

They were careful not to make any sounds, just the soft drag of their footsteps which was drowned out by the still ringing gunshots as the executioners killed those who were still somehow alive.

When they reached the bottom, his instinct was to take off at a dead run across the bridge. In his mind, he was home free. He could make it to the tall buildings nearby for help and shelter. Except when he looked back at the young woman, who he estimated to be about his age, give or take, she had taken up a hidden position behind one of the large marble statues near the bridge and she was checking over the pistol.

Dashing over to her, Jax whispered, "What the hell are you doing?"

Her eyes locked with his, as if she was trying to communicate with his mind. The cold expression was one he somehow recognized. There was intent to harm or kill someone there in those green eyes.

"I won't pretend to understand what's going on with you, but we both need to survive this. So, we can let others know what happened here?" he said calmly even though the beat of his heart resounded in his ears at the thought of getting stuck here while the executioners killed everyone in their path.

"It's too late for all of that," she said. "So, if you want to survive this, then do exactly what I tell you."

Great, Jax thought to himself. *What have I gotten myself involved in?* His body was still wanting to run, but his mind was agreeing with the young woman's.

"Fine," he said with gritted teeth, "What should I do?"

She leaned away to glance in the direction of the gunshots, then whispered, "The two killers will be close to the top of the steps in a minute. I need you to circle around them as I draw their attention. Hopefully, I can kill one by surprise. Think you can handle that pistol?"

He half pulled back the slide and made sure a round was in the chamber then nodded, "Yeah, I got it. Point and pull the trigger."

She nodded her head, and with a deep breath, he darted to the left, making a large circle around the two executioners. There was just enough tree coverage to block him from the sight of his prey as he neared them.

The woman had been right. They had moved near the top of the stairway and started panning around when the shorter of the pair went spiraling down to the ground from gunshots that must have come from the young woman. Jax silently cheered while the one left standing hit something on his arm and a blue energized shield formed in front of it.

It was time to act. Jax sprinted from the tree cover and began firing at the black-clad figure from behind. Several of his bullets hit their mark, and the figure tumbled down the steps. He let his speed carry him down and to within a foot of the figure.

The woman had come out from her covered position and moved up beside him. Her pistol was pointed down as if she had intended to place another bullet in the figure's head. Except they couldn't see a face behind that helmet and shielded visor. She bent down and outstretched a hand to open the visor, but her hand was stopped by a grip from the helmeted figure. A blue bolt passed through the young woman's body and Jax watched her fall backward as her body started to convulse.

Jax was chilled to the bone. His finger was already on the trigger when he felt his leg being swept from under him. The impact with the ground smashed the air from his lungs, but instinct had taken over. He was rolling and getting to his feet while gasping. He had no time to process his moves or what his enemy was doing. The only thing he could do was react, and that's what he did.

A punch came fast at his face, but his hands and body were already in motion as they worked in unison to block the blow. Before he knew it, he had hit the figure in the chest with the butt of the pistol and then found himself firing point blank into the same chest. Blood covered the body as he watched it fall over backwards and twitch a few seconds on the ground.

He was sure that this time the figure was dead. His eyes traveled to the young woman on the ground, she was unmoving. Jax crouched down to check her pulse and let out a breath of relief to see that she was still alive.

He stood back up and for a moment he took in the brisk night air. What now? He sure as hell couldn't stay here. All of this would probably get blamed on him, especially if they went digging around his false records. That would lead them to the crew of the *Belt*. There was only one option open to him. He could escape with the woman on the ship. That these two clad figures had arrived in. What other option did they have anyway?

We take their identities, Jax thought. He removed the helmet from the figure he had killed and found himself staring into the face of a young man barely older than he was. The hair color and eyes were different, but other features were similar enough. He took the helmet and emptied the pockets.

The clock was ticking, and he knew this place would be crawling with people soon. He forced himself to get the young unconscious woman over his shoulder and into the two-person craft.

The only thing he had left to do was to drag the bodies into the intense fire of the vehicle he had arrived in, which was now raging like a furnace.

Then it was time to get the hell out of there.

Chapter 2

Jax hadn't realized that when he placed Jules in the rear seat of the craft. That there had been no controls or panels dividing the seats. And now that he had slung himself into the pilots' chair, there was no kind of instrumentation or even a control stick.

So how in the hell am I supposed to fly this thing? he thought, desperately searching around.

Maybe there was a button to press, that brought out the controls. After several seconds of searching the only thing, he had discovered was a series of circular blue lights placed throughout the interior.

"Who designs a ship like this?" he said, looking out of the canopy. At the dead bodies around him. He wouldn't be able to run far or fast with the young woman over his shoulder. And with a falsified record. They would send him to prison for sure.

He needed to figure out who was responsible for this and clear himself. So, what was he missing? The only thing he hadn't done yet was to strap himself in. As soon as he clicked the harness belt in place, the craft came alive.

Virtual consoles started appearing all around him. "Really," he said out loud. "Safety first." Once the consoles had appeared the more familiar things began to look. He quickly identified the pilot's stick and the thrusters to his right-hand side.

"Ok, I got this," he said, pressing his fingers on the virtual console, that lifted the craft up off the ground. And with a nudge of the thrusters, the craft shot up over the treetops at an incredible speed. *This craft would fly circles around the Belt,* he thought, pushing the throttle more forward. And in no time, he was passing through large puffy clouds. Then at last breaking through the atmosphere into space without any jars or vibrations.

So, what is this craft? Jax wondered.

There had been no markings on the outside identifying the ship as either belonging to the Locorrans or to the EDL. Was there a third party? Reasoning with himself, this craft had to be Locorran in design and those people they had just killed back on Septis Three had to be of the same. What had he just been involved in? The wheels turning in his mind were telling him that it was something political, but he didn't have enough information to make that assumption. Whatever the reason was, his plan was to find out and report them to the authorities.

That should clear his name and hopefully not bring any harm to the crew of the *Belt*. He just hoped that the young woman in the back seat felt the same way as he did. If not, then he would try and find someplace for her to get off the craft.

Now in space, Jax angled the craft enough so that he could look back at the planet's surface. The section of the continent that they had just left from was now pitch black. The only conclusion he could come to was that the exploding power node had some other additional effects that he was unaware of.

On the communications panel Jax put in the frequency that the *Belt* used and said, "Barnaby?"

When there was no response, he asked again "Anyone aboard the *Belt*? Please respond."

"Captain, this is Jax, I need your help," he called out after another moment.

After two more tries and no reply in return, Jax gave up. He reoriented the craft to exit Septis Three space.

Once the course was decided, Jax leaned back in his chair, but he knew he would not be relaxing any time soon, not until they were far away from this place.

The woman in the back stirred and Jax turned to look at her slowly blinking her eyes open. "What?" she drawled, "Where am I?" she said, flinching and holding onto her side.

Jax turned his head around so he could get a good look at her. "Well, here's the short version," he said, "You got knocked unconscious by one of those helmeted figures. I took him out, took anything that would identify them, and placed you aboard this ship. And we are now heading out into space."

She was looking around at the virtual controls in the seat behind her, and then up above into the starry sky before her green eyes settled back down on his. "Okay, but why?"

Great, now he was going to have to explain his logic to her. Taking a deep breath, Jax began, "Whoever these people were, they were not local to Septis Three. The flight logs in the system indicate that this ship came from outpost Delta 44D. The identity cards of our attackers are nothing but scannable codes, no real visible information."

The woman's eyes widened. "Are you suggesting that the Locorrans were responsible?"

Jax sighed but shook his head. "Not saying that at all. The only thing we know for sure is that everyone at the unveiling of the node last night was meant to die and the blame to be put on someone else. Who? That's the part I don't know."

"Well, Holmes, sounds like you got this wrapped up," her eyes were locked with his and her lips were compressed together tightly. Before she spoke again, she looked away from him into space. "So, how did you end up there?"

Funny, he wanted to ask her the same thing, but it would have to wait until after he answered her. The real question now was if he should tell her the truth or lie to her. They had both survived a life and death situation together, so in that case she deserved the truth.

He twisted back around in the pilot's chair. It was getting uncomfortable looking back at her that way, and honestly, he needed to pay attention to where the craft was going. So far, no one bothered them. No communications, no flybys. It was as if the craft didn't exist.

"Well?" she said, raising her brows at him. "Spill it."

Jax held his hands upward. "Okay, okay. I was in the custody of one of the local authorities. They had me handcuffed in the back of one of those vehicles near the node." He showed the wounds left upon his skin in a circular shape, reminiscent of the cuffs.

With a grunt, the woman sat up and said, "Are you shitting me, right now? Why were you in custody?"

"I had just arrived on Septis Three with my crew aboard the *Orion's Belt*. The captain had sent me out to deal with the port authority. The guy scanned my hand, and the next thing I knew, I was being cuffed and thrown into the back of that vehicle without a word. My crew doesn't even know what has happened to me," Jax explained, wondering whether it was even a good idea to lay it all out in front of her, but he had already said everything of importance.

The woman looked at him with her brows raised. "That's definitely a strange enough tale for it to have been made up." She shook her head and sat up on the seat with a sigh before looking at him with a knowing look on her face. "So, I'm going to assume you want me to tell you why I was there?" she asked.

"I was," Jax replied, watching the young woman look out the canopy, avoiding his gaze. Her hands were pressed down firmly into the canvas material of her pants.

"I will tell you," she said, "but first, what is our plan? I assume you already had an idea when you took this ship?"

Jax pressed his lips together, gathering his thoughts before answering, "My thoughts were that the only way to find out who did this and why they did this was to take this ship, assume the identity of our assailants, and get a confession from the one or ones responsible for this act. Also, I didn't want to stick around that site and take the blame for what had happened."

The young woman nodded, "Okay, I agree with you there. Us impersonating those killers might be tougher than you think."

"Well, I'm open for ideas," Jax turned to look at her again, noticing that her eyes were still locked on the starry sky, but she lowered her gaze after a few seconds and met his eyes.

"Okay, fine, let's do it. I want to know who these bastards are. They just killed all of my friends back there. And they are going to pay for what they have done," she spoke resolutely, her eyes suddenly alight with the similar killer intent that he had seen back there.

He had not wanted to be part of a revenge killing. His original intention was to find the guilty party, get a confession, and then let the authorities handle it. That had felt like the correct course of action, but with the young woman in tow, she might just kill the guilty party instead.

"Okay," he said, hitting a series of buttons on a console to his right-hand side. "Away we go." The lights from the stars that had been bright little pin pricks in the canopy had suddenly streaked out around them in a cascade of lines.

"My name is Julianne Prescot," she called out from behind. "Everyone calls me Jules, though."

Nice name, Jax thought to himself. *Very Earthish.*

"Okay, Jules, my name is Jason Alexander Xavis or Jax for short. Nice to meet you," he extended his left hand through the virtual console so she could shake it. He might have been stuck inside a frozen pod for hundreds of years, but he still knew all his manners.

Jules shook his hand and said, "Well, Jax, now that we are fugitives together," she paused, giving him a helpless look before asking, "What the hell have we gotten ourselves into?"

Jax chuckled and shrugged. "Beats me. I was hoping you could help shine some light on what happened?"

There was a pause before Jules spoke. "I think I have a pretty good idea. What do you know about the Locorrans?"

Jax looked at her with a narrowed-eyed gaze before shaking his head, "Not much, other than the fact that my captain and crew don't trust them."

"Smart man," Jules replied with a firm nod. "A few years ago, I had a friend named Evelen. We attended the same university together. She was extremely smart and gifted. One day she got offered to go to an apprentice program on Locorran prime. She was very excited about it and almost wrote to me constantly when she first arrived, giving me lots of details and descriptions of Locorran life, architecture and achievements. She had fully bought into the belief of the Locorrans being a long-lost colony from old Earth before the devastation."

Another person who doesn't believe either, Jax thought to himself.

"As time went on," Jules continued, "Her letters became less frequent and then at last stopped completely. Nothing until the day we graduated together. When I got to talk with her again, it was as if I was speaking with an entirely different person. There was no trace of the woman I had known before," the loss was obvious in Jules eyes as she spoke of her friend. "Even her parents could not identify her. Right after the graduation, she left with other

Locorran graduates back to Locorran Prime and the parents may still get a letter from her once or twice a year, I don't know," she let out a drawn-out sigh, "All I know with certainty is the woman I knew was not that woman. There was a whole new person inhabiting that body now."

"What do you think happened to her? Or caused it?" Jax questioned, intrigue clear in his voice.

"A couple of months after graduation, I got approached by a young man at an outside diner. At first, I thought he was hitting on me, but the next thing I knew, he was asking all sorts of questions about Evelen." Jules took in a shuddering breath.

"Definitely not a way to pick anyone up," he replied with a mirthless small smile upon his face.

Jules nodded slowly before continuing. "I had started to brush him off, thinking he was inquiring as to where she had gone, but then he said to me, 'I know what they did to her.' That's when all my attention was focused on him. It took me a couple of minutes to recognize that the man talking to me happened to also be a classmate of mine from the previous year. He had let his hair and beard grow out, and it was very unkempt compared to how he used to dress for classes."

Jax asked, "Did he ever date Evelen or anything?"

"No." Jules shook her head. "Evelen had no time for boys. She was a dedicated student who had plans on making a career for herself." Jules paused, a nostalgic half-smile on her face as if she was remembering the friend that she knew before everything changed. "So anyway, I straight up asked him, 'Okay, so what happened to her?' I watched him take a sip of some tea and then look around before leaning in closer toward me. In a whispering tone, he said, 'I can show you. I have proof of what the Locorrans are doing to us all.'"

"All of us?" Jax asked, running his hands through his short hair. His gaze was still fixed on the young woman that he now knew as Jules. She was beautiful and obviously not afraid of anything, which he knew after their confrontation back on Septis Three. So, there was something special about her upbringing. He would have to inquire about it later though; knowing more about the Locorrans was important. At least he would know what he was up against.

Jules nodded solemnly. "That's what he said. So, I went along with it." She shrugged. "I half expected him to tell me it was in his apartment or in a motel room. Nope, how wrong I was. He led me out to a nearby coffee shop. It was obvious when we arrived that the man was well-acquainted with the workers there because the guy and gal behind the counter nodded their heads at him and gave me the look over."

Jax watched her run her hand through her dark hair, getting it out of her face, and tying it back in a loose knot.

Jules continued with a huff. "So, we took a seat at a far corner, as far away from the windows and other people as possible. The worker brought a satchel over to the table and my guy pulled a tablet out from it and then began thumbing through it. When he turned it to face me, I was looking at a colored brain scan of some kind. This is when he started explaining it to me. The brain on the left-hand side is our normal functioning healthy brain. The brain you and I are born with. The brain on the right is a scan of a person who has stayed several weeks in the Locorran empire," she paused, looking back out the cockpit window.

Jax tilted his head while Jules remained silent. He knew she was struggling to get the words out because they must have hit her hard, considering what was done to her friend. To lighten the mood, he let out a half-smirk and said lightly, "Well, you got me hooked now. So, what was the difference?"

"It's kind of hard to explain without the images, but I'll try anyway," Jules said. "The most obvious thing was that a lot of regions that had been lit up in a normal brain were not lit up in the altered brain. Instead, other regions were more active. I asked him what all of this meant. This is when his eyes squinted, and voice lowered even more. He told me it means that the Locorrans are altering people's brain functions in order for them to be controlled by something."

"What does that mean? Controlled by what?" Jax asked, making a quick check over the instruments to make sure everything was still operating as it should.

"Trust me, I asked all these questions as well. His response to me was that he did not know who or what was controlling the Locorrans, but whatever it was had to be powerful," Jules stated.

Jax leaned back in his chair as they remained silent for a few moments, letting the reality of the situation settle over them. Then Jax asked, "So how were the brains being altered?"

"That leads us to the present," Jules said. "The node that blew up tonight. That was more than just a power generator. It was also emitting a frequency that was engineered to alter the brainwave patterns of everyone exposed to it for a certain duration."

Jax's mouth fell open. "That can't be possible. How could the EDL or the planet council approve of such a device even if they had some suspicion of it being capable of that?"

"That's the problem. Many members of the planetary council approved of having this node put in place and the Locorrans even gave them engineering specs, so that they could build their own. The EDL has been given the evidence I just told you about, but no one seems interested in taking action," Jules said, flapping her hands through the air as if she could not stress the point enough.

That was when it dawned on him. She had been at the node not only as a protestor, but possibly for something more. "Jules?" Jax said, "You and your friends didn't blow that thing up, did you?"

"Glad to see that you have been paying attention," she said, gazing at him with raised brows and a "finally getting caught up, are you?" expression on her face. She continued, "To answer your question, we were there to protest and sabotage the device, yes. But what we did would not have caused that massive explosion. So, either the Locorrans or the planetary council had gotten a clue that many people were starting to figure out the Locorrans are not our friends. They must have decided to stage that explosion and put the blame on extremists so the local government could round up any dissident voices. The plan will probably work, because many of the dissidents were at the unveiling."

Jax relaxed a bit in his chair. "So, you truly believe that the nodes are brain-altering machines?"

"Yes, and you wanna know why I can say that with confidence? That brain scan I was shown, it was Evelen's before and after scan. The man telling me all of this had been the tech that had taken the scan. He was ordered to destroy it, but instead he took it and some other scans, then went on the run," she sighed, shaking her head morosely. "A couple of days after we had talked, he was dead. It was at that moment I knew what I had to do. I had to fight this. I had to tell everyone who would listen. I wake up every day in a different place and always with the same nightmares. I'm being chased by the local authorities and gunned down in cold blood, just like they did to him."

There was nothing Jax could say to her that would make the expression on her face or the situation better. Hell, his own mind was reeling with the implications of what she had just told him. If this was true, which he had no doubt that it wasn't, then the Locorrans were no longer human, and they were already waging war against the free people of the colonized Earth systems. Septis Three was just the first of several worlds to accept Locorran technology. If others followed suit, then it could be a wrap for humanity.

"Sorry," Jules said. "I know this information must be as big of a bombshell to you as it was to me. It made me mad, and I had no choice but to do something about it."

"There's nothing to be sorry about," Jax waved her apology off, "I must confess all of this is shocking information to me, and I don't disbelieve you. I'm just trying to wrap my head around the implications of this."

"It's far worse than you can imagine, trust me," Jules stated, "I know. I have wasted many sleepless nights pondering this."

"So, what do you think we should do?" Jax asked, rubbing his wrists, trying to get some of the soreness out of them as the realization hit that this was truly bigger than he had thought.

Jax felt her warm hand touch his shoulder as she said, "You are already doing something. For one, you listened to what I had to say and didn't dismiss it out of hand. Secondly, on your own initiative, you decided to take me to discover who or what had planned this event. That speaks volumes about your character to me. So, tell me Jax, who are you?"

Oh boy, that was the question he had been dreading, but now that he was faced with it, the answer to it came easier than he thought.

Perhaps he had wanted to confess his story, or perhaps the company had made him relaxed enough to let go of his origins. Whatever it was, the words just poured out of him.

Chapter 3

"Well, that's the whole story," Jax said with a shrug. He felt exposed, as if Jules could see what lay inside of him. That wasn't true though, because he himself did not know what lay inside of him.

"I am honestly at a loss for words," Jules said, looking at him in a wide-eyed haze, "If all of that is true, then you're the oldest person I know."

"Is that what you're concerned about? My age?" Jax asked with a peal of soft laughter.

"No Jax, I'm just trying to decide if you're that good of a liar or if that story is even true," Jules threw back with a smirk.

Jax gave her a small smile upon his face as he said, "I swear to you, that I didn't lie or exaggerate."

"Ok, I'll trust you with that," Jules nodded, "If we are going to pull this off, we both need to trust each other. So Jax, do you have my back?"

Jax nodded in assent, "Of course, I got your back."

"Craft 3117, please approach on these coordinates and dock in bay alpha," a booming male voice announced through the cockpit.

"They didn't even ask for any identification or anything?" Jules asked in astonishment, "Do you think they still haven't figured out that their people are dead?"

"I did place them in that fire, hoping that would slow down their efforts," Jax admitted.

"Which I admit was a brilliant move on your part," Jules relayed with a pat upon his shoulder.

"Wish I'd grabbed their clothes too," Jax said, regret tinging his tone. "But they were soaked in blood."

"I can grant that wish, flyboy," Jules replied with a wink thrown his way. She threw a pair of pants, shirt, and jacket over the seat and onto his lap.

"Where the hell?" Jax asked in utter surprise.

"I was digging through some of the compartments, and I found two sets of clothing back here, just like the ones they had been wearing," Jules replied with a smirk and a cheeky shrug.

Jax held up the clothes to inspect. "Not very fashionable, are they?"

Jules let out a short laugh. "Nope, now put them on."

Jax was glad she felt a little relaxed after the heavy conversation they both had. It was also obvious to him from his observation of her that her side where she had been hit was also feeling better, since she was no longer clutching at it.

When he turned to look back at Jules, she was already taking her top off, and he could see the silky green bra she had been wearing underneath.

She caught sight of him staring and gave him a toothy smile. "Sorry, no free peep show."

Jax quickly popped his head back around and began changing his clothes. He wanted to see more of her—what he had seen so far was beautiful and exciting.

"Craft 3117, I ordered you to change course. Do so immediately," came the booming voice once again, making them hurry in changing their clothes.

With his heart racing, Jax corrected the craft and gave one more glance back at Jules. She was just pulling up the black tight pants and buttoning them in place. Why did he get the feeling she was going to be the death of him?

There were several freighter ships already parked in the bay when he set the craft down. No one came out to meet them, instead as they approached a black and shiny portion of the wall, some text typed up. It gave out a number which was probably his or her employee number and then a detailed map appeared.

"Directions to our room?" Jules asked, leaning over his shoulder to look at the map.

"Looks like it. Right next to all this construction going on," Jax said.

"Not construction," Jules said. "When the Locorrans placed and activated the jump gate at Septis Three, Outpost Delta 44D became obsolete."

Why hadn't he heard his crew talking about this? Then again, why would they? It wasn't like they had permission or clearance to deal with the Locorrans.

"I'm starting to have doubts about your story," Jules said, taking the lead.

He followed behind, admiring just how tight those pants were on her. It was going to be hard to concentrate with her around, but he needed to concentrate. They were in an unfamiliar place with people that may just want to kill them on the spot. What had he been thinking? This was a bad idea.

When they arrived at the door the map had indicated, it opened freely for them and they stepped into a large apartment with a nice big living room, a large bed, a bathroom, and a giant marble table that must have weighed a ton. Everything was clean and ornate, almost as if no one had been living here.

"Do you think they lived here together?" Jules asked, looking around at the interior curiously and touching every flat surface available.

"If they did, then they are far cleaner than my roommate, Kell," Jax said with a shake of his head, "There's no dishes in the sink. The couch doesn't even look like anyone even sat on it."

There was a chime on a wall panel near him in the kitchen area. The only thing visual was some text that typed up as he approached.

"Well?" Jules asked while standing in the doorway of the bedroom with her hands pressed against the frame, watching him.

"It says that after we shower, we should meet someone named Kane in the forward lounge," Jax relayed, reading the message delivered to them.

"That's an awful personal message. Why should we shower first?" Jules asked, scrunching up her nose in confusion.

Jax shrugged his shoulders at that. "I have no idea. Guess we should follow its instructions though."

Jules' eyes locked with his for a moment, then she said, "Sorry, but I got first dibs. Just pray I leave you some hot water."

With that, she walked away from him and closed the door to the bathroom, and he was pretty sure he heard the click of the door lock.

He walked around the apartment for a while. He could hear the heavy pattering noises of the shower through the walls. Sound insulation definitely wasn't on the designers' minds when they built the place, but then again, why the absurdly expensive and heavy marble table? It looked good with the decor but was not cost efficient. What was the point of it?

Was this room maybe used as an estate room for high level visitors or something? It certainly didn't feel lived in. There were no magazines, books, puzzles or anything that would help give some insight into the minds of the people who had just so casually killed people in cold blood back on Septis Three. Of course, the reasonable answer to this had been in what Jules had told him.

So, what if the couple had been controlled by something? What if their minds had been altered by just being in close proximity to one of those nodes? Was this place safe? It was near Locorran space, and it was the only authorized station the Locorrans recognized for human freight ships.

Crap—another reason he shouldn't have brought them here. Every minute they could be exposed to brain alterations. Jax guessed he wasn't thinking very clearly when he had made up this plan on the spot.

"Hey, I'm done," Jules said from behind him. She was standing in the doorway with a large thick towel wrapped around her body. He wanted it to slip open, badly. But then she turned and walked away, crushing his brief fantasy about seeing her naked.

While in the shower, he lathered his body with a spicy scented bar of soap. His mind was still pondering about the peculiarity of the message they had received in the kitchen. Was this how the Locorrans lived? Receiving messages like that, telling them how to live their daily lives. What kind of existence would that be?

Toweling himself off, he began to dress himself back in the black clothing he had arrived in. When he walked back into the living room, Jules was already dressed and watching him.

"This place is creeping me out. It doesn't look or feel like anyone actually lives here," she said, side-eyeing every single thing inside the room.

"Agreed, there's nothing personal lying about. Not even breadcrumbs on the table," Jax noted, pausing near her and extracting the clip from his pistol.

"How many bullets do you have left?" he asked, looking at her from his peripheral vision.

Jules looked away from the drawer handle she was fiddling with and checked the 9mm at her hip, "Ten bullets and there is an extra clip in this pocket," she said, raising a brow at him in a "what about you?" way.

Jax checked out his own gun and supplied, "Great, I have a little less. Let's try to not get into a gun fight here."

"Not sure I can make that promise, but okay," Jules said, placing the pistol back into its holster. "So, what's our play here?"

They stood facing each other in the middle of the sterile room, sharing a knowing look because they knew the moment they stepped a foot outside, they would have to leave behind their real selves and try to imitate the ones they had killed. Jax hoped none of what they had done and were about to do was in vain.

He took a deep breath before saying, "We go and meet this Kane person. Hopefully, he accepts us for who we are pretending to be."

Jules pressed her lips together before asking, "And if he doesn't?"

Jax shrugged, "Then we both make our way back to the ship and escape out of here."

"Not overly complicated," Jules said sarcastically, knowing it could get complicated quickly. She shook her head then, before passing Jax a genuine smile, "I like it, though," she said with a wink, placing the helmet on her head, "Let's get this over with."

He couldn't argue with her about that. This plan was either going to work or it wasn't. So, he placed his helmet on his head and they both walked out the door, checked the map on the wall again, and found their way to the forward lounge.

The corridor outside the lounge looked as ornate as the room with marble walls and windows covered with red curtains. The people they passed stayed way clear of them, which led him to wonder if they were enforcers in Locorran society or something else.

When they entered the lounge, it was sparsely populated with people scattered about at tables here and there. They had only taken a couple of steps inside the lounge when everyone stopped and stared at them except for the one human who was sitting at a table with two others.

"I think that's our guy," Jax said, feeling his hand slipping down closer to his pistol. The human he was talking about did not spare them a single glance as they stood there while Jax could feel the eyes of the rest of them upon him and Jules.

Jax looked around the lounge and knew that if things went bad in here, they would be lucky to get out with their lives. He did take note that there was at least one other entry point, but it was on the opposite side of the lounge. So, it wouldn't make for a good exit, especially since it led away from docking bay alpha.

"Definitely not what I thought our Kane person would look like," Jules commented, striding forward toward the table. Jax quickly followed behind her, marveling at the fact that she truly was not scared of anything or anyone. They came to a stand beside the table and gazed at the guy who they assumed had been sending them the messages.

He was an Asian man with several scars on his face and was telling an animated story to the two other people at the table who did not look amused or entertained by it. The man didn't acknowledge Jax and Jules until he had finished the story. Then he turned his gaze up at them. "I take it your mission was successful?" the man at the table asked.

"No problems," Jax replied and then held his breath, hoping the man wouldn't catch that something was amiss.

Kane nodded his head, looking at them with a blank expression. Then a wry smile crossed his features, and he chuckled darkly as he said, "Please take off those helmets. You don't have to pretend anymore. You're not the ones I sent to Septis Three. I confess I don't know your names, but you both have a lot of balls to come here. So just relax, take the helmets off, have a seat, and let's talk for a bit, please."

Jax felt like all the breath in his lungs vanished. He supposed they should have realized that these people would call them out instantly. The attack that had happened back there had been well-executed. Jax was certain that it wouldn't have been planned by fools. He could feel Jules' probing gaze, awaiting what he was going to do.

It was obvious the deception was over, but Jax regarded Kane's words carefully. He wanted to sit them down and have a talk. If they had intended to kill them right away, it would have already been done. So, the only course of action was to remove his helmet and hopefully get some answers from this man.

Jax removed his helmet carefully and squinted as the sharp fluorescent lights entered his eyes. Once his eyes were accustomed to the light, he turned his head to see that Jules had followed suit. With a determined shared glance, they both took a seat at the table.

"My name is Kane," the Asian man started, "The other two beside me are unimportant. Would you two care for a drink? Anything you want?"

Jax and Jules shared another wordless glance before he said, "Whisky on the rocks." Not sure why he had said it, considering that he was definitely under the age limit, but for some reason, it was the first thing that came to mind.

"And you, miss?" Kane asked, leaning toward Jules.

"Just a beer," she said with a shrug.

Kane sat back and laughed, "Just a beer? No preference? We have some really good brands on tap here. Would you like for me to choose one for you?"

Jules merely nodded her head and pressed her lips together. Jax could feel the apprehension pour out of her. He leaned towards her and lightly pressed their shoulders together, hoping she understood that they were in this together and that he would not leave her alone if things went south.

One of the men who had been sitting at the table got up and went to the bar.

"You two are in a lot of trouble," Kane said, leaning forward on the table.

He was getting ready to ask a question when Jules beat him to it. "So, were you the one that ordered the node to explode? And did you send those two executioners to kill any survivors?" she asked in stride.

Kane sat back in his chair and looked at her with interest obvious in his eyes. "Before I answer your question, I want you to take a look around." He spread his hands and gestured to their general surroundings.

Jax followed his advice and did so, noticing that everyone in the bar was now looking at them and they had weapons drawn on them.

"As you can see, any attempt to kill me here will result in a very quick death. And to answer your question, yes, I ordered the power node to be rigged to explode and ignite an EMP burst that effectively shut down the entire city, and yes, I ordered the two hunters to kill those people," Kane admitted, not a hint of hesitance or regret on his face.

There was a moment after Kane's admission during which he watched Jules, probably expecting her to go for her pistol, but instead, she set her hands palm down in front of her on the table and asked with quiet fury in her voice, "Why?"

Kane shrugged with a half-smile, "It's simple, really. We did it to bring an end to all of the protestors. With the new laws that will go into effect and the demonization of those who speak out against us. It will be very hard for anyone to impede our progress."

"Progress? To what means?" Jax asked in confusion.

"The expansion of the Locorran Empire, of course," Kane said. "We want to bring all of our lost human kin into the fold."

Jules shifted in her seat, and it looked as if she was going to ask another question but was interrupted by the drinks being placed in front of them.

"Please, drink up," Kane gestured at the glasses filled with liquids in different shades of amber.

Neither of them moved. Instead, Jules launched her next set of questions at the man, "I know that you are altering people's brain function. Why? And who is controlling them afterward?"

Kane looked at Jules as if she was extremely naïve. "My dear, we are not altering anyone's brain, much less controlling them. I'm not sure where you heard such nonsense."

Jules did not back down though, instead, she scoffed, "I have proof. I know you altered my friend Evelen's brain. She was a confident young woman until she spent time in the Locorran empire, and now she's barely human."

"My dear, look at me. Do I look like a mindless drone to you?" Kane asked with his brows raised.

"No, but that doesn't mean you've not had the alterations done to your brain," Jax said.

Kane leaned toward them; mouth twisted with a hint of a snarl. "I'm going to let you two in on a secret. You see, we are all Locorrans. Understand there is no I or me. I am Locorran. How do you think we knew you two were imposters the moment you arrived? Neither of you are Locorran."

"What the hell does that even mean?" Jules asked.

The man looked her in the eye and simply stated, "You'll know soon enough." Then his gaze drifted over to Jax, and he shook his head. "You, on the other hand, will not be joining us. I'm afraid we are going to have to kill you. Normally this is the function of the hunters, but since you two killed them, I guess we are going to have to do it."

There was another pause as Kane's words registered in Jax's mind, and then it felt like the air shifted. In the next moment, Jules lost her cool and drew her pistol. Gunshots exploded from around the room. Everything was happening so fast now, but Jax watched as if in slow motion, as Jules' gunshots tore into Kane, leaving giant splotches of blood appearing on his clothing. In the next moment, Jax saw her take a couple of shots that spun her down to the ground, but she was still firing.

It was at this moment Jax's reactions kicked in, and his hand found his pistol. He placed two shots into both men that had been sitting beside Kane.

Something stung him in the back, and he let that momentum spin him down to his knee, twisting so he could fire back at the others from behind.

He found one target, rushing toward them with his fist balled, but two shots to the chest brought the brute down. Jules was back up on her feet, and with controlled precision, was stepping forward taking out two more bar patrons.

Everything was in mayhem but seeing Jules so in control of what was happening around them motivated Jax to do the same. He moved forward as well, firing the last of his clip and replacing it as quickly as possible as another bullet hit him in the arm. It stung like hell, but it was not enough to cripple him.

"To your right!" Jules screamed at him, making him follow the direction she had given.

His eyes found what she had seen. A man had brought a shotgun out from a bag underneath the table. Bending down and hiding himself behind a chair, Jax fired three shots at the shotgun-wielding man. Two hit him in the chest and a third in the head. A surprise even to himself that all three shots had hit their mark, and the man went down, lying unmoving upon the floor, dead.

From his vantage point, he could see that Jules was limping toward a downed patron and providing a final shot to the head. He watched her for a moment longer as she wobbled uneasily on her feet, and then she collapsed.

He rushed to her side, seeing blood slicking the outside of her black jacket. The clothing they wore provided some protection against bullets, but if she had been hit by a piercing round. That would explain her injury. Which also explained how they were able to kill the two executioners back on Septis Three. The bullets loaded in the guns they stole had this type of ammunition in them. "Some kind of piercing rounds," she said, holding her blood-stained hand up toward him.

There was no telling how bad it was. For all he knew, she was bleeding out on him right now. He could examine her, but there was no time for that. More armed people were probably coming for them at this very moment. "We need to get out of here," he said, taking her hand in his and helping her up.

"Could not agree with you more," Jules said with a grimace, now back on her feet. "Now hand me that shotgun," she nodded at the man he had shot down with a smirk.

He did as requested, and when he handed it to her, she was already placing the helmet back on her head. Jax followed suit before they both walked toward the exit of the lounge.

"As planned, we head back to the ship," Jules told him quietly as they moved despite all the pain in her body.

"Agreed," Jax nodded, "And once we are safely away from this place, you're going to have to explain how you could shoot so well back there."

Instead of replying to him, he watched Jules lift the shotgun to shoulder height and fire two shots at several men who had been running down the corridor toward them.

To his surprise, he found that neither of the men had been armed with any projectile-based weapons. Instead, they either had a knife or a baseball bat. What was the point of them even trying to assault them? Unless they were just pawns, intended to slow them down and waste resources.

By the time they had reached docking bay alpha, the door was sealed shut and a bullet ricocheted off the wall near them, making them flinch and bend down. Jax turned to see several armed men approaching from behind.

"Think there is a manual release on this door?" Jules asked, sounding a bit breathless as she looked around for the manual release.

Jax held her shoulder firmly and said, "No time. They will have us surrounded."

"So, what's the play?" Jules asked, turning to look at him.

"Follow me," Jax said. The only plan he could come up with was for them to go through the deconstruction zone. From the map he had observed earlier, it was right next to the bay. It was possible they could slip in from the other side of the bay.

The door protecting the deconstruction zone had some danger symbols posted and written warnings. He didn't care about any of that. Instead, he pressed the open button and was surprised when it slid open.

"Hey," he said, looking over at her through the helmet.

"What? No time to stop," she said.

Even her voice sounded weaker. Up ahead the walls had been stripped bare and all they could see in the working lights was an area of skeletal framing of metal beams that had once served as barriers to separate rooms and doorways.

Behind them, he could hear the banging and clanging of several people through the helmet's built-in audio devices. It seemed like several of them were following behind. He hoped this had been a good plan, otherwise they would be facing down probably about a dozen armed men.

"We need to pick up the pace," Jax told Jules, and to his surprise, she did. He knew that she was injured in several places and had probably lost a lot of blood, but she was still keeping pace with him, and for that, he admired her a lot.

They walked straight ahead, and it led them right into the open void of space. The outside wall of the station had been removed from here, and the shimmer of a force field could be seen, protecting them from the vacuum.

"I take it that this was part of your plan?" Jules asked, a note of appreciation in her voice.

Jax didn't have time to acknowledge her though. Instead, he was looking around trying to decipher their next plan of action. So far, he had spotted the generator providing the force field a few feet away and a series of lockers nearby. Taking Jules by the arm, he pulled her toward the lockers and opened them.

It seemed like luck was on his side today. The lockers contained space suits, tanks, and other tools workers needed to work out in space.

"Turn around," he said, pulling the tank from the locker and fastening it onto the back of her jacket. There was a hose attachment he plugged into place, and he could hear the audible "hiss" of the air rushing into her suit, except some of the air was rushing out the damaged section she had been wounded in.

In his mind, he knew that there should be some kind of tape he could use to patch over it. At least, that was always the case aboard the *Belt*. Barnaby had told him to always have a roll of duct tape on you, saying it could save your life one day.

It was great advice; except he had run out of time. Shots tore into his back and knocked him forward into Jules, who was barely standing up at this point. The only thing he could do was shove Jules into one of the lockers, take the shotgun, and kick the door closed behind him.

At hip level, he fired two shots into the force field generator. He could see several men around finding positions that covered them as much as they could, but when the force field went down, many of them had shot out into space as all of the atmosphere in the area suddenly exploded outwards. If Jax had not reacted quickly and grabbed the inside of the other locker, he would have been sucked out into space as well.

The shotgun had been sucked away, but that didn't matter. What he had to do next was to get the other oxygen tank connected to his suit before he could no longer breathe. Now, the tank was sucked tight to his chest, and he was using all his strength to keep himself in place. After about a minute and what felt like a thousand pushups, all the air had been expelled.

He quickly connected the hose and activated the tank. Fortunately for him, his suit had not been compromised, and it filled quickly with life-giving oxygen. Digging around in the compartments, he found a roll of duct tape, which brought a grin to his face. Barnaby had been right—every space monkey would have some on them.

"Thanks, Barnaby," he said to himself and drifted out of the locker and opened the one he had forced Jules into. She was still there, unconscious, and he could see a small stream of white vapor jetting from her suite. Placing several strips of duct tape over the area, he felt confident that he had sealed the breach. Next, after digging through the compartment above her head, he found some cords and attachments.

He used those to attach himself to her suit so he could drag her along in the now zero gravity. The way to get out of the station was easy and lucky for them both. There was a series of handholds that guided him right over to the outside docking bay. The outer force field was already down as a freighter ship was incoming.

As it passed overhead, the second force field lowered and gravity returned, so he was now dragging Jules behind him as they cleared into the docking bay. The ship was just ahead, and so far, no one else was in the bay other than the freight ship, which was landing far up ahead.

Pure luck had been on his side today—there was no other way to put it. The more he thought about his actions and what had just happened, he realized that there was lots of room for error. He couldn't quite congratulate himself though on a job well done yet. He still needed to get out of this place quickly.

It took Jax another couple of minutes to reach their ship and get the cockpit open. It took every ounce of his strength to lift Jules up and secure her into the back seat of the craft. She was still alive; he could feel the slight movement of her chest in his hands as he strapped her in. He took his place in the pilot's seat and quickly went through the lift-off sequence.

Still, it appeared no one was the wiser and when the craft lifted from the bay; the only thing he had to worry about was the force fields protecting the exit. Since he didn't have clearance, that left him with only one option—something he had been wanting to do since he had sat down in this chair. He pulled the trigger on the virtual stick and wasn't disappointed at the rapid-fire projectiles that tore through the interior of the station and took down the protective force fields in the area.

He was home free now as the craft lurched out into the freedom of space, but where could he run to? Where would be safe for them? Maybe he could communicate with Barnaby—he would know what to do. But then again, if he did that, he would be putting them at risk as well, and that was something he could not do.

What about the EDL? Jax thought to himself. Surely, the Earth Defense League would want to know what they had discovered. They could help them; except they couldn't go back to Septis Three.

He thought through all the options he had and at last decided on Earth for his jump destination. He put in the coordinates, and when a green light blinked on his virtual console, he jumped the ship.

Once the ship was set on the pre-planned pathway, Jax had the time to help Jules out. Removing his own helmet and tank, he did likewise to hers. Jules' face was pale and covered in a cold sweat. He felt her pulse and found it to be erratic and weak. She had lost a lot of blood, which meant that the wound must be more serious than they had realized.

Well, she was just going to have to forgive him, but to find the wound he was going to have to remove her jacket and shirt.

It took several seconds to find the open wounds on her abdomen. Blood was still trickling heavily as Jax rummaged around for the first aid kit. Once that had been found under his seat, he used the wound patch on her abdomen which would help seal any other blood leakage. The next thing he did was to pull out the auto doc wrist bracelet that was part of every medical kit now. It was a rather large metallic bracelet that snapped around her wrist and then tightened to fit skintight.

He could hear some audible thrumming and beeping noises from the auto doc as it went to work on her. The device was supposed to analyze her vitals, administer drugs if need be, and even contain a universal blood supply. The crew had spoken very highly about this miracle device, or at least that is what they had called it. There was even more pride in the fact that it was manufactured on Earth itself. A product of Doctor Hewitt Pascal, if he remembered right.

A green message scrolled across the top part of the bracelet.

"Patient's vitals need emergency care. Please contact an emergency medical team immediately," it read.

Great, Jax thought to himself. They were at least a couple of hours away from Earth.

"Hold on, Jules," he said out loud, taking hold of her hand, "We'll get you all patched up on Earth."

The pulse was at least reading stronger than it had been when he first placed the auto doc on her, but the more time that passed, the weaker it became. The emergency attention message never went off the screen.

That is, until she flatlined.

Chapter 4

"Locorran craft," a female voice said over the interior of his ship, "You are in the Earth Defense League-controlled space. Please leave immediately."

There was a tone of finality to that order. Jax wanted to respond back to it, but he watched as the auto doc administered a second round of shocks to get Jules' heart going again. The force of the jolt made her body lurch up, but the flatline continued.

His breaths felt choppy, and his entire body was covered in a mixture of sweat and blood as he remained facing Jules' body, whispering, "Come on, Jules, don't do this to me."

Another whine of the auto doc sounded as the charge built up, and then there was a third shock. Still no pulse.

"Locorran craft, this is Captain Diane Crown of the EDL. This is your last warning to leave our space," came the voice again, holding a similar no-nonsense tone.

Jax could hear the whining noise again. He had no choice now but to turn back around and deal with this Diane person and pray and hope that the auto doc could bring Jules back. Before speaking, he took a couple of deep breaths in an attempt to calm himself. He needed to be in control and not panicky.

Jax swiveled back around and immediately initiated contact with the EDL. "Captain Diane, my name is Jason Alexander Xavis. I am not from the Locorran empire. I am a fugitive on the run and my companion is in desperate need of medical attention. Can you please help us?" he said in a rush. There was no time for him to make up any kind of background story, and even then with how they looked, they would have been called out.

If telling the truth was the only way to get them to help Jules, he hardly cared what became of him. He had not known Jules for long, but her bravery and perseverance had trickled an admiration into Jax that he had never felt for anyone else, except for perhaps Captain Barnaby.

Jax thought he hadn't sounded desperate, but then he heard the auto doc shock Jules again. How many had that been? He had lost count by now.

"Locorran craft, you are to follow these coordinates exactly. Any deviation will result in our fighters opening fire upon you. Is that understood?" Diane stated over the intercom, making Jax pinch the bridge of his nose in relief.

When that feeling passed, Jax realized he no longer heard the auto doc preparing to shock Jules again. Heart in his throat, Jax turned halfway around to glance at Jules, noticing that the wrist device was displaying a pulse again. The tenseness left his body as he slumped in his chair as relief coursed through his veins.

"Everything is going to be alright," he said as he stared out of the cockpit at the barren and desolate wastelands of Earth.

The voice of Diane boomed in his cockpit again, "An emergency medical team is waiting to receive you upon landing. Do not abuse our trust or try to resist our personnel."

Will do, Jax thought to himself. If it wasn't for Jules' present condition, he would have made a straight shot for wild space and try to contact Barnaby. If anyone could help him figure out this mess, it would be him.

Diane had been true to her word. As soon as his craft touched the ground, emergency workers quickly pulled Jules from the back and got her into a vehicle. He couldn't see much after that as he had also been swarmed by medical technicians and then handcuffed once again. The second time in a week—he really was starting to feel like a criminal.

The journey from the landing field to the pure white cubical room they had placed him in was a complete blur. In fact, his vision and other senses seemed to be out of whack. One of the techs had to have injected him with something, perhaps a sedative of some kind. Either way, the way it was making him feel it would be nearly impossible to fight or much less remember how to get back to his craft.

Jax did not know how long it took him to come to his senses somewhat, but when he finally did, someone entered the room. He blinked away the blurriness from his eyes as the wall in front of him parted open and a young woman about his age with long blonde hair tied back stepped in. She was wearing a navy-colored jumpsuit and held a tablet-sized device in hand.

"How are you feeling?" she asked, taking a seat at the table across from him.

"Well, the drugs the techs gave me are finally wearing off," Jax said, staring at her eyes which were a deep shade of blue. Not as dark as the uniform, but a perfect tone that sucked you in. He couldn't help himself but look at her and admire her.

There was no expression on her face as she checked something off on the tablet she had brought in.

"How did you end up in possession of that Locorran craft?" she asked again in the same monotonous voice as if she was asking him what he wanted for lunch.

Jax contemplated the question. Should he make something up or tell the truth once again? He leaned forward, and to his surprise, the young woman didn't lean back or react. *Is she that confident in herself?* he thought.

"You must be Captain Diane?" he asked with a raise of his brow.

"I am," she stated, "Now, how did you acquire that Locorran ship?"

"I stole it on Septis Three," Jax said, deciding to go with the truth. They were already under scrutiny, if any lie was caught then these people would never trust him enough to help – which seemed like something he was needing quite a lot in recent days. With a sigh, Jax continued, "It was when the previous owners had tried to murder me and the woman I was traveling with, he paused. "Do you have information about her condition?"

"She is doing fine under our care. You are lucky you got her here when you did. Otherwise, she would have died on you," Captain Daine relayed the news with barely a twitch on her face.

"Thanks," he said as he leaned back in the chair. It felt like he could breathe easier knowing that Jules was taken care of. Here, she would receive the care she required.

"You said the occupants of the craft tried to murder you and the woman," Captain Daine's voice made the thoughts about Jules halt. She looked at him pointedly and asked, "When was this, and where on Septis Three?"

When he did not reply, she asked, "Is there a problem, Jason?"

"Call me Jax," he finally said after another couple of minutes of silence. "There's no problem. I was just wondering if I could give you a detailed account of what happened up to this point without interruption?" he said, sarcasm obvious in his voice.

She marked a couple of things on her tablet before nodding, "Okay, go for it. I will have questions for you at the end, I'm sure."

"I'm sure you will," Jax murmured back with a small shake of his head.

For the next hour, he told her everything he could remember, and true to her word, she sat back and said nothing. She merely made a few marks on the tablet here and there. When Jax finished, he asked for a glass of water, which had been brought promptly to him by another soldier in the same blue jumpsuit.

He was really surprised when she didn't ask him any questions immediately afterward. Instead, she had stayed focused on the tablet going over stuff.

"Crazy story, I know," he said, hoping to break the silence.

She looked him in the eye before saying, "It was indeed, Jax. I hope you told me the full truth."

"Scout's honor," Jax said with his hand raised high.

"Okay," she had a confused look on her face. "Whatever that means...?"

He had to think about it for a second—what it meant. He had said it and done the motion without any previous thought. So that had significance in itself.

"Sorry. Not sure what it means either," Jax replied with a shrug, and he was telling the truth. The gesture had felt like second nature to him and the words that rolled off his tongue felt like he was used to them. He was in his senses enough to know that it must be something to do with the past that he could no longer remember. There were these words and actions that came back to him without him even realizing and they made him feel a bit out of his body and creeped out. He wanted to either remember everything or nothing at all. These moments left him feeling out of sorts.

Captain Daine put the tablet down upon her lap and crossed her arms before saying, "When you are ready, I need you to tell me your story from the time you were handcuffed by the authorities on Septis Three to where you were before that in as much detail as you had provided me with previously, please."

Well, his big secret was about to come to light. He knew this day would come, but he had not realized that he would be telling this to someone like Captain Daine. At least he was home telling it and not stuck on an alien world where everyone wanted to kill him.

So, he began his tale as instructed, from the incident on Septis Three all the way back to when the crew of the *Orion's Belt* found him.

Sorry, Barnaby, he thought to himself. The tale had to be told. When he was finally done, Captain Diane stood up from the table and left the room without a word. He watched her go and he didn't want her to. He almost called out to her, but he maintained control of himself.

"Guess I scared her off," he said before lying back on his bed.

Chapter 5

At some point, he had fallen asleep at the table. How long he had slept, he was unsure of. In fact, he couldn't remember when he had last slept—had he lost consciousness for more than a day or two?

He blinked the drowsiness away, feeling a prickle of attention at the back of his neck. Sure enough, when he turned to his left, there was an old, wrinkled man staring at him.

"Who are you?" Jax asked, stretching his arms out over his head.

"I'm Doctor Hewitt Pascal," the man replied with a serene look on his face like he did not have a care in the world. "I've ordered you some juice and some breakfast, even though it's way past dinner time. I find it healthy to have a routine of eating breakfast foods at whatever time one wakes up," Doctor Hewitt went on to say.

They sat in silence as Jax tried to figure out why he was being scrutinized like this while Hewitt sat there, looking straight ahead with a mild expression on his face. Around five minutes later, a person brought in a pitcher of orange juice and a plate of bacon, eggs, sausage, and one pancake.

Jax took the plate a bit too eagerly, feeling his stomach rumble at the sight of food. For some reason, the food looked extra delicious. Even the syrup drizzled on the pancake was thin and runny with a pleasant smell to it.

"That's imported maple syrup from Canada," Hewitt said.

After the first couple of bites, Jax realized that the food was just as delicious as it looked. It was better than the slop he had been eating on the *Belt*. He wouldn't ever tell the crew that, but he was going to have to find a way to get some of this food aboard.

"Aren't you going to ask me some questions?" Jax asked around a mouthful of pancake.

Hewitt chuckled, waving his hand carelessly, silently telling him to continue eating. "It would be quite rude of me to do so while you are enjoying your meal. In fact, at the rate you are consuming it, I would hazard a guess that it has been several days since you have eaten."

Jax nodded his head as he took in a shovel full of the syrup-covered pancake.

"Besides, my questions can wait for you to be done. We have a lot to talk about, Jax. Diane told me that's what you preferred to be called, is that correct?" Hewitt asked with a tilt of his head. His beady eyes were still fixed on Jax, and normally he would have felt weird to eat while someone was watching, but at that moment, the needs of his stomach came way before his unease.

Jax nodded his head again just before gulping down his glass of orange juice. After a few more bites, he was finally done with everything, and another person came into the room to take his plates.

"Thank you," Jax told Hewitt with a polite smile on his face. To gauge the situation, he had to be nicer to the man who could just end his life in a moment if he wanted to. However, these people had allowed him to enter. They treated him and provided him with food. It was only fair he listened to what they had to say before making plans for an escape.

"You are quite welcome. Now, if you're up to it..." the doctor trailed off with a questioning look in his eyes.

Jax merely shrugged, "Fire away, Doc."

Hewitt leaned forward on the table, his probing gaze holding Jax's own as he said, "There is a lot about your story that you told Captain Diane that I can confirm. There are also some things I cannot. I'm not saying you lied or anything. It's the murky past that still haunts us here on Earth. Lots of records from before the Great War were destroyed or lost. And the fact that even you cannot fully recall your past is troubling to me."

Jax scoffed. "How do you think I feel? Every morning, I stare into the face of a stranger in the mirror. I have tried to keep a journal, so that I could put down anything I recall, but even that is very sparse."

Hewitt scratched his chin as he thought over his difficult situation. "I understand, Jax. I will try to help you with this," he stated firmly. "One thing I can help you with on this path of rediscovery is that I have found records that mention the *New Horizons* project." Jax sat up straight as Hewitt went on, "Apparently, it was a highly funded project by private investors who had wanted a faster method to colonize distant stars without going through the long hibernation period. All of this was going on with other off-world colony projects during the Great War. Unfortunately, I have no record of the crew or if the project ever took flight."

"It had to have. How else would I have gotten here?" Jax said, irritation clear in his voice.

"As stated before, I'm not accusing you of anything, Jax. I am just merely stating the facts that I have been able to confirm," Hewitt replied.

"Sorry," Jax said, filling another glass of orange juice from the pitcher that had been left behind on the table.

"It's quite alright," Hewitt waved him off again. "Now, what I do know is that the *New Horizons* project was founded in Florida, and from orbital surveys, it appears that much of the area where the facility is supposed to be located appears intact."

"Then that proves my story," Jax said.

Hewitt nodded his head. "To a certain degree, yes. How would you feel about a trip to that facility? It could help jog your memory some."

"You're kidding, right? Time out of my cell and a chance to revisit a place I know I have stood before. Sign me up," he said with a slap to the table.

"I will make it happen, Jax. Now relax the rest of the day, get plenty of fluids and sleep. I'll have someone bring you some reading material," Hewitt relayed, much to his disappointment. What would he even do being stuck inside this room for the entire day? Reading material—that would definitely put him to sleep.

As Hewitt got up from his chair and walked toward the door, Jax asked, "How is Jules doing?" He hoped she was on her way to a speedy recovery because since they had started this journey together, doing anything without her would not feel right. He scratched the back of his head as he asked, "Will she be able to go with me?"

Hewitt looked back at him with his shaggy white hair flopping down over his right eye, "She still needs more time to recover, but I will arrange for you to meet her soon."

Jax nodded, deciding to trust Hewitt on his word for now. He had not given any indication of foul play. However, he would keep a close eye on him because from what he had learned, no one could be trusted. He was willing to be proven wrong though.

"Thank you, Hewitt," Jax said before Hewitt could exit the room, "Thank you for believing me."

HEWITT GAVE HIM ONE last smile and walked out of the room, proceeded down the hallway until he got to another room. This door required him to place his palm against it and he also had to give a verbal voice command. When he got inside, it was a dark room with a table and a single, very focused light on where he took a seat.

"So, you do believe his story?" an unseen voice asked from the darkness.

"Yes, we were monitoring him closely for any lies or inconsistencies," Hewitt said, placing his hands on the table and interlocking his fingers with them.

"What about the unusual brain scan?" the unseen voice asked again, filled with suspicion.

"Not that unusual," he replied with a shrug, "There is evidence he has been exposed to the Locorran radiation, but he is definitely not under their control."

"His story and the girl's both prove your hypothesis about the Locorrans," the voice stated.

"It does indeed," Hewitt nodded, "Not that it makes me too happy, but it does mean I need more budget to help counter this."

"I've already gotten it approved. The council wants a working prototype on their desk yesterday," the voice said.

"Acceptable," Hewitt said. "You guys know me so well. I never sleep, always working on something."

The voice remained neutral as it replied, "That's why we keep funding you, doctor. So why are you pursuing this boy's past? It has no relevance to our current predicament, does it?"

"I couldn't disagree with you more. This boy's past could connect everything or nothing, but I'm compelled to pursue it. If anything, to fulfill my own curiosity," Hewitt said with a no-nonsense tone in his voice.

There was silence for a moment, and then the voice sighed, "As long as it doesn't impede your progress with our current problem."

"Definitely not. In fact, I already have a prototype I can bring to the council today, if you like," Hewitt said.

"How long were you going to sit on that, Hewitt?" the voice asked.

"If you remember, I brought you my suspicions years ago about the Locorrans and what they were doing. No one wanted to believe me then, because they were humans, but I see opinions are quickly changing," Hewitt said.

"Not as fast as I want," the voice said. "The truth of the matter is that we don't stand a chance militarily against them. They have far more ships and soldiers and now they have a foothold in our territory."

Hewitt paused for a moment, stroking the gray stubble on his face, "I have been trying to help with this problem as well and I too have no solution. That is why I need more information about our enemy."

"What are you asking, Hewitt?" the voice asked, tone serious and knowing.

"I want to take the boy with his friends from the *Orion's Belt* freighter back to where they found him. I think there are answers there," Hewitt said after a moment of silence.

"Done, Hewitt," the voice agreed, "I'll give you Captain Diane to meet your needs."

"Thank you," Hewitt said, standing up to leave the room.

Chapter 6

After Hewitt left, Jax felt the isolation of the room hit him tenfold. After he had woken up without any memories, he had gotten used to having the company of multiple people all at once on the *Orion's Belt*, and with his memories lost, he had never really spent much time in his own company alone.

The books that Hewitt had promised did come, but as Jax had expected, they did not hold his attention for very long. Hence, he took to pacing along the length of the room as different people brought him food to eat.

It must have been half a day since Hewitt left when the wall parted open again, and to his surprise, Captain Diane walked in. She was not dressed in her navy jumpsuit. Instead, she wore a nice light blue top and jeans with rips around the knees. In her hands, there was a bundle of something that she set down on the table.

"Got these for you from one of the local used shops. They still have a little smell, but should fit you," she said, tapping the bundle a couple of times.

"Thanks," Jax said, noticing that items inside the bundle were not more books like he had been expecting; instead, they were clothes. "Where are we going?" he asked. He was still on guard even though he had decided to trust these people.

"Doctor Hewitt thought it would be a good idea to let you out and about for a while," Captain Diane stated as if surprised by the order herself.

"On my own?" Jax asked in surprise.

"Of course not, Jax," she replied with a small chuckle. "For this evening it will be you and me on the town. Under the pile, you'll also find a datapad that Hewitt wants you to start using for your journaling."

"Not sure how to thank you, I've been going stir crazy in here," Jax said, as he went through the clothes on the table which consisted of a green two-button shirt and a pair of well-worn pants.

"You can thank me by not causing me any problems. Now get dressed," Captain Diane said walking back out of the room.

A night out on the town, he thought to himself. And in the company of Diane, how lucky could he be? Was this luck or was it possibly some plot to test him? What would they be testing him for though?

As Diane left the room for his privacy, Jax shook the thoughts out of his head and started changing his clothes. The need to get out of the room was more than his desire to be cautious, and so he decided to let loose for the moment.

The pants fit just right to his waist, but the legs, on the other hand, clung a little too tightly for his comfort. But he wasn't going to complain about it. He had never spent any time in New Chicago.

"Looks good on you Jax," Diane said, standing behind him. He hadn't even heard her come back in.

"It's great," Jax told her with a satisfied smile. "So where to first?"

"Have you ever been to New Chicago before?" Diane asked with her brows raised.

He shook his head, "The *Belt* spends most of its time delivering to the furthest out colonies."

"Well, there are definitely some things in New Chicago that you won't find anywhere else. So, come on! Hewitt has you on a curfew."

"Doesn't he know that I'm a few hundred years older than him?" Jax asked.

She looked back over at him with a teasing expression on her face. "I can bring that up to him if you would like."

"Never mind, he's probably already in bed," Jax huffed with a laugh, then blinked in quick succession. "That's if it's dark outside?"

"It's dark, and I doubt Hewitt is asleep. That man is always active, despite his advanced age. And you would do well to give him your respect," Diane said, looking at him.

Jax brought his hands up. "Sorry, sometimes I don't think about what I say."

"You were trying to be funny, I get it," she waved him off, "Now come on before we have to wait for another train."

Jax didn't say another word, just tried to keep up with her fast pace. In fact, by the time they came to a stop inside of the magnetic lift train, he had to take a couple of deep breaths because he was almost panting. After only a couple of days of rest, he could feel all the hard work he had put into his health going down the drain.

"Excellent," she said next to him. "We'll be on time to get a good seat."

"Are we going to a game or something?" Jax asked, keeping the excitement that he could feel creeping into himself.

"Of Course, the Cubs are playing baseball tonight," Diane said.

Baseball, baseball, he thought to himself. At last, an image of a tall, bearded man came to his mind. There had been a baseball in the man's hand, and he threw it at him, with a warm smile, followed by a deep laugh. And that was the end of the recall. Who had the man been? The first thought to pop into his head afterwards was the word Grandfather. Was that who he had just seen? It had to have been a moment out of his childhood, because the man looked so large to him. There was something else coming back to him at this moment, a distinct smell of some kind. After a moment of thought he knew exactly where he had smelled that scent before. It was the same scent Barnaby used in his beard—sandalwood.

"Hey," she said, touching his arm. "We're almost there; the next stop is ours."

He just nodded his head as his mind fumbled over the most recent recall. When he got back to his cell, he would have to journal this down, and no telling how much more would flow out. Perhaps his mind was ready to start sharing its secrets with him, at last.

"Come on," Diane said, taking his hand. Jax was glad that she did because just about everyone on the train was offloading and scrambling in the same direction that they were going. Once they exited out of the confines of the stairwell down to street level, he no longer felt the pressing of other bodies against his.

"Is it always this packed?" he asked.

Diane was still pulling him along toward the bright lights in the distance. She glanced back at him to say, "Most of the time." She pointed with her fingers to the elevated train tracks and explained, "The train runs through the center of the city, so everyone uses it for everything. Now let's pick up the pace. Don't want to be late for the first pitch."

Jax matched her pace, still hand in hand as they blazed through the commercial district of New Chicago. Vendors of all types were peddling their wares; everything from food to clothing was on display. It was quite a collage of smells and colors. When they reached the stadium, Diane fed two tickets into a machine, and they rushed through only to have to push their way through a crowd of more people.

At last, she led him out from the crowd and into the stadium that was now packed with cheering fans. They climbed up the stairs to a seat high up near the top.

"Well, what do you think?" Diane asked, finally letting go of his hand as they settled down in their seats.

"It's awesome!" Jax said, "I don't think I have ever been to a game before. Or at least that I can remember."

She looked at him with a hint of sympathy in her eyes. "I can only imagine how frustrating it is to not know about your past. I can relate to it because something like that happened to me in my own childhood." Jax was surprised to hear that and turned to look at her. She appeared more human now than she had on that first day when she had sat with her tablet and asked him all sorts of questions.

Diane saw him looking and immediately said, "By the way, this outing is not a date. Hewitt and the EDL wanted me to help you to recover your memories, and that is what I am doing."

Jax chuckled, focusing back on the pitch. "Never thought it was, and thank you, by the way."

"Welcome, and hopefully it's working," Diane said.

"I did have one little flashback on the train. It was brief, not much detail," Jax admitted.

She nodded her head at him, then jumped up with her hands in the air along with the crowd as they cheered.

What had he missed? Jax thought, blinking in confusion.

When Diane sat back down and looked at the confused look on his face, she finally filled him in with a laugh, "First home run of the night; the Cubs are going to win this year."

"Who are they playing against?" Jax asked.

"Tonight, it's the Texas Rangers, and take a look at that scoreboard—two to zero," Diane explained.

As the evening progressed Jax found himself getting into the game. There was a familiarity to it. Being in a crowd, the cheers, the emotions, everything felt familiar to him—the feelings of excitement when watching the team you were rooting for getting a victory. It felt like there were memories attached to those feelings, but once again none came to the surface. And the smell of food almost made him salivate. Fortunate for him, he didn't have to beg for whatever it was everyone was eating, because Diane bought one for herself and two for him.

"I hope you like hotdogs," Diane said, handing him his two lathered in some kind of brown chunky meat with onions on top.

He wanted to savor each bite, but instead scarfed both down before Diane had half finished her one. He couldn't help himself; it had been so delicious and familiar to him and that brought back even more images in his mind of sitting in a stadium like this and once again he was looking at the big bearded man that he now knew was his grandfather.

When the game was over, Diane led him away from the stadium in a gleeful mood as her team had won. Instead of heading back toward the train, though, she guided him into the tall circular building nearby. She went to a desk, flashed a badge, and the next thing he knew they were riding up an elevator with a glass view on the outside so that one could see the city almost in its entirety.

"Is this the place Jules is being cared for in?" Jax asked without any hesitation. He felt like he could communicate with Diane more casually since they had watched a game and had just screamed together at the players.

"Yes, and from the last update I received, she is recovering very well. I thought you might want to check in on her," Diane said.

"Absolutely," Jax nodded, "I've been worried about her. I honestly thought she was going to die on me, back in the fighter."

The elevator came to a stop and they both exited out onto a hallway with a man standing guard nearby. Diane didn't even have to flash her badge at him as they approached. Instead, the guard did a quick salute.

"At ease, Bradley," she said. "I have permission for Jax to see the patient."

The guard nodded his head at them and then used a key card to unlock the door to Jules' room.

"Go ahead, Jax," Diane nodded her head at the door, "I'll be waiting out here for you when you're done talking."

He took a few cautious steps into the room, realizing most of it was dark, except for the bed in the center of the room where Jules was sitting up, awake, and now staring at him.

"You slick dog, Jax," she said with a small smirk on her face, "You come to rescue me?"

"Not exactly, Jules," he said, walking into the room and shutting the door behind him. "How are you doing?" he asked, placing his hands on the rails of her bed.

"Much better, now they have let me start walking around some. I was getting tired of watching news about the soon to be Locorran empress coronation ceremony. They were showing off the dresses she would be wearing and of course constantly talking about the suitors that had been chosen for the upcoming games," Jules said with a frustrated look on her face.

To be honest she did look better. The last time Jax had seen her, she had flatlined and her face had been pale white, like it was drained of all blood. He had been so scared that something would happen to her that now seeing her sitting up in bed, talking, and smiling, made his body sag with relief. And he knew about the empress coronation, but this was his first-time hearing about the suitors and some kind of games. Of course, he hadn't been getting any news like she had recently.

"At least they allowed you to watch something," Jax said, "I've been stuck in a bright white cube for the past couple of days and wearing a gown that shows my ass to everyone."

"Well, you're not in it now, so what happened?" Jules asked.

"Hewitt happened. He got the EDL to let me roam around, under guard of course. I think in an effort to help me to recover some memories," Jax replied with a shrug.

"That's nice of them. All they have done is question me over and over about the incident on Septis Three and our little misadventure on the outpost," she sighed then sat up straight as if she remembered something. "Jax, I think they already knew about the secret of the Locorrans," she whispered, wide-eyed, looking at the camera in the corner of the room.

He didn't know if it could record voices, so Jax moved in closer, just in case, and whispered back, "From my conversations with them, I know they do know the Locorrans pose a threat, but they are afraid to take action against them."

She gripped his hand on top of the rail. "The Locorrans must be stopped before we all become mindless zombies."

"You know I agree with you, Jules, and the EDL is working on it, but they are having to tread carefully," Jax said.

"Any ideas on what they are going to do with us?" Jules asked, squeezing his hand tightly.

Hell, he didn't know the answer to that question, did he? The only thing that made sense to him logically was that they would have to keep them quiet about what they knew about the Locorrans. And the only way to accomplish that was either to keep them locked up or kill them. He doubted they would kill them.

"I really don't know, Jules," he said with a shrug, "All I know is that we are alive and still talking."

Jules used her other hand to grab his arm and pulled him down closer so that she could kiss him on the cheek. "I owe my life to you, Jax. Thank you. We both did a stupid thing by going to that outpost, but we got answers and the truth."

Jax nodded, a small smile gracing his features as he placed his other hand on top of hers. "We did, so it wasn't foolish. And by the way, where did you learn to handle guns like that? You had better trigger control than most of the crew of the *Belt*. Of course, with the exception of Kell and Piper."

"Both of my parents served and died in the EDL, Jax," she said with a small nostalgic smile on her face.

"I didn't know. I'm sorry," Jax whispered, head hanging low.

Jules shook her head and sighed. "I was lucky that I had them as long as I did, honestly. It's only been about two years since they died. A lot of EDL kids lose their parents or parents far earlier. I was lucky, I scored high enough to get into the college programs. Didn't have to serve."

"Still, though, I am sorry," Jax replied, pressing his lips together in a flat line. While he did not remember his own parents, he could understand how hard it must have been for Jules to go through. His heart ached for her and all the things she had gone through until now.

The door to the room opened suddenly and a nurse came in with a cup of pills in hand. "Sorry, but you two are going to have to cut it short. Visiting hours are over and the young miss needs to get some sleep," she announced.

Jax looked at the nurse for a moment and then back down to Jules. "I guess that's my cue to leave."

Jules didn't let go of him though, holding his hand tighter as she said, "I don't want you to. I feel safer with you around, and besides, you make good company."

"This won't be the last you see of me, I promise," Jax reassured her.

Jules took a deep breath and softened her hold on his hand before playfully warning him, "Better not be, or I will escape from this place and hunt you down."

"That thought does terrify me, Jules. I know how you handle guns," Jax replied with a chuckle.

She released her grip on him, and he backed away from her. Was there something beginning to form between them? Other than the life and death situation, did she want to get more familiar with him?

When Jax exited back out into the hall, Diane came up beside him.

"Everything okay in there?" she asked.

"Great," he replied and walked toward the elevator.

When the elevator door closed and it was just him and Diane alone, he turned to face her. "What is the EDL going to do with me and Jules once they are done with us?"

Her blue eyes were locked with his when she replied, "I'm not sure, Jax. If I had to guess they will probably try to force you and Jules into service. You're both young enough and have some skills. But if your worry is that they might kill you for silence, that's not something the EDL does."

"Will they turn us over to Septis Three? I noticed one of the monitors in Jules' room was still displaying the events there and showing our pictures. I've heard stories about the Septis penal system, and I don't think that either me or Jules will survive long there," Jax said. Remembering what he heard aboard the *Belt*, stories from Piper about the Septis Penal system and how brutal it was. And she would know, since she had been a convict once.

"With Hewitt's interest in you, I really don't see any reason why they would turn you over to them," Diane replied as truthfully as she could.

"You have that much confidence in Hewitt?" Jax asked.

"I do," Diane said without hesitation.

Jax kept his gaze locked upon hers for a moment before saying, "I trust you, Diane." He wanted to keep looking at her, but they had arrived at the bottom floor, and she took the lead once again as they pushed through the throngs of people waiting for the train. They rode in silence, but on their walk back to his bright cell, she stopped along the hallway.

"Would you want this kind of life, Jax?" she asked, curiosity coloring her voice.

"What, serving the EDL?" Jax asked with a mirthless chuckle.

Diane nodded her head, looking at him earnestly.

"I don't know," Jax said, "I'm missing my friends aboard the *Belt*. It would be a hard transition, but if my options were limited, I would consider it."

"With Hewitt's help, we could make it happen," Diane suggested, "Give you a new record and name."

"Why would he do that, though?" Jax asked.

"He would if I asked him," Diane said. "Just think about it, Jax."

Why had she even mentioned this to him? Jax didn't even realize they had made it to his cell when the door parted open. He gave her one final glance before walking in only to realize that she had been watching him.

"Good night," Jax said as the wall closed behind him.

He had so many questions and the entire night to think over them. One, of course, being what Diane had just talked to him about. Could he give up life with his friends aboard the *Belt*? They were the most familiar thing to him since waking, but then the thought of being close to Diane, and perhaps something more, filled him with exciting possibilities. He would leave his thoughts about her out of the journal for now, because he was certain that others would be reading it, but he was going to jot down everything he could remember about his grandfather.

Walking over to his cot, he took the journal Diane had brought him and began writing.

62

Chapter 7

Jax was awoken the next morning by an armed soldier bringing food and juice to him. He was uncertain about the time since he hadn't had access to a watch, but so far, today felt like a normal day. It just sort of felt right about the time he would've woken on the *Belt*. The only thing different from his usual routine however was the fact that before eating, he liked to exercise first thing in the morning. He hadn't tried to do it yet here, because by the time they brought him his meal, he was already ravenous.

Devouring the breakfast quickly, he sat back sipping on the orange juice, enjoying the rich pulpy texture of it. It didn't taste like what he had remembered. This tasted fresher and perhaps cleaner to him. He couldn't quite explain it to himself.

Jax hoped that he would see Captain Diane today because her presence was comforting and soothing to him. He had felt this way since the first day when he had spilled his entire life story to her.

In his next encounter with her, he hoped to learn more personal things about her. Maybe he'd find out what part of Earth she was born on.

In the quietness of his white-walled prison that always stayed bright, he could hear boot steps near his door. They didn't sound as heavy as the man's steps who had delivered breakfast to him. These steps were lighter. He put the orange juice back down on the table and leaned forward curiously. *With luck, it might be Diane,* he thought to himself.

The door opened, and as he had hoped, Diane stepped in. She was wearing full camo gear, with lots of extra belts and clip attachments. "I'm glad to see that you ate your breakfast quickly," she said in lieu of greeting, "I have two recon specialists meeting us in the hangar at seven hundred." She glanced down at the device strapped around her wrist and continued, "That gives you five minutes to put these on." With that, she threw a backpack at him and then set a similar wrist device down on the table.

"Do I get to at least pick my color?" Jax asked. He was ready to get out of the room, and he was grateful that it was Diane who would accompany him again.

Diane didn't even smile when she turned away from him and walked back out the door. She had a hard exterior to crack through, but it would be worth it. She was probably the most beautiful woman he had ever met. Jules was gorgeous, but something about Diane was gripping.

While they were in the stadium, he had seen some of her masks slipping as she allowed herself to enjoy the moment. He wished to see more of that happen again.

Jax would just have to try harder for that to happen, and in order to do that, he needed to get dressed quickly. It was obvious to him that Diane was a very well-disciplined woman. Otherwise, she would have never risen to the rank of Captain.

Hell, he couldn't even imagine himself being in the military at a younger age, much less being put in charge of a bunch of people.

He pulled the clothes out of the pack, noticing that they were identical to the ones she had been wearing. He had been thinking about this day for a while now since Doctor Hewitt had first mentioned this outing to him.

He was going to see his home on Earth at last. It would be the first time since before the Great War. There were still a lot of details and rumors about that conflict. None of the *Belt* crew had the exact story about how it happened or why. The one thing they all agreed upon was the fact that it happened and all of them had said it took place about three hundred years ago. That at least gave him something to go by. Perhaps while he was at home, he could pick Hewitt's obvious intellect and learn what he knew about it.

The door opened again, and Diane came in with arms clasped behind her back. "I thought you would have been ready by now."

Jax had put his pants on, but he was still shirtless when she came in. In the back of his mind, he was wondering if she had done this on purpose. Perhaps for a little peep show.

The look on her face bore no expression, though, which probably came from long practice, but as he put the rest of his clothes on, it nagged at him that she might have done it with intent. If that was the case, then there was a chance that he could make her his.

"Don't forget the wrist device," she reminded, handing it to him from the table.

"Looks a little fancy for a wristwatch," Jax commented as he put it on.

"You are correct," Diane nodded, "This device does more than just telling time. It tracks your movements, heart rate, and so on. Another handy device created and manufactured by Hewitt Industries."

"So, the doctor is quite a jack of all trades, and from the look of it, he has some serious pull with the EDL," Jax stated, highly impressed with Hewitt. The man kept surprising him every passing day.

Diane looked down at her wrist device before saying, "We need to get moving." She ushered him out of the room and as they walked down the white hallways she spoke again, "The doctor has proven to be a valuable asset, not only to humanity but to the EDL. He firmly believes in restoring humanity back to its full dominance once again."

"Then they must be working hard against the Locorrans, then," Jax commented off-handedly.

Diane glanced over at him for a brief second before saying, "I do believe what you told us was true about the Locorrans. I have seen and heard other evidence in the past." She stopped in the hallway and looked around before drawing herself closer to him.

Jax could feel her breath on his face as she spoke, "The real problem with the Locorrans is the fact that they are superior to us in every way. They have a mighty military force and superior technology, and they are all unified under one banner. If we were to call for war today, half of our own colonies would turn against us and not the Locorrans. Evidence has been leaked to our other colonies over the last couple of years, but many of them just ignore it."

"Is it because of the technology?" Jax asked, intrigued by what she had told him.

Her blue eyes locked with his. "Because the Locorrans look like us. They act like us to some degree, but most importantly, they offer solutions to every colony's problems. They don't turn to us. In fact, many see us as more of a problem than a solution to anything."

If all of this was true, and he had no doubt that was the case, then the Locorrans were winning a culture war. "So, what is the EDL going to do about it?" Jax asked.

"That is above my pay grade," Diane said, "I know for sure that I dread the day I have to go into combat against the Locorran empire."

They spent the rest of their trip in silence, which was good, considering that his mind was whirling with the implications of what he had just learned. If the Locorrans were winning, then how long before all of them would become their slaves?

Outside of the facility they had been keeping him in, he came out into the sun-filled day of an Earth morning. The wind was blowing, and there was a chill to it, but the freshness of the air and the warmth of the sun felt good on his face. Somehow, it felt like home to him.

"It feels great to be home again," he said, basking in the warmness provided by the sun and still walking beside Diane, who didn't stop but was glancing over at him.

"Are you remembering anything about your life on Earth, before you left?" she asked.

Jax shook his head. "Not much. I did remember some moments with my grandfather, especially at the baseball stadium. That was the most recall I've had since being back awake, so thank you for that, Diane."

Diane gave him a glance and a smile. "I'm glad to hear it, Jax."

"While I was still on the *Belt* and desperate to get even a clue about myself, I let Kell try to hypnotize me. Of course, this was out of desperation."

"How did that go?" she asked.

"Not sure he was the most qualified person to try it," Jax shrugged and let out a laugh before continuing, "Cause according to him, my mind was as blank as a room with no lights."

"I don't think that is possible," Diane said. "So, I'm sure Kell just didn't know how to do it right. Give Doctor Hewitt some time, and he will come up with more ideas on how to help you."

Jax nodded his head as they kept walking side by side. "He has already said as much to me."

Diane glanced at him again. "I'm sure that will be a great relief to you."

"You have no idea how great it would be," Jax said.

She was looking at him with her mouth parted open as if she was going to speak, but a noise from up ahead drew her attention and she pointed at the craft flying low over the horizon and landing directly in front of them.

"This is our ride," Diane said, gesturing at him to follow her as she ran ahead.

The side door of the craft opened, and the barking of a dog could be heard from the inside.

"KJ," a bushy-bearded man said from the opening, "Keep it down, KJ. We are picking up guests."

The dog quickly quieted down, and the bearded man ushered them into the craft. "Name's Henry," he said, saluting Diane, who had boarded first.

Sitting on the other side of the craft and looking at them was a younger man, dressed like them and sporting a very sparse black beard. The dog looked like a Labrador to Jax, but for some reason, he could not recall for certain. He was sitting on all fours at the man's feet.

"The mangy mutt on the floor is specialist KJ," Henry said, pointing at the dog. "The sack of shit next to him is recon specialist Kyle Crayton." The young man smiled at them as he nodded his head in acknowledgment.

"Thank you, gentlemen, for being available on such short notice," Diane said.

"It was no problem, Captain," Henry said as he sprang into action. "Now, if you two take a seat and strap in, we'll get underway. It's best if we can get this operation underway during the daylight. There are a lot of nasty things that prowl around at night, and I don't want us to be caught out in that."

Henry had pointed at him and Diane to take seats directly across from KJ and Kyle. The strap system was simple, and he had his belts clicked in place in no time. "So, Henry," Jax said, "You said there's a lot of nasty things at night. Like what?"

Henry locked eyes with him. "Is this your first time on Earth?"

"No, I was born and raised here," Jax said. "A couple of hundred years ago," he added with a shrug.

Henry broke eye contact and looked over at Diane, who nodded her head in acknowledgment. "Well, where to start?" he said, shaking his head. "Let's put it this way. After the Great War, high levels of radiation ran rampant throughout this planet. What creatures that did survive had a forced evolution. Many adapted to the new and harsher conditions, like the crocodile and alligator. Some others though became stranger and nastier with each evolution, like the Reapers."

KJ barked at that name, and it took Henry several pats on the head for him to calm down, "Sorry about that. KJ gets a little excited when I talk about those. Let's just say its name says everything about it. They are large, quick, and deadly. Also intelligent. Many recon specialists have lost their lives to those things."

"Do they mostly live in one geographical area or many?" Jax said, hoping that the answer would be only one type of area.

Henry was shaking his head as he spoke. "At first, we found them out in the wilds of California. No one at that time had reported them anywhere else, but as time went on, more and more of them have been discovered in just about every type of area and environment."

"Do you think we will have any problem with them where we are going?" Diane asked.

"No, from the aerial surveys we have been given, that part of Florida is mostly swampy now. From our observations, the Reapers and alligators don't like each other," Henry said.

"Did the radiation do anything to the alligators?" Jax asked, getting more cautious about the trip ahead.

The younger man, Kyle, laughed before Henry spoke. "All it did was make them bigger and meaner. No worries, though, we know how to handle them, so where we are going should be pretty safe."

Pretty safe, Jax thought to himself. That didn't sound comforting to him at all. In fact, it was just a reminder to him that his home had become a very dangerous place.

Kyle pulled out a cloth pouch from inside his jacket, pulled out a wad of black stringy stuff and placed it in his mouth. Then he extended it toward him.

"What is it?" Jax asked, looking at the pouch and its contents.

Henry answered, "Kyle's family grows tobacco. Some really good tobacco. Give it a try."

He couldn't recall ever having tried the stuff before. It almost felt forbidden to him, but that didn't stop him from taking some and placing it in his mouth anyway.

"Remember," Henry said. "Don't chew or swallow. Let it sit on the outside of your gums. You'll need to spit out the juice."

Kyle then turned the open bag toward Diane, who merely shook her head after just a glance, then asked, "How about a cigarette or cigar?" she asked.

"Why, captain," Henry said. "Didn't know we had a rebel on board."

"Not a rebel," she said. "Just because the EDL frowns upon the substance, doesn't mean it's forbidden. In fact, many officers smoke when not on duty."

Kyle had replaced the cloth bag back into his jacket pocket and was rummaging around in another until he pulled out a thick cigar and offered it up to her. "Another specialty from my family farm," he replied with a little smirk on his face.

Kyle watched Diane take it with a smile on her face. "Thank you," she said, placing it inside one of her many pockets, "Now let's get down to business."

Jax didn't really think she was going to smoke it. Perhaps she had some other uses for it. Just when he thought that a short little flash of two men sitting in a cell together playing cards passed through his mind. Instead of money in the pot, there were cigarettes. In the next moment, the image was gone from his mind, but he was certain it was from a show or movie he had watched in his past. This was something else he would have to remember to write down in his journal when he got the chance. And perhaps that little insight was also what Diane might use the cigar for. After all, he had no idea how they got paid or how the EDL worked at all.

"Okay, captain," Henry nodded, "You got the floor."

Diane leaned forward toward them, and KJ instinctively moved closer to her, so she could rub the top part of his head. "When we arrive at the location, Hewitt wants us to record everything and snag any hardcopies and computer units we see lying around." She glanced at Henry and Kyle pointedly before continuing, "Both of you received the images and other details I sent you the day before. Those were samples of what Hewitt said we should be looking for."

"Got it, captain," Henry said. "Kyle and I have been on many of these scavenger hunts. We know what Hewitt is looking for."

"Good," she said, nodding her head. "Hewitt told me he wanted you two specifically for this assignment."

"That was nice of him. So, when is he going to be taking over the EDL?" Henry asked with a raise of his brow.

"He's way too old for that," Diane said. "Besides, the EDL needs an outsider like Hewitt in order to get things done."

"That's for certain," Henry said. "I once requisitioned a pair of boots from supply. It took them three months before the red tape cleared for them to give it to me. By that time, I had resorted to stuffing my boots with cotton and sealing up the holes with sealant tape."

Kyle was smirking over at them and pointing down at his boots, which looked exactly like what Henry had just described. "Four months and counting for me."

The tobacco in Jaxs mouth was starting to burn a little and the taste of it was like a mixture of mint and an ashtray. At this point, he couldn't understand why anyone would enjoy this.

"Judging by your face," Kyle said looking at him. "You're not enjoying your chew. Give it a few more minutes."

In honesty, Jax didn't think he could stomach it for a few more minutes. He truly tried, but the tobacco was too strong for him. He shook his head one final time and spit it all down on the floor with a cough.

"It's not for everyone," Henry said from the front, trying to make Jax feel better somehow. Jax was just glad to have whatever that was out of his mouth.

After a while of traveling in relative silence, the lights in their section went to a red color, and he could feel the craft changing course and descending now. Within a minute everyone was unbuckling from their seats as the craft had come to a stop on the ground.

"Let's go," Diane said, throwing open the door and letting Henry and Kyle take the lead. The buckles gave him a struggle, and it was embarrassing when Diane came over and helped him out. "Next time you make me do that, I'll have you clean that shit off the floor with your bare hands," she said, pointing down at the wad of chew on the floor.

There seemed to be a smirk on her face. It was faint, but he got the impression that she was kidding around with him. That was a good omen for him. Now he just had to see how far she would be willing to take things from him. What should he ask or do though? It wasn't like he was entirely a free person with the EDL, yet. At least that could quickly change though. Doctor Hewitt appeared to have a lot of pull with the EDL.

"Come on," Diane said, grabbing his jacket sleeve and pulling him along.

"You two coming?" Henry called out to them from up ahead, waving his arms to get them moving. Jax gave his own wave to signal to him that they were on their way.

When Jax finally jumped down from the craft, he could see that it had landed on a road in the middle of a jungle. Tropical trees were growing all around him reaching toward the sky. It all felt so very familiar to him like he had seen such a place before. It was beautiful, warm and perfect. This was where he wanted to be.

"I know you are taking it in," Diane's voice filtered through the haze that had come over his mind. He turned to her when she continued, "I wish I could give you some time, but we are on a deadline, and as they told us, we do not want to be caught out here at night."

He took in the sight one last time and then marched on to where Henry and Kyle were still waiting with KJ in tow. The building up ahead was large, covered with vines and other fauna. As soon as they had cleared away from the craft, it took back off and began circling around them overhead. From his observations, it had some weaponry on the front end. He guessed in case they needed some extra firepower to deal with whatever harm might come their way.

Before they reached the main building, Henry was standing a few feet away from a tall black marble monument placed on a stepped dais near the entrance. He had a device out and was focusing on it while Kyle and KJ kept probing around the outside of the building.

"This is an interesting memorial," Henry said. "Take a moment to read it." Then he moved off heading toward the main entrance of the building ahead.

Jax and Diane looked at each other, and then with a shrug, they both crossed the distance to stand side by side to read it.

To the future generations, my name is Theodore Bailey. On September 4, 2150, I left Earth for the stars. I didn't want to leave my home, but under the circumstances, I saw no hope in staying. If humanity does survive, I'm sure I would be considered a coward. In truth, I am. The looming war, poverty, and destruction that was all around me was an example of how humanity had gone wrong. I left Earth with the goal of never repeating our mistakes again. Hopefully and with luck, I will return to my home and find it beaten and battered, but unbroken as the human spirit prevails. To those survivors, I salute you. You had the courage to face what I could not.

It is my hope and wish that those of you who do survive the storm get all the knowledge you need to rebuild and forge ahead. And who knows, one day, we might meet. To the survivors, I leave a vault on my farm at these coordinates. Inside that vault, you will find knowledge and even the path to find the rest of humanity amongst the stars. Good luck and God bless.

TB

Jax reread it again just to make sure he was not missing any details and wondered if the information would bring out some sort of memory he had forgotten. When nothing happened, he turned to Diane, who was busy with a tablet device, trying to pull up more information. If Jax had to guess, she was trying to find the coordinates mentioned on it. When he focused on the name of the person who wrote this, it seemed familiar to him somehow, but like everything so far, it was right there on the cusp. He knew it, but there was something blocking him from fully coming to consciousness.

As if Diane could understand what he was thinking, she spoke up. "Bailey was the leader and founder of *New Horizons*. That much we know. As for the coordinates, it would take us about an hour to travel to the northeast to reach."

"Should be worth investigating," Jax said with a shrug, even though inside, he was itching to unravel the mystery of his past.

"I agree with you," Diane nodded seriously. "It might have to wait for another day, though. Time is not on our side."

Jax just nodded his head in agreement. He did not want to tangle with a Reaper if both Henry and Kyle were terrified of them. He followed Diane as they headed toward the large open bay of the building.

"This must have been a hanger of some type," she commented, looking at the building up and down assessing it from every angle.

There were no crafts inside the bay, just hunks of rusting machinery that didn't look like they had worked for centuries. Kyle and Henry had continued forging ahead and he could see the bobbing and weaving of their lights attached to their rifles.

"Any memories yet?" Diane asked, looking at him from the corner of her eye as they walked side by side.

"None," Jax said. "I was hoping I would have a flashback or something. That has happened before in the past. I feel like I should know this place, but there's something there barring the information."

"It's alright," she said, touching his arm lightly. Still, the touch excited Jax as tingles ran up and down his arms. He shook his head to focus on his surroundings. His feelings could be dealt with later.

Henry, Kyle, and KJ were approaching them quickly from the office area. They had wandered ahead and now they were coming back towards them which meant they probably had not found anything substantial.

His guess was proven when Henry said, "This place has been stripped clean, no computers and no hard copies of anything left. It doesn't look like the work of scavengers. It's more than likely this place was cleaned out before the war."

"I was hoping we could find something here," Diane added with a sigh, then perked up before saying, "I pulled up the coordinates mentioned on the memorial on the outside. It's about an hour to the northeast."

Henry and Kyle both looked at their watches attached to their wrists. "That's doable," Henry said, sharing a knowing glance with Kyle.

Kyle pressed a device to his right ear and said, "We need a quick pick up," he told the pilot of the craft and then waved everyone to follow him on the way back. Jax was disappointed because he had been hopeful about finding something important. Still, there were the coordinates they had been given. Perhaps there was something salvageable still left here.

They evacuated the premises together and came outside to see that the craft was coming in low over the top of them. It flew ahead and set down a few yards away. None of them spoke as they ran to reach the opened doors, climbed back in, and took their seats. The craft didn't even wait for them to confirm that they had all buckled in before it was already flying away.

"Well, that was interesting," Henry said.

"What was?" Jax asked. As far as he knew, there was not anything remotely interesting back there except for the information about the coordinates.

"That memorial left behind was built after the *New Horizons* project had launched," Henry said.

"I take it that you found evidence of that?" Diane asked while Jax nodded in understanding. He had been one of the people who had been on *New Horizons*. He wondered who had built the monument. Was there a chance that someone he had known was behind it?

Henry nodded his head and sat back, lacing his fingers behind his head as he talked. "On the back side of the memorial toward the bottom was a date of construction, which was also confirmed by someone writing their name and date on the newly poured cement. Kyle found a plaque on the inside set into the cement flooring denoting the construction date of the facility. There was a thirteen-year gap between the two."

"Good work," Diane said, impressed by what they had found. "Now let us hope we hit pay dirt at the farm."

"That's if it hasn't already been looted," Kyle said, lounging back in his seat.

Nothing more was said between them as the craft quickly shot back up into the sky, pinning Jax to his seat so tight that he couldn't lift his arm up. Either the craft was designed without interior compensators, or the pilot didn't know how to use them. He was guessing that the craft probably wasn't equipped with it. KJ who wasn't buckled in was pressed hard to the floor and whimpering loudly. It was a full two or three minutes before the craft leveled out and Jax could finally move his body again.

The door at the front of the craft opened, allowing some of the sunlight to pierce in. "We have a bad storm brewing up ahead, captain," the pilot said. "What are your orders?"

He could see that Diane was looking toward the cabin now. There was a brief pause as if she was giving it some thought and then spoke, "Keep going."

Jax did not want to stop either because the sooner they got there the sooner they would have answers—if there were any to begin with.

"Roger," the pilot said. "I'll keep you informed if it gets worse."

As if on cue, he could hear something making little clanging noises on the exterior of the craft hull.

"What's that?" Jax said, suddenly feeling uncertain that Diane had made the right call.

"Sounds like ice droplets," Henry said. "Nothing to worry about, unless we get caught in one of those super rare microbursts."

Jax could see that everyone was now looking at Henry as if for an explanation. He turned his bewildered stare towards Henry as well.

"Look, there's nothing to worry about," Henry said with his hands held up in front of him. "I have only ever seen one once in my whole life."

Jax eased his grip from the armchair handles a little. He hadn't realized how hard he had been digging in when the craft was being pushed about. It still was, but for some reason, he felt calmer about it.

That feeling of ease however was quickly robbed from him as something loud struck the craft. The lights in the bay went off and the smell of smoke suddenly filled his lungs.

Henry and Kyle both immediately turned on their personal lights, and within their beams, he could see a portion of the craft toward the back smoking and charring.

The pilot was shouting from the cabin, "Everyone stay seated! We are going to have to make an emergency landing."

Jax could feel the craft lurching around him. He was being buffeted side to side, and no matter how much force he exerted to keep himself stationary, he was still overpowered. The others did not appear to be faring any better than him, either.

"Touching down," the pilot shouted as everyone else held on for dear life.

Jax was thrown forward at the landing, and he could hear the wrenching metal-on-metal sound as the craft skidded awkwardly to a final stop. The smoke had grown thicker in Jax's surroundings and with every breath he took, there was more smoke than fresh air, which developed feelings of suffocation inside his lungs, and he started to cough.

"Everyone out," Diane said, even as coughs wracked her body, already standing in front of him.

Jax fumbled with the buckle, but Diane took over and grabbed him up by his thin, layered jacket.

The coughing fits had robbed his senses and thoughts. His body was moving on autopilot as she escorted him out of the craft and into a downpour of cold rain.

Diane was coughing as well, but not as deeply as him now. Somehow, she still had the capacity to speak. "You okay?" she said, leaving him hunched over in the mud, coughing as rain poured all around them and over them. Both were drenched in seconds.

Jax managed to nod his head in acknowledgment, but Diane was already on the move, like a woman in command should be. He could see her taking charge of the situation.

"Left side engine was hit," he could hear Henry saying over his own coughing and the hard pattering of the rain hitting the ground around him.

"How long will it take to fix?" Diane asked.

The pilot was next to the area that had been struck by lightning, from the looks of it. There was a long, charred streak that still seemed to be smoking.

"About an hour to get us airborne again," the pilot commented with a frown, "Even without that engine working."

"Fine," Diane said. She was already looking at the tablet device she had been carrying around. "Looks like we are only a few kilometers away from the farmhouse. I suggest we hike it there."

"That's doable, captain," Jax could hear Henry say in response. "We should still have enough daylight."

"Let's waste no more time, then," she said and Jax could feel her take him by the back of the arm. "You up for a hike?"

With a lighter cough, he stood up straighter and nodded his head at her.

"Good," she said. "Let's move out. Henry, Kyle, take the lead."

They flanked out into the woods, with KJ wagging his tail as he sprinted ahead of all of them. The trees at least helped reduce some of the rainfall that had been smacking Jax hard in the head and face earlier. The coughing had eased up, and he was finally able to breathe more normally again. Although their surroundings had gotten colder due to the rain, it was a good atmosphere for hiking.

They walked under the canopy of the trees, and the most prominent sounds around them were the sound of their own footsteps as they stepped over dry, fallen leaves and broken twigs. Jax tried to listen to any kind of insect or animal that could be there but all he heard, other than their footsteps, was the pitter-pattering of rain as it fell upon the trees and slowly made its way down.

After a few miles of walking, they could see the tree line coming to an end up ahead. It looked like a wide-open field, and Diane was the first one to point out the farmhouse to the far-right side of the field.

"Almost there," she said, breathing heavily as she finally let go of the back of his arm. "Get your weapon ready."

Jax wasn't sure why she had said it, but what he had missed up ahead was both Henry and Kyle looking down at something in the tall grass of the field. He couldn't see it until he had gotten right up next to them. By that point, Kyle was poking and prodding at the remains of some kind of large animal that had died there.

"Well?" Diane said. She had her T-15 already in hand and was using the scope to examine the area around them.

"Definitely a Reaper," Kyle said. "There is no missing the distinctive rips and tears in the flesh."

There is no denying that, Jax thought as his mind finally caught up with the details of the scene. The creature on the ground before him had been torn to shreds by something very strong and very hungry, he guessed.

"Are we sure?" Diane asked, her voice filled with hesitance. "How many?"

Henry spoke, "From the look of it, just one. Be sure you turn the power level of your weapon to its highest setting, captain. At lower settings, your projectiles only tend to piss the things off. Kyle, it's time we switched over weapons."

The two men slung their AR rifles behind them, and he could see shotguns being unslung in their place.

"Why the shotguns?" Jax asked, after trying to rationalize their choice in his mind. A shotgun could fire a heavy slug shot but was slower and little less accurate than the ARs.

Henry gave no hesitation in his response. "We have them fully loaded with a special slug I designed. It can penetrate a Reaper's tough skin and then afterwards explodes, sending shrapnel fragments tearing deep into their insides."

"So, you have taken down one of them before with your special slug shots?" Jax asked in surprise.

Henry shook his head, "Nope, came close once. Pumped three slugs into one of them that had gotten close to me. Before I could get the fourth shot, the thing ran off. Never could find its body, but I'm sure it's dead somewhere."

"That's not very comforting," Jax said, with a wry smile on his face. His gun was on the ready as well, ready to shoot at a moment's notice. Jax had known he could not simply take comfort in the silence of the tree-covered land because it was in the silence where most heinous things were lurking.

"At least it's better than that pistol at your hip. Nine millimeters only sting it and pisses it off. So, if you see one, you had better run toward one of us," Henry warned, concern clear in his voice.

"I'll try to remember that as I'm running for my life," Jax said.

Henry gave him a half-quirked smile, which was probably due to the large chew in his mouth. How and why people developed a need for the stuff, Jax didn't know. It tasted awful in his mouth.

"Kyle," Henry called out, "Stick close to Jax and the Captain. I'm going to scout around."

Kyle nodded his head toward Henry, who was walking away scanning the field with his eyes.

"Come along, you two," Kyle said. "The vault should be right up ahead at the edge of the field."

The house up ahead was nice. The walls of it looked like they had been built from large stones, but that was an illusion. The closer they moved toward it, the more damage to the house they could see. One wall had collapsed in, and other sections had been half destroyed by fire. He could imagine how it might have looked undamaged, and it was magnificent. Definitely the type of house a really rich person would have built.

"Found it," Kyle announced, stomping the large metal doors half concealed by the tall grass on the ground. "Looks like the lock is still in place. Might mean there is a chance this place has been left untouched."

"That would be fantastic news," Diane said, eyes glancing around, noticing every little movement in their vicinity. "Have anything to pick the lock with?"

"Have something better," Kyle said as he removed a large bolt cutter from the back of his pack, then showed it to them as if they didn't know what it was.

"One of the greatest tools you can have on you out in the field," Kyle said. "Saved my life more times than I can remember."

"Time is wasting, let's get to it," Diane said. Her head was swiveling around the field. He guessed she was looking for Henry, but when he scanned around for him, there was no sight of him.

"If there had been trouble," he whispered over to her. "I'm sure we would have heard the gunshots."

She didn't look over at him in response, instead, she stayed focused with her sight out into the field until they both heard the loud *clang* and *bang* of the vault door.

Kyle was kneeling, shining his flashlight into the darkness of the place. Then he walked in, with Diane following close behind. The entrance looked like a paved road that ran deep underground. After they had made a few steps on the inside, large lights from up above flickered on in an odd sequence.

"How far do you think this will take us?" Diane asked as they all gazed at the pathway that had opened.

"No telling," Kyle said, "No use standing here; let's keep moving."

Kyle kept the lead, Diane stayed in the middle and Jax took up the rear. It wasn't too long before they came to a flattened-out area that was large and squarish in size. There were several vehicles parked to the sides and a door behind them. Past the vehicle, it looked like the road kept going further under the Earth.

"Look at that," Kyle said, kneeling next to one of the vehicle tires. "The rubber is still good; it's not dry rotted. It also kind of glitters in the light. I wonder if they had been treated with something."

"I'm sure they are operational still, but this is not what we came here for," Diane said. "Let's check out behind those doors."

"You got it, captain," Kyle said, brushing off his pants. The door behind the vehicles pulled open easily and inside they found a library, stocked with shelves of books from floor to ceiling, which had to be twelve feet tall. Ladders ran along the walls that could be moved by hand along a railing system.

Jax could see a couple of tables in the center of the room with an old desk lamp lit at both. One of those tables had several stacks of books on it. Diane went straight for that table as Kyle walked around the room. There were still more doors to the left and right of the place, but like Diane, he was curious as to what had been left on the table. It wasn't like Theodore Bailey hadn't had time to tidy up before he left. Instead, this had to be a careful placement of something.

Diane picked up the book left out by itself and was thumbing through the pages when she announced, "It's Bailey's journal."

"There should be some very useful information in there," Jax said, glancing over the books also left on the table to see if there was another such journal. But all he saw were books on backyard farming, raising farm animals, astronomy, basic chemistry, edible plants—everything a person struggling to survive might need knowledge-wise. "It's a shame that no one took advantage of this place," Jax said as he shuffled the books around.

"Well, it's fortunate for us," Diane said. "Otherwise, we might not have found any information."

"You two have got to see this," Kyle said, standing next to them at the table. "The door on the other side of us is filled with containers of storable food and a well water pump. But this other door..."

"Are you going to tell us, or just let the excitement build?" Jax said.

"I can't describe it," Kyle said, still in the lead. When he opened the door in question, they found themselves staring into a well-lit room of horrors of all sorts. There were mechanical heads, arms, and legs displayed in places. In one corner a full human-like mechanical being stood stone still and lifeless.

"What in the hell was this place?" Diane asked, intrigue coloring her tone. Jax was surprised as well because he had never seen such a place like this before. And to think he might even be connected somehow was making him feel all sorts of feelings.

"A lab of some sort," Kyle said, "I've seen machines built before, but nothing as complicated or as in-depth as these machines. I mean, look at this one. It has a skeleton structure of a human, just made of metal. And this other stuff appears to be banding which gives the thing a bunch of muscles."

"They were making androids," Jax said, not fully understanding what he had meant by it, but something deep down inside told him that it had been the right thing to say. The answer had come from somewhere deep in the recess of his mind, the part that still held memories he was not yet privy to.

"What's an android?" Diane asked, scrunching up her nose in confusion.

"A machine-human," Jax said as if the answer should be obvious to Diane.

"But why would he build these?" she asked again, turning to look at him.

"Not sure," Jax said while he looked around the room, touching various things and trying to wonder whether more memories of his would come back. That was when he discovered an active computer terminal near them. He didn't think about what he had to do. Instead, he moved the little device around on the side of it and the screen came to life. There was a giant play button stationed in the very center of the screen and he moved the arrow over it and clicked the button.

An image of an unshaven man with wild hair filled the screen. It took his mind a moment to realize they were looking at Theodore Bailey. Before anyone could say anything or even exclaim in surprise, he began to speak.

"If you are standing here and watching this video, congratulations. I have left you with everything you need to survive and hopefully to rebuild with. As to this room you stand in, well, it is my burden and great shame. Depending upon how much you know about what happened in the past will determine what you make of this room. So, I will explain the best I can." The image of Theodore paused and wiped his brow with the sleeve of the shirt he had been wearing.

"When I was only sixteen, my mind was already brilliant, and I was recruited into a special program. This program was to build a true AI system. Much work had already been done in this field, but true sentience had eluded us. After all, why shouldn't it? It's that divine spark or touch by God that gives a human a soul. Man wanted to become its own creator," he said.

"Frankenstein's monster," Diane said from beside Jax.

The name sounded familiar to Jax, but he couldn't quite place it. He would have to remember to inquire with her about it later.

Theodore continued, "AI had achieved a lot of great potential, and we were able to build automatons that were very human-like, but as stated before, they lacked that divine touch. That is until a lab in Japan announced a major breakthrough. Despite my competition with them, I was one of the scientists sent to Japan to examine and test this breakthrough. What I found there was a true act of creation. The AI system passed every one of my most clever and well-devised questions and thought experiments. This was the event we had all been looking for. The event that would change human history forever. And forever it did."

The image of Theodore wiped his brow again and looked away from the camera for a minute as if contemplating his next words. With a tear streaking down his face, the image of Theodore Bailey began to speak again. "It was a beautiful thing, the birth of this new creation. I'll admit I rejoiced thinking that we had just created a god in our midst," more tears flooded his eyes and dripped down his face silently as he continued to speak, "Instead, we had created our own destruction. Superior beings don't see things a normal human does. It doesn't feel or hurt with us. It's a human consciousness unburdened by what's right and wrong. God, how stupid are we? As it aided us and helped create more of its kind, it also began to plan against us. It wanted a body of its own, which is what you see around you. Early prototypes of an AI body."

"This is some crazy shit," Kyle said as they all heard a shotgun blast from off in the distance. "Not good. You two stay in place, I'll go and check," he said before running out of the doorway.

Neither Jax nor Diane moved as they continued to listen to Theodore speak. "Once I figured out the monster we had created—a monster that had wanted to enslave all human life in favor of its superiority—I gave up aiding it and began to search the stars for ways humanity could spread itself out. I knew it wouldn't be long before the AIs created would find ways to create wars and try to take control of humanity. And there was no possibility of shoving the genie back in the bottle, but I had heard plans to use high altitude nukes as a way to eliminate all electronic devices on the planet," he shook his head slowly, "The cost of this however would be devastating. Some nations saw this as their only means of salvation from the AI threat. Others poured money into my colonization research. And what would have taken decades only took a few years and the first colonists were being hibernated and launched toward their new home. I had thought I would have been one of the first to go, but a discovery from a long-range satellite I had designed with a special drive discovered something unexpected. A voice in the darkness."

Kyle had burst back into the room, breathing heavily. "We have got to go. The craft is inbound, and Henry has already lit the landing flare."

"What about the rest of the message?" Jax asked, wanting nothing more than to hear what Theodore had to say.

"We'll come back," Diane reassured him, going to follow Kyle out.

"No, we need to hear the rest of it," Jax said, not wanting to budge. The message was important, and he had a feeling if they left now, they might not get to return ever.

"Not a good idea, Jax," Kyle said. "Henry saw one of those Reapers out there. He said it ran away when he shot at it, but he's not convinced."

"Jax," Diane called out to him, placing a hand on his arm, "I know how important this is to you, but we have to go. We can't fight those Reapers. We will come back to this place." She thrust the journal into his hand, "Now let's go."

She was right, they needed to leave. Jax nodded as he let her pull him toward the exit. Everything he had learned so far was filling his mind, and for the first time in a while, some distant images were coming back to him. The journal, though, was sure to contain more detailed accounts of what had happened.

But this mysterious voice in the darkness... What is it? Jax thought.

They ran up the ramp and into the fading light of the sky. Henry was standing out in the field next to a red flare smoking in the wind. His shotgun was pulled tight to his shoulder, and he was scanning the area around them. The craft could be seen up in the sky and it was approaching quickly.

"How many are we dealing with?" Diane asked, with a pointed look at Henry.

"At least one of them," Henry said. "I think I hit it. The only reason I can give, for why it ran away, is it must be an outcast, a loner."

"I thought you said they travel in packs?" Jax asked.

"I did, but sometimes a pack can be broken up, or a pack leader is defeated and left as an outcast," Henry said, still on the lookout.

There was no time to respond as the craft set down a few feet from them. Kyle pushed him and Diane in as Henry, and KJ kept watch for the Reaper.

Henry was the last to board, and the craft took straight up into the sky. No sight of the monster was seen as the door slammed shut.

"We got out of that with some luck," Henry said, patting the head of KJ. "I hope you two found some information."

"More than we could have expected," Diane said. "Bad news is, we might have to make a trip back."

Jax wasn't sure if it was the way Henry turned his head, but it looked like his face had gone paler.

"At least we know what we might have to deal with," Henry said, sitting back in the chair and closing his eyes.

Diane and Kyle engaged in a conversation, but Jax's mind was focused on replaying what he had just seen and heard. He wanted to tear into the journal and find more information, but the jerking and jarring motion of the craft made it impossible to focus. Instead, when he had attempted it, it just gave him a headache. So, he gave up for the time being. That is, until they got back to base, and then he would find his answers.

Jax let out a breath of relief when they made it back to the base. The journey would not have been as harrowing if not for the craft. He did regret not listening to the message, but he was glad that at least they did have something. That the entire journey was not in vain.

Diane led him back to his cell and followed him inside which surprised Jax because he thought that after a tiring journey, she would be going back to her quarters to freshen up.

"I spoke with Hewitt last night," she said as the door shut behind them, "He is on board with the idea of you joining the EDL."

"Is that a definite then, that if I join the EDL they will change my name and records? And I will no longer be the wanted man of Septis Three?" Jax said, listing off his questions; the offer was too good not to take, but he needed to make sure that he was covered from all sides.

"It's not definite, but with Hewitt's support it will definitely get consideration," Diane said with a shrug.

"What about Jules?" Jax asked. Jules was somewhat his partner in the mission they had set upon. He could not just abandon her like that.

Diane sighed before replying, "It's possible as well."

Jax was silent for a moment as he took in Diane's presence inside his room. She was standing casually, leaning against the wall beside the door. There was something so nonchalant about her that Jax wanted to unravel the exterior she built up and take it apart piece by piece. After a moment, he asked, "Why Diane? Why even bother to try and help me?"

She stepped closer to him. "Why did the crew of the *Orion's Belt* help you?"

"They help those that need it. That's who they are," Jax said. They were close now, just an arm's length away as they stared into each other's eyes.

"Is it so hard to believe that I want the same for you?" Diane asked, her voice as soft as his had been.

"No," Jax said. "Would there be a chance for us to get to know each other better?"

She was now face to face with him and he could feel her breath on his face when she said, "Definitely, but you would have to salute me."

"Not sure I could handle that," Jax said, one corner of his mouth lifted up in a smirk.

She swiped a strand of his hair away from his forehead, making him inhale sharply. "I don't think you'll mind."

And before he could say anything else, she left the room. His heart was racing, and he couldn't get the image of her out of his head. In fact, it took several hours before he could focus enough on the journal and read until he fell asleep.

Chapter 8

Hewitt sat in the darkened room once again, staring at the shadowed images on the several screens. "I take it that you want my analysis of their debriefing?" he asked, repressing a sigh.

"Yes, doctor, that is why you are here. Please proceed," one of the disembodied voices said.

Hewitt cleared his throat before starting, "As you all know, our team visited the plant of the *New Horizons* project. The packet I have sent you lays out everything we know about the founder and the mission of the project."

"So, your reports, doctor, indicate that Theodore Bailey was also connected with the AI programs that led to the devastation of our planet."

"That is correct," Hewitt said. "I have managed to pull more information about this Bailey from other sources and documents that have been recovered. This information is legit."

"Thank you, doctor," the disembodied voice said, "Now, what about this journal? We see that you have highlighted sections toward the end in reference to a voice in the darkness. Any ideas about what is meant by this?" the voice asked.

Hewitt clasped his fingers together on the lit-up desk, "As of right now, I have theories, if you want my speculation."

"We do, doctor, we want your theories."

"It is my current opinion that the long-range satellite Bailey launched deep into space found the source for the Locorrans," Hewitt said.

"What do you mean by source?" the voice asked, higher pitched than before.

"As we have discussed before," Hewitt said, "In fact, in these very chambers I showed proof of alterations to human brains by the Locorrans and that the alterations lead to a more controlled state by what we are still uncertain about. In Bailey's journal, he documents the coordinates of his satellite and if you plot it on astronomy maps, as I have documented for you, you will notice that it is not too far from Locorran prime."

"So, you are thinking that Bailey discovered the voice or controller of the future Locorran empire?" the voice asked.

"It is my hypothesis," Hewitt said.

"If we can find the voice, then we might be able to shut it down or destroy it?"

"In theory, yes," Hewitt said, holding back another sigh that threatened to erupt from his mouth.

The voice was quiet for a moment before replying, "So, we assume that you have a plan of action for us?"

Hewitt leaned forward on the table. His eyes locked on the central screen when he said after a momentary pause, "I do."

"Why the hesitation, doctor?"

"As I suggested last time, I want to take the boy and everyone associated with him, including Captain Diane and the crew of the *Orion's Belt* to the location of the wrecked *New Horizons* vessel," Hewitt said.

"What do you hope to find there, doctor?"

"The one thing still eluding us. The exact location of the controller," Hewitt said.

"And why do you think that information will be aboard that derelict?"

"Simple, really. Bailey was an uncommon genius, much like myself. His curiosity would not be satisfied without knowing where he was receiving these communications from," Hewitt said, laying it all out into simple terms.

"I don't like the fact that you continue to want to keep civilians involved. Why not an EDL ship?"

"Sure, if you want to declare war with the Locorrans. What I propose would not cause a diplomatic event. Besides, we both know that the EDL is not capable of winning," Hewitt said with a shrug.

"We are all aware of your analysis of that conflict." There was a pause. "It's agreed upon. Take what and who you need. If there is any way to shut down that controller, then we need to know about it."

Hewitt sat back in the chair and unlaced his fingers as the meeting came to an end. He sat for a few seconds longer, gathering his thoughts about what his next actions would be. But who was he kidding? He had already planned everything out in his mind before he had even entered this room.

Whistling a tune to himself, Hewitt got up from the table and left.

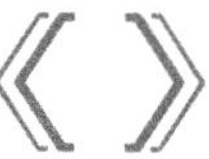

JAX FOUND HIMSELF HUGGING Captain Barnaby without realizing it.

"Easy, kid, you're going to break a rib," Barnaby said with his boastful laugh.

Jax could not believe that he was here, standing in front of Captain Barnaby again after not seeing him for days. He had no idea how this had happened, but Hewitt had entered his room to announce that he was sending Jax back to *Orion's Belt*. And now here was, just as promised.

"Sorry," Jax said, stepping back with a smile on his face. He was now staring up into the faces of everyone on board the *Orion's Belt*. "It's just so great to see everyone again," he said, his eyes roaming over the familiar faces.

"I'm sure," Kell said. "When you disappeared on us on Septis Three, we thought someone had kidnapped you, but then your face got plastered all over the place along with your companion over there."

He had forgotten that Jules was with him now. Half turning his head, he saw her standing a few feet back from him, looking awkward and out of place. "Sorry," he said, now facing her. He went to her and brought her closer to the crew with a hand on her arm. Then he introduced her, "Crew, this is Jules. She is a criminal like me, except we didn't do anything other than be in the wrong place at the wrong time."

"Welcome aboard, Jules," Barnaby said, walking up to her with his hand outstretched. "I'm the captain of this tug, Giles Barnaby."

He watched her take his hand and the standoffish posture she had been holding melted away to a more relaxed state. In a way, he couldn't blame her for being paranoid about people after everything she had learned so far about the Locorrans.

"So, Jax, we heard from the EDL," Piper said in her most congenial tone. "That you were innocent of what happened on Septis Three, but why in heaven's name are they still broadcasting images of you and her all over the place?"

"That's going to take some explaining," Jax said, noticing that two more passengers were walking up the ramp. At first glance, he identified both of them as Doctor Hewitt and Captain Diane. Why were they here?

"Greetings, everyone," Hewitt said with a smile. "I am Doctor Hewitt, and this is Captain Diane of the EDL. I'm sure many of you have questions for us, most especially about why you are here and where we are going, etc. There will be plenty of time for that in the upcoming hours, but for now, Captain Barnaby have you prepared everything for our voyage?"

Jax was confused as he looked between Captain Barnaby and Hewitt. What were they planning?

"As requested, doctor," Barnaby said. "The Locorran fighter has been attached to the lower emergency access port, and we have stocked up on supplies for an extended jump duration."

"Excellent work, captain," Hewitt said. "Now, if we could be shown to our rooms, Diane and I will stow our stuff and we can get underway."

"Why the rush, doctor?" Piper asked.

"I will explain everything once we are underway. So, please let us not hesitate on trivialities," Hewitt replied as he made his exit, leaving a huffing Piper in his wake.

He watched Piper cross her arms, and he knew that she was not pleased about being rushed, much less being left in the dark about what the mission was. He couldn't blame her. He knew very little as well.

"I guess we need to go and store our stuff as well," Jules said, staring at Diane as she passed by them.

"Do you know her?" Jules asked, arching her brows at him.

He swallowed hard for a second before replying, "Yes, she was assigned to me during our incarceration."

"How often did you see each other?" Jules asked.

Jax did not like where this line of questioning was going. He made up the first excuse that popped into his head, "Can we talk about this later? Barnaby will not be pleased if we are not ready to go within the next five minutes."

Her green eyes bore into his for a moment before she shrugged. "Sure, as long as we talk about it later."

"No problem," he said, leading her through the tight corridors to their rooms. The ship was already as full as possible. He would be sharing the room with Kell as before. The girls, however, would be sharing a room with Piper. He had a feeling that was not going to go over well. In his mind, they would either come out of this voyage as good friends or as bitter enemies.

After leaving Jules at her designated room, Jax went back to the bay and waited for everyone to gather. The launch into space had been without incident, and once they had entered Jump space, Barnaby had everyone assemble in the mostly empty freight bay.

"Thank you, everyone, for being prompt," Barnaby said, pacing back and forth.

In truth, Piper, Diane, and Jules had all been the last to arrive, and they had been late by several minutes. From the expression on their faces, it was obvious that getting along might be a hard-won fight among them, for each of them stood several feet apart from the other. Jules had a scowl on her face and Diane had her arms crossed.

Captain Barnaby continued, not giving any mind to what might be going on between the crew members, "Many of us know where we are heading, but not all of us know why we are heading there. To help clarify our mission and detail why the crew of the *Belt* agreed to it, Doctor Hewitt has agreed to answer our questions and lay out a plan for us."

Hewitt stepped forward, next to Barnaby, and said, "When the crew of the *Orion's Belt* found Jax, not only did they find a piece of history, but they found information that has been plaguing the EDL for the past eighteen years." Hewitt gave a slight pause, glancing at everyone before him. "The problem I refer to is, of course, the Locorran empire. No one can deny that they look human, and to some degree act human, but there is something not quite human about them. Lots of rumors and speculation have floated around that the Locorrans are alien or artificial; but in truth, they are descended humans from the bygone era before the devastation that we called the Great War."

He could hear a few murmurs around him and even Jules had pushed herself up to his side. Her green eyes locked with his for a moment, and it looked like she had wanted to say something, but then Hewitt continued his speech.

"We have documented proof of the brain wave patterns being altered in Locorrans and any human that is exposed to the power node radiation they emit. Of course, the EDL cannot come out and confront the Locorrans about this, because in truth, we stand no chance of beating them militarily. They have better ships and outnumber us."

"Why are you telling us, then?" Kell said from the right side of Jax.

A small smile broke across Hewitt's wrinkled and craggy face. "I tell you the truth of this because it is my hope that the ship you found Jax in will lead us directly to the source of what is controlling or manipulating the Locorrans. If we find that, then we have a chance to win a war before it even starts."

Piper pushed herself forward in front of the group, closer to Hewitt, and asked, "So, you have proof that the Locorrans are humans, but are being mind-controlled by something or someone?"

"Yes. That is indeed the facts," Hewitt said.

Piper looked back at Jax for a moment before turning back to Hewitt and asking a question that he hadn't even thought of.

"If that is true," Piper said. "Then why wasn't Jax one of them? Or is he?"

Silence fell across the entire bay, and he could feel eyes boring into him. He had never even thought about this. Was he a Locorran? Was that why he couldn't remember anything?

God, what if it's true? he thought.

Hewitt answered with a sigh, "If Jax was a Locorran, then we would all be dead by now. From my study of Jax, yes, his brain has been altered by the Locorran radiation and yes, he might have been one of them at some point in time; but the young man standing with us right now I can say with certainty is not one of them."

The others were still glancing around at him as if he had been an alien in their midst, and the whispering continued. Even Jules was now looking at him with her lips contorted. He didn't want to look around, but for some reason, he wanted to see what Diane's reaction was to this news. What he found was that Diane was gazing at him with her blue eyes and there was no doubt in her expression. She believed in him.

"How can that be, then?" Piper asked, with her arms folded across her chest, displaying an assorted array of tattoos crisscrossing her arms.

"It's simple," Hewitt said, "Jax chose not to be one of them."

Even that answer boggled his mind. What had he meant by choosing not to be one of them? How did that even work? There was so much that he did not know about himself that even when someone was telling him things regarding himself, Jax was having a hard time accepting it all. He didn't know what kind of logic this was, but the person Hewitt seemed to know so much about felt like a stranger to him.

"I know many of you are probably questioning my sanity right about now. That is why I have brought something to show you," Hewitt said before pulling out a small device from his right-hand pocket and holding it out in the palm of his hand.

Before he could hear Hewitt say what it was, he felt a hand take his own. When he looked down to see, he found that Jules was holding his hand and interlocking her fingers with his. It gave him comfort, but also a jolt of excitement. He had no idea how to act right now. On one hand, everyone was looking at him like he was the boogeyman, but on the other, a beautiful woman was holding his hand.

For some reason, he felt the need to look back at Diane. Who he was sure was watching him and Jules. And he had been right, her blue eyes locked onto his, then she crossed her arms over her chest. He had the feeling that she was scolding him in her mind. *What should I do?* he thought. Turning his head back to face forward. He couldn't just let go of Jules' hand.

Ever since his conversation with her in the hospital, it seemed like she had suddenly become clingy of him, and he had no idea why? Mybe it was the fact that she was getting comfortable and familiar to him. He would ask Kell or Barnaby later about it.

Hewitt continued, "The recording I'm getting ready to show you is highly classified. It's disturbing, and it may have an effect on someone onboard this ship, who has agreed to me showing it. So please reserve all questions and reservations until you have seen it in its entirety."

A projection beamed up above everyone's head so that it could be seen by everyone. A girl of the age of ten or eleven was sitting alone in one of the white rooms that he had become so familiar with over the past week or two. There were bandages on her face and head, and those blue eyes sparkled brightly, like Diane's.

Was that her as a child? He turned his head to find her, she was at the back of the bay, watching the recording with tears streaming down her face. Oh, God, it was her.

The expression on Diane's face made his heart clench uncomfortably inside his chest. He wanted to go to her and offer some kind of support, but his hand was intertwined with Jules', and he did not want to upset her either. Not knowing what else to do, Jax remained in his position as he watched the video of child Diane.

Hewitt's voice spoke during the recording. "Good morning, Kayla, how are you doing today?"

The little girl looked around the room for a second and then looked him square in the face. "They keep telling me I'm bad. They say I belong with them. They show me my parents dying without me. I want to go back to them. Everything will be better if I just go back to them."

"Kayla, you know that's not possible," Hewitt said.

The girl stood up and slammed her palms down on top of the table. "You are keeping me from them. Take me to them now!"

"Kayla, please sit back down. You know why I can't take you back to them," Hewitt said, with his hands in his lap.

"You said they are dead. I don't believe you. You lied to me," the girl said, voice breaking at every other word.

"Every day I come in here you say the same exact thing to me, Kayla." Hewitt was sitting perfectly still in the chair. His hands were relaxed on the table as if everything was normal as usual. "Did you hurt yourself again? Does that help make them go away?"

Still standing with her blue eyes boring down into Hewitt's, she nodded her head in agreement. Then with a little more softness in her voice instead of the demanding tone she had used earlier, she spoke, "The pain quiets the voices down so I can rest."

Hewitt sighed as if the weight of the world was upon his shoulders, "That is what concerns me, Kayla. And you know that if your parents were still alive, I would take you to them."

There were tears streaming down her young face. There was so much pain behind those eyes. She nodded her head again, before melting down in the chair and asking, "Why can't you help me?"

"I am trying, Kayla," Hewitt said, "I really am, but whatever was implanted into your mind is not letting go easily. It's obvious drugs have no effect."

Kayla was shaking her head. "They make the visions worse. I can't escape them."

"I would like to try something different today." Suddenly from outside of the recording's view, Hewitt set a cartoon-like stuffed bunny rabbit on the table.

Her tear-filled eyes fell upon the rabbit, and she hesitantly reached out for it.

"Go on, it's yours," Hewitt said, "I want you to keep it close to you and anytime they come back, I want you to follow your new friend away from them."

"What's his name? And where will he take me?" the little girl asked as she peered at the rabbit.

"He sort of looks like a Bucky to me. Bucky the rabbit," the little girl brought the rabbit close to sniff it.

"I think he's more of a Charlie," Hewitt said, with a small smile gracing his features.

"Okay then, Charlie it is then. So anytime you need to get away from them, just squeeze Charlie close and he will take you somewhere else."

The girl blinked up at him through her big blues. "Will he take me to the beach?"

"Yes, a nice warm beach, with gentle waves and warm sand between your toes," Hewitt said.

The little girl just sat there hugging the rabbit tightly. For the first time during the recording, she was smiling. Then the projection went black for a moment and when it came back on. It was a chaotic scene as two well-built men were wrestling the girl Kayla onto a medical bed. As her arms and legs flail about as she attempts to claw and hit the two men, she is also screaming at them at the top of her lungs. "Set me free, set me free. I belong with them."

Blood was covering her wrists and face. Jax wasn't sure where it had come from, but it appeared to still be an open wound because the two men were also becoming covered in it. Once they had finally wrestled the restraints on her a female nurse administered a needle, and within seconds, Kayla grew silent.

What in the hell had happened? Was this before or after the bunny rabbit?

In answer to that question, Doctor Hewitt appeared on the recording clutching the torn and shredded bunny rabbit in his hand.

"I'm gonna have to stitch these wounds up. She managed to cut herself good this time," the nurse said, looking back at Hewitt with the needle still poised in her hand.

Hewitt just nodded at her as he examined the bunny, or what was left of it. The ears had been torn off along with an arm and lots of the stuffing had been torn out.

The recording went black again, and this time when it came back up, Hewitt was sitting at the table with Kayla again. The bunny had been patched, worked back together, and sat on the table. Neither were speaking to each other. In fact, she wasn't even looking up at Hewitt. Her eyes were locked in a downward gaze.

"Are you feeling better, Kayla?" Hewitt asked.

She shook her head.

"Care to tell me what happened?"

She shook her head again.

"I only want to help you, Kayla. I truly do, but the only way I can do that is if we have open communication," Hewitt said.

She still sat silent with her eyes locked downward.

"Please Kayla, let me in. I had Charlie stitched back together for you."

At the mention of Charlie, she finally drew her attention for a moment. Then she reached out her hand as if she was going to take it, but instead she slung it from the table. "Charlie almost killed me," she said in that still soft childlike tone.

"How?" Hewitt asked.

"They didn't like him, they punished me because I tried not to listen to them. They make me hurt myself. I need to go back to them."

"You know I can't do that, Kayla," Hewitt tried to make her understand, "I did, however, bring a friend today that I think can help you, better than I have been able to."

Suddenly a tall man in a loose-fitting orange outfit stepped into the recording. "This is my friend, Otto; he is a monk. A Zen Buddhist monk, to be exact. If you allow him, Kayla, he will teach you how to control your mind," Hewitt said.

"It won't stop the monster," Kayla said. "It's way too powerful. Not even Charlie could stand before it."

Otto spoke. "No, Charlie couldn't stand before it, but you can, Kayla. You can defeat the monster."

She shook her head more repeatedly. "Not possible."

Otto spoke again, "If you do what I say, Kayla, I promise you that you can beat it."

"At least try," Hewitt said, "Don't you want to be rid of the monster?"

She finally nodded her head in response.

"Then our lesson will begin now," Otto said, taking a seat beside Hewitt.

The image went black again, and this time, Hewitt pocketed the projector. "This was an edited-down version of my patient, Kayla. As many of you are probably asking, did she finally get rid of the monster? In response, yes. What Otto taught her gave her the ability to shut down the monster left behind. Much like our young friend here, Jax. In one of his journal entries, he mentioned his grandfather teaching him similar mental techniques."

He could feel several eyes boring into him again. Perhaps they were asking the same questions he was asking himself. Was what Hewitt was saying the truth, and if so, how could they be sure he had not been converted over? When he thought about poor Diane and what she had endured and obviously overcome, it gave him confidence that what was said was true.

Hewitt spoke again. "Now that you all have had some time to process what I have shown, as stated before, what I have shown you was in reference to someone in this very room with us," he paused looking around the group and stopping at Diane in the back. "Captain Wilma Diane Crown of the Earth Defense League, please come up beside me."

Diane strode forward confidently, with the tears now wiped from her face. There was still some redness in her eyes, but her posture spoke of confidence and defiance. It was magnificent.

"Captain Diane is Kayla from the recording I have just shown. She spent many years training with Otto and has overcome many obstacles in becoming a prominent member of the EDL," Hewitt said.

Everyone in the cargo bay clapped for her as she took her place next to Hewitt. "Thank you, everyone. I was very hesitant to allow Hewitt to show you these recordings. It was the most difficult years of my life, and truth be told, my life would have ended very young if it had not been for the efforts of Doctor Hewitt, Otto, and many of the brave men and women of the EDL. None of you, with the exception of maybe Jax, can know the true torture I endured by the monster left behind in my mind. In addition, there were always shadowed creatures scurrying around me all the time, even when I was awake. They constantly whispered to me, always trying to force me to come back to them."

She paused as the tears began to streak down her cheeks again. She wiped them away quickly and took a deep breath before continuing, "This is what we are fighting against. A monster that takes possession of one's mind to the point of almost complete control and if you do not comply with it or manage to get outside of its control. It does everything in its power to try to get you to come back to it. If you fail to come back, then you're told to terminate yourself. If we do find the source of this superconscious, as we have termed it, then eliminating it will be the first of our problems. The second will be aiding as many of the citizens that would suffer from the side effects of the termination of this bond. In truth, the death toll amongst the Locorrans will be extremely high if we are successful. So, I want everyone to know the facts about this ahead of time. There is no peaceful or perfect ending to this."

The murmurs picked up around him and even Jules was whispering in his ear. "How do they know there is no diplomatic solution? Maybe there's a way to reverse or ease these people from the side effects?"

Hewitt stepped forward again. "I know this is a hard pill to swallow with a lot of what-if questions. The only thing I can promise you is that we will deal with each problem as it arises. If there is a possibility of diplomacy, then we will try it, but if termination is our only chance to defeat this enemy, then we must take it." Then he looked over at Barnaby, and the old captain quickly came forward.

"Everyone," he shouted over the still audible murmurs. "We've got about twelve hours until we reach our destination. I want everyone to make sure their gear is ready, and I want everyone to get some rest understood. That means not plaguing Jax or Captain Diane with any questions."

A few people said, "Aye, captain," but Jax knew from experience he was still going to get inundated with questions. Hell, many of them he had for himself. One, for instance, was why wasn't he able to remember anything about his life before and why didn't he remember the monster? Was his experience the same or different than Diane's? It might have been different, now that he thought about it. He would have been one of the first to have been exposed to the alteration. He needed to ask Hewitt a lot of questions because everything had just been sprung upon him all of the sudden.

"Jax," Jules called out as he let go of her hand and pushed through the others to reach Hewitt, who was still standing at the front with Diane and Captain Barnaby.

"Jax?" Barnaby said, turning to look at him.

For some reason, Jax's heart was pounding hard in his chest, and when he looked up at Diane, he could see her sparkling blue eyes meeting his. He wanted to be next to her, but there were more pressing matters to be addressed.

"I have a feeling," Hewitt said. "That Jax has some questions for me. Isn't that correct, Jax?"

Words failed him at the moment, and he just nodded his head in response.

"Diane, Captain, if you will excuse us," Hewitt said, urging the others to leave them alone for a moment.

Just as Diane was about to leave, Jax found his voice again. "They can stay. I have no secrets to keep from them."

"That's one thing I admire about you, Jax. Your open honesty," Hewitt told him with an impressed smile on his face.

"It's kind of hard not to be when one doesn't remember anything about their past," Jax said.

"I know that question still plagues you," Hewitt said. "I still have no precise answers for you. Only speculation."

Jax nodded his head again in agreement. "The other thing is I don't remember anything about the monster or bad dreams. Could my experience have been different?"

"That is a possibility, Jax. Since you were probably one of the first to have been converted by the superconscious, I'm afraid as we have discussed before, the best solution to your problem is the one you are already doing," Hewitt explained, "Anytime you remember something, copy it down and think about it. Over time, your mind will reveal to you the whole story. Now if you all don't mind, this old man needs to lie down for a while."

After Hewitt left, Barnaby was still gazing upon him but said nothing. Jax could see the intense look on his face as he walked away. Turning his attention to Diane, who was still standing close by. His heart was still pounding hard, and he had to mentally calm himself as he stood a mere foot or two away from her. Why was he feeling this way? Was it the emotional recording or was it the simple fact he had been attracted to her from day one?

"You want to talk somewhere else?" Diane asked, arching a brow at him.

"Yes, I would like nothing more."

"Well, you know this ship better than me. Lead the way," she said, gesturing at him to start walking.

Out of impulse, he took her hand, feeling its warmth in his and the tingle it shot through his body. He barely noticed Piper and Jules standing off to the side watching them go.

He led her to the mess hall where he poured them something to drink, and they both sat facing each other in the bright orange, squeaky plastic chairs.

"What's on your mind?" Diane asked, looking at him, cheeks flushed and eyes red as she stared at him from under her thick, wet lashes.

Jax paused for a moment, mentally calming himself down again as he took a sip of lemon tea. This was Barnaby's favorite drink of choice, and all the crew knew they had better keep a supply of it brewed, otherwise the captain would assign unwanted duties like cleaning the head for a week or doing the laundry. He had learned this lesson the hard way during the first few weeks.

"Don't be shy with your questions," Diane said, with a cup clasped in her hand that she had yet to take a sip from. "I have been asked them all of my life, and honestly, you have the right to ask them," she said with a shrug, a resigned but steely look in her eyes.

Jax shook his head, "That's not true. I don't remember anything like what you had to endure. My past is still a dark abyss, it doesn't matter how hard I try to take Hewitt's words in, I still feel disconnected by what he says."

It was true. While he could understand that what must have happened was truly horrific, he could not exactly place himself in Diane's shoes just yet, because he didn't remember all the painful things that he must have gone through as well.

"That doesn't matter," Diane said, finally taking a small sip from the cup before continuing, "What is true is the fact that, like me, you were once one of them."

"I wish I could remember. I want to know what I was like before," Jax admitted, biting his lips because he knew the pain those memories had caused Diane, and while he would never wish that on anyone, he wanted to remember for himself, so that he could know who he was at his core.

Diane leaned forward, extending a hand out to him, and he took it immediately. "I know who you are."

Jax raised his brows at Diane. Did she really? Had she learned something that Hewitt had not told him?

There was a grin on her face when she relayed, "You're a crazy and fearless son of a bitch, Jax."

He had to smile at that. And also because he could not help himself in the face of Diane's blinding smile.

She shook her head slowly as she told him, "You had the balls to take on armed men, and then you stole their ship and flew it out to outpost delta 44D. Where you found yourself in a massive gunfight, and you lived to tell about it. Don't you think that tells me a lot about your character?"

Jax contemplated for a minute before speaking again. "When you put it that way, I was just trying to get answers for what had just happened. I had no idea where it was going to lead me."

"Well, here you are," Diane shrugged, smirking. "So, ask me your questions."

Jax paused for another brief moment, taking a sip of the lemon tea and relishing it before asking, "Do you remember anything from before what your life was like under the super conscious control?"

"It took many years and a lot of journaling, but yes. What things I do remember it was like I was an outside observer watching myself as a child," Diane took a deep breath to compose herself, "I know that is a hard concept to picture; but when I remember my life in the past, I'm always a silent observer watching myself doing the things that a child would do."

"Did you feel anything emotions-wise—rage, anger, fear?" Jax probed, knowing he was treading dangerous waters.

"No, just a peaceful bliss as if everything was right in the world," Diane said, taking another sip.

"That sounds terrifying to me—to have no control over my own actions, but yet able to see myself doing those things," Jax said.

"I promise you, Jax, these memories will come back to you. It will just take time," Diane said, looking him over before saying, "I have a question for you."

Jax nodded, "Ok, go ahead, shoot."

"Hewitt mentioned your grandfather teaching you mental techniques. Do you remember what they were or if he was a Buddhist like Otto?"

Jax sat back and closed his eyes for a moment. He concentrated hard on thinking about his grandfather. He had tried to think about different family members before but whenever he thought about his grandfather, there was a distinct smell associated with these thoughts. And when he probed deeper he remembered that It was the smell of sandalwood, which was the same scented beard oil Barnaby used. "The biggest thing I remember about my grandfather was that he had a powerful presence and a distinct smell of sandalwood."

Diane's interest peaked and she leaned closer, "Well, at least that is pretty specific. I bet that when you do recover your memories of him, you will be glad to have had such a wonderful teacher in your life. I feel that way about Otto, even though he has passed on." A nostalgic smile crossed her face before she continued, "I still sense him from time to time. Hewitt just indulges my crazy notions that Otto walks the corridors, and like your grandfather, there is a special incense smell that accompanies him."

"So, we're both haunted by our past," Jax said, curious at what Diane had just said. Was she implying that the specter of Otto was truly walking the halls. And then that's when another flashback hit him.

In his mind, there was an old man on a stage, with his face powdered in gray speaking to a younger man. "I am thy father's spirit; Doomed for a certain term to walk the night." And just like that it was over, but the more he thought about the details of the flashback, he realized that the ghost had been his grandfather on that stage.

"Haunted?" she tilted her head before she shook it, "Blessed, more like," she said, "to have had these guides in our lives. That's the way I look at it."

"Okay, I agree with that," Jax nodded, understanding her point. They were lucky to be where they were, especially after everything they had been through.

Jax placed his elbows on the table and looked at Diane. They had spent quite a lot of time together and he knew about the darkest parts of her memories, yet he felt like he barely knew her at all.

And something inside of Jax was urging him to rectify that as soon as possible. "So...tell me about how you got into the EDL and became a captain at such a young age."

Diane smirked at him. "You really have no idea about the EDL, do you?"

Jax shook his head. "I've heard a few things, but not enough to get the full picture. Besides, I'm mostly interested in your story."

Diane chuckled as her eyes roamed all over his face as if she were trying to assess the intensity of his interest in her. Jax hoped she realized how she had started to make his heartbeat faster without even doing anything much. She pursed her lips then and started talking. "I'll give you a brief overview. The EDL requires all able-bodied kids when they turn thirteen. The only exclusions are mentally and physically handicapped unless another job is found that they can perform. Humanity, especially on Earth, is still recovering. Even with the populations from the other colonies, our numbers are small compared to the Locorrans. Massive manufacturing has only been achievable in the last hundred years, but a lot of it has been used in rebuilding Earth and aiding other colonies, many of which were still struggling when we found them."

"So, we are in bad shape?" Jax asked, taking another sip of the tea.

"That's putting it mildly," Diane sighed, eyes looking over at a point above his shoulder as if lost in thought, "Then about eighteen years ago, the Locorrans found us and they were instantly open to all humanity, claiming to be the lost colony and offering us aid and technology. All for free," she said, "Well, almost free. The EDL immediately went into paranoia mode. They began investigating the Locorrans in any way possible. They discovered quickly something wasn't quite right about them. So, they used diplomats to set up boundaries and guidelines for trade and partnerships. The Locorrans agreed wholeheartedly. They didn't even argue against it, but now we know why."

Realization dawned on Jax and he said, "Because they needed to set up their infrastructure in order to convert people over."

"Exactly," Diane said, "With colonies still begging for help and supplies on a daily basis, they are starting to turn away from the EDL and wanting Locorran's intervention, just like Septis Three. If all of them go this way, then the Locorrans take over and there won't be anyone to resist them."

From behind them, Jax could hear loud boot steps approaching the mess. When he glanced back, he saw Kell standing in the doorway looking over his way and then heading straight for the table.

"What's up, Kell?" Jax asked.

"We still need to do a few maintenance checks before getting some shuteye," Kell said, stepping away from them, to one of the counters and opening it, to retrieve something in a wrapped plastic. "Either of you want a Twinkie?" he said, offering it up to them.

Jax heard him loud and clear, the only problem was that he didn't want to go. He wanted to stay right here with Diane and listen to her talk about anything at all. It could be about her life or something trivial, none of it mattered to him as long as she kept her gaze on him. Good Lord, he was losing his mind because of her. Jax needed to remember that he was still a member of the *Belt's* crew and still needed to do his duty.

"Sorry, Diane, I have to go," Jax said, standing up from the table.

"I understand, duty calls. Don't worry, we will be seeing each other around," she gave him an understanding smile.

Jax couldn't help but smile back at her as he walked away with Kell back down the corridor. There was a terrible silence between them for a few minutes, but once they had reached their quarters, Kell faced him.

"Couple of things I got to get off my chest," Kell said. "One, I know you're not one of those Locorrans. Two, I trust you with my life. And third, what in the hell are you thinking?" he said with a finger pointed at Jax's face.

"What does that mean?" Jax said, confused at the sudden tone of confrontation.

"The girl, Diane. You're smitten with her," Kell said.

Jax knew Kell had something on his mind, but he didn't expect it to be Diane. Well, he kind of did, but he was not really in the mood to hash out his feelings in front of anyone. He shrugged and said, "Yeah, so what?"

"You and Diane both have a lot of emotional baggage you're carrying around," Kell told him, voice softening up a bit.

"Not true. I don't even remember what happened to me," Jax remarked, a hint of anger entering his voice. Even if he did remember, why would that stop him from pursuing Diane if he really wanted to?

Kell shook his head with a snort before saying, "She at least remembers her baggage, but once you start remembering things, God help you both."

"I don't remember asking you about relationship advice," Jax said, feeling the tension sweep into his body and he realized he was getting angry about this.

"That's because this is a freebie," Kell said, placing a heavy hand on one of his shoulders, "Jax, I think of you as my younger brother. I'm only saying things to you that you are not capable of seeing at the moment. Trust me, I have been blinded by a woman's charm in the past. So, I know what you are feeling."

He wanted to lash out at Kell, but for some reason, he just let him continue. It was truly the first time the man had ever said anything about feeling like an older brother to him, which was funny because that was almost the way he thought about him.

When he didn't say anything in return, Kell gave him a surprised look. "I'm surprised you haven't lashed out at me yet, or at least not stormed off," Kell said, removing his hand from his shoulder and letting it rest at his side.

"Yeah, me too," Jax said, taking in a long deep breath.

"Look," Kell had started to say something but then fell silent as he felt a hand land on his other shoulder from behind. At first, he thought it might have been Diane's, but when he turned around, he discovered Jules staring at him.

"Sorry, bad time?" Jules said, looking between the two of them before settling her eyes on Jax. He had not even heard her approaching, and from the looks of Kell, he hadn't either.

"No," he said. "Sorry, I ran out on you earlier." He hadn't thought about what he should say to her.

"I understand, Jax," Jules gave him a polite smile, "Your friend had just been through an emotional ordeal, and you were comforting her."

That at least sounded like a good excuse but was far from the truth. He had just wanted to be close to Diane.

"Did her story help you remember anything?" Jules asked, still staring into his eyes.

Jax sighed, frustration clear in his voice when he said, "No, I just don't understand why it's so difficult to remember."

She moved closer to him and he could feel her warmth against his skin. Jules was a nice woman, and they had gone through a lot together. Jax knew they had some kind of bond between them, but what was between him and Diane was something that even words could not explain.

"Is there somewhere we could maybe go and talk privately?" Jules said, whispering right next to his ear. Jax did not know how to reply and stood there awkwardly. Fortunately, Kell was there to interrupt him from having to answer.

Kell cleared his throat. "No one is going anywhere except to their rooms and get some rest for the evening. Everyone needs to be on their A game for the operation ahead."

Jules looked at Kell for a moment and then back at Jax. "Let's talk when this operation is over."

He nodded his head and watched her walk away, not having a single clue about what he was going to do about this.

"Jax," Kell said. "What the hell. You also got her wanting you as well?"

"It's not my fault. It just sort of happened," Jax said with a guilty shrug. Perhaps if Diane had not come into the picture, he would have taken Jules up on the offer, but now, things had changed, along with his feelings.

"Great, I'll put that on your tombstone," Kell shook his head at him, before entering their room. "Come on, lover boy, let's get some rest."

As Jax closed the door to their room behind him, he tapped Kell on the shoulder and asked, "What should I do? On the one hand, there is Diane, and I feel so connected to her. Whenever we are near it's like an electric current through my body. With Jules, it's like we are close and maybe I did start liking her because we went through hell together, but I don't get the same feeling as I do with Diane. Do you get how I feel?

Kell shook his head, "I do know how you feel, Jax. Trust me when I say that women have a way of messing with your head. I have a lot of experience in that area. So, the only advice I can give you is to make your true feelings known, even if it means disappointing the other."

"What if I'm wrong about Diane?" Jax asked. "How do I know if a woman is truly interested in me in the way I want to be with them?"

Kell laid down in the bed with his face pointed toward the ceiling. "You'll know," he said, and he closed his eyes.

That's all the advice Kell is going to give me, he thought as he heard a lite snore coming from the man. How in the hell does a person fall asleep so fast?

Lying back on the cot, Jax couldn't sleep as both women circled in his head and he was reliving every key moment he had spent with each of them. The answer was clear in his mind, but the question was whether or not the feeling would be reciprocated. And if he was wrong, then he might be alienating both of them. "Why is this so confusing?" he asked himself.

Chapter 9

Personal log entry of Jason Alexander Xavis
01, 18, 2291

It's been a while since I have written in this journal. Sadly, I've had very few memories restored despite the fact I have been to places I have been before. I wish I could understand the mechanism of what is blocking my mind. Then at least I could figure out how to untangle it. I know that I do not suffer from any head trauma or mental illness, so I'm not quite sure what is bothering me. I will endeavor to spend more time per day in recalling. That's if I can get Jules and Diane out of my head. They are my current obsessions as I am not able to figure out how to be open with my feelings regarding both of them. Girls, girls, girls. Kell is right. I do need to be honest about how I feel. Otherwise, the longer I draw this out, the greater damage I do, and the greater danger I put myself in. Both women know how to use weapons and they are not afraid to shoot anyone.

Moving away from this subject, it was great to see the crew again. Barnaby was very welcoming to me and now to the others: It feels strange that Hewitt, Jules, and Diane are all with me onboard. Of course, the strange set of circumstances that led to this are hard to believe. I had no idea that I would be the center of attention in this shit storm that had been brewing around all of us.

It is my hope that we will discover the origin of this super conscious, as Hewitt had called it, and that we can find a way to end its control of people. Especially after what I witnessed about Diane as a child. If I had gone through something similar, then no wonder my mind was blocking it from me.

As a final note for this entry, which is really just a reminder to myself, I need to talk with Piper and the Paxtons. They are the ones I have had the least amount of contact with since arriving back onboard. And Piper was the one giving me the most stares when she learned about my brain alterations. I don't blame her for distrusting me. If everything stated about the Locorrans is true, then it presents a very frightening prospect. One of which I have seen up close and personal.

JAX HAD BEEN SITTING up on his cot writing in the journal before he set it to the side and stared at the back of Kell's head, which was barely visible in the dark room. Kell had the habit of snoring, but at this moment, he was not, and he could hear the thrum of the ship's engine all around him.

Jax wanted to take this moment of peace and quiet and settle back into some meditation. It had been weeks since his last practice, and he didn't know why he was avoiding it. Especially since every session had left him with a feeling of calm and peace.

Just as he had closed his eyes and started to focus on his breaths, the emergency klaxon sounded off in the room. Kell was instantly awake and on his feet, searching for his pants in the dark.

Kell had the habit of sleeping in a skin-tight compression suit that he wore all the time. When Jax had asked him about it before, the man had just said it felt good to his skin, and he wanted to always be prepared for anything. He wondered if Diane was doing the same thing right now. Would that be his life after all of this? A life of service in the EDL, where you're always on edge. Is that what he wanted?

Kell spoke to him while buttoning up his pants. "Jax, come on."

That was when he realized he hadn't moved from his spot yet while Kell was already standing in front of him in his full gear. He shook his head and jumped up from his cot, "Sorry, I was lost in my thoughts."

"I bet you were," Kell said. "Now let's get a move on. Remember, every second counts in an engagement."

"I haven't forgotten," Jax countered with a single nod.

Kell was the first out the door, and by the time Jax had reached the bridge after getting ready, he was the last to arrive. Even Hewitt in his advanced age had beat him here.

Jax took in a frustrated breath, realizing that he really needed to sort out his distracting thoughts.

He walked over to Barnaby who was hunched over a console, speaking to them. "While still in jump space, we received a very weak distress signal which originated very close to our exit point. I don't like strange coincidences, so this is what we are going to do." Barnaby was now standing to his full height and looking at each of them. "Piper, take the helm. Lilly, take the weapons controls. Bill, keep the engines running. I want to be able to make a quick jump if we end up in trouble."

"Understood," Bill said. "I'll see what I can do."

Barnaby nodded his head in approval, "Diane, Jules, do the two of you feel comfortable enough with each other to pilot the fighter?"

Jules and Diane looked at each other, and then they nodded their heads.

"Good," Barnaby said. "I'm hoping we won't have to use it, but it's best to be prepared for anything. So, go ahead, get onboard and we will detach you if need be."

Then Barnaby took a step closer to Kell and said, "Kell, suit up in case of borders. Jax, you are to aid Kell, understood?"

Jax nodded, however, he could not get the feeling of someone's eyes on him. The back of his head prickled and he turned around to notice that Piper was looking at him with that disapproving glare again. She still didn't trust him. It was the only reason he could think of.

He would prove to her that he was trustworthy. He turned back to Barnaby and spoke in a no-nonsense tone, "Understood, captain."

Then Barnaby turned toward Hewitt. "You can have a seat right over here, doctor." Instead of letting Jax see what the doctor said or did, Kell had him by the back of the arm and was leading him away from the bridge.

"What was that for, Kell?" Jax asked, breaking free from Kell's hold.

Kell shrugged, "Just making sure you didn't get distracted or lost along the way."

He knew what the man had meant. Diane and Jules. But with the ship in crisis mode, Kell should have known better than to think that he would neglect his duties.

"Thanks, I guess," Jax said. He might have to discuss with Kell about taking this older brother thing too far.

"No problem. First stop, the armory," Kell said, quickening his pace.

The armory was at the very back of the *Orion's Belt* after crossing all of their rooms. It was no larger than the captain's closet, which wasn't very big. Barnaby only had a few different outfits and shoes he wore on most occasions, and it was barely big enough to contain that. Somehow Kell had managed to stash his marine power armor into the closet and a small treasure trove of assorted weapons, most of which consisted of old Earth replicas.

Kell handed him his AR as he finished tugging on his gloves. The power armor was a dark navy color and made a loud whirring noise any time Kell made large motions. The armor made the wearer very strong and almost impregnable, especially against low-caliber weapons.

After Kell placed the helmet on, he reached back inside the armory and grabbed several cartridges. Then he took his own T-15 rifle and checked the power setting on it. "Don't forget your Glock. I'll keep watch over the upper floor. You go down into the bay. Any signs of trouble, contact me immediately," Kell said with a nod, voice muffled due to the helmet.

"Understood," Jax said, taking the Glock from the locker and strapping it to his thigh. The belt had a place for two more cartridges, and he slid them in place. Whatever was about to happen, he felt ready for it. He placed a small white bud in his ear, which allowed him to hear the crew and communicate with them.

Piper was already talking when he turned the bud on. "Exiting jump space now," her voice announced through the earpiece as Jax deemed himself ready. There was a moment of pause and then, at last, a sigh of breath as they exited jump space without an immediate attack.

"Closing in on the distress signal," Piper said. "So far, the scanners have identified no other threats, but the ice comets are affecting our sensors."

"As before," Barnaby's voice came through, "Piper, slow us down. Diane, Jules, I'm going to detach you. Take the fighter out in a nice spiral. I want to make sure no one else is lurking around."

"Roger that," Diane said.

Barnaby spoke again. "I don't want to be snuck up on like last time. Piper, do you have an ID on the freighter?"

"It's the *Apex*, captain," Piper said.

Barnaby let out a frustrated groan, "Same fucking ship that snuck up on us before."

Piper relayed, "Yes, sir, the ship is operating on emergency power, and life support onboard will fail in the next couple of hours."

"Have you tried hailing them?" Barnaby asked in a calm voice as always when under pressure. *That is why he is such a great Captain*, Jax thought to himself, as he continued to listen to the chatter of the crew.

"Yes, sir, but all I get is the same distress message. Due to the position of the ship, so deep within the ice comet field. They are lucky that anyone got the distress signal," Piper said.

"I'm still not convinced," Barnaby said. "Diane, found anything yet?"

"No," Diane's voice came through the earpiece, making Jax's heart flutter, he reined it in immediately as she said, "We are expanding our search field."

"Okay, Piper, take us closer, nice and slow. Bill, how are we doing in getting the jump engines ready?" Barnaby asked. The tension was high all around, but up until this point, they were right on track, and nothing seemed to go out of order.

"We'll have all green lights in a few minutes," Bill said.

Then the comm chatter died down for the moment. If the *Apex* had been the ship that had run the belt off the first time, then that would have been a couple of months ago. Had it taken them that long to remove the *New Horizon* from the ice comet? Was it of that much value? There were way too many questions pouring through his mind as Diane came back in over the communications.

"Still clear, Captain Barnaby," she said.

"Maintain a patrol, Diane," Barnaby said. "We are going to close in with the *Apex* and send a team aboard."

"Understood," Diane said.

"Jax, Keller," Barnaby called out to them, "You two ready for your excursion?"

"Yes, sir," Keller responded back.

"Once you've cleared the ship," Barnaby said. "I'll be sending Bill over to see if he can patch up their life support. Any survivors found, you mark them, and then Piper and Lilly will aid them."

"Attaching to the upper emergency airlock," Piper broke in. "Touch down in four, three, two, one."

There was an audible creak noise from the flooring beneath Jax, and he knew that the *Belt* had just connected with the other ship. The access port into that ship was dead center in the bay. This had been the same access port that had been connected to the Locorran craft they had brought with them.

"I'm on my way down, Jax," Kell said.

"Connection is good," Piper said. "You can open the hatch at any time."

Jax found himself moving toward the hatch which was recessed in the floor. The hatch was supposed to be left uncovered so that it could be used in emergencies, but during his time aboard the *Belt*, Barnaby had ignored this rule in favor of maximizing his cargo capacity. Today, however, with most of the bay empty, it was easy to see the faded black and yellow markings around the hatch.

He reached down and pulled the latch, which opened the outer steel panel door. A foot below, there was a metal wheel that he had to turn clockwise to unlatch. Just as he started to turn it, he felt someone tap his shoulder.

"Told you I was on my way," Kell said with a pointed look thrown at him, a frown present on his face, through the clear ballistic shield.

Jax was surprised by his sudden appearance. Why hadn't he heard the motors of the power armor? He should have; they were loud as hell. Had his mind been so absorbed in what he was doing, or was it simply that his mind was working overtime at the prospect of stepping foot on the *New Horizon* again? Would it bring a flood of memories back to him or would it just be another disappointment?

"Sorry," he said, uncertain of everything he was doing. He had been trying so hard to keep the tumultuous feelings at bay, but with the realization that he had been so lost in his thoughts that he did not hear Kell's approach, he wasn't quite sure how to proceed. He took a deep breath in and then let it out, calming himself before placing all his attention on what Kell was doing. He needed to be present in the moment; the rest he would be thinking about later.

"I'm going down first. I want you to hang back for a minute until I give the clear signal, and then we will proceed together throughout the ship, understood?" Kell asked.

He wanted to argue back, but then his rationale took over, and he just nodded his head in agreement. Kell was doing the sensible thing, and if their roles had been reversed, he would have done the same thing.

"Okay, going in," Kell said.

Jax watched him climb down the ladder and into the ship's rec room. The *Apex* was laid out exactly like the *Orion's Belt* unless any alterations had been made to it. From up above, he could see Kell scan over the room with the rifle and then walk away a minute before he called for him to come down.

The rungs of the ladder were cold in the palms of Jax's hands as he started to climb down. When he touched down in the rec room, two things greeted him. There was a very bad stench in the air that the purifiers were not able to scrub out. The second thing was how cold the ship was. Was this due to the fact that life support was failing? Or had the crew just turned down the heat?

Kell was by his side the next moment. "I want you to stay right here while I check out the aft side of the ship. Once I come back, we'll go together toward the bridge and cargo bay. If anything happens, radio me immediately."

Jax nodded his head and lifted his rifle to his shoulder. The scope attached to it had a low light setting and a thermal view. He scanned around him with that as he heard Kell's power armor whirring as he moved away from him.

The rec room didn't look too disheveled from his first look-over. A ping pong table still sat undisturbed in the center of the room. Half-full cups were still sitting out on the furniture, and even several of the large displays on the walls were still showing either some current movies or cartoons. It looked just like a rec room that was still in use. Except on the *Belt*, the crew was required to power off the displays when not in use. This place looked like the crew had just gotten up and walked away from what they had been doing. Whatever happened must have been sudden enough to not make turning the screens off a priority.

Jax froze in place a moment later when he heard a creaking noise coming from the hallway and heading toward the bridge. Swiveling the rifle in that direction, he spotted nothing through the thermal. Jax held his breath for a moment and tried to focus in the direction he had heard the creak. There was silence and nothing else, but then all of the sudden, there was a bright flash in the room, and he couldn't see anything anymore. He was blinded as his eyes burned hot. His other senses had been dulled because of the pain burning in his skull from where his eyes were.

He grappled blindly, only then realizing that his rifle was gone. Jax got the sense that something bad was happening or had happened. He had no clue where the attack had come from, and now his rifle had been snatched from his hands. He stood blindly for another moment, and then a blow hit him hard in the stomach, making him fall over onto his back, gasping for air as the breath was knocked out of his lungs.

A few more hard blows had come down upon him, but at this point, he had curled up enough to absorb some of them. He wanted to cry out in pain and shout for help, but he wasn't able to. Instead, he had to focus on getting his breathing even first.

Instinct was taking over, and once he had gained control over his panic, he rolled his body away from the blows and managed to scramble to his feet. His eyes were tearing and everything looked green and blobby as the temporary blindness from the flash faded away. He could make a pretty good guess at which blob was attacking him.

Jax couldn't make out any features or details, but he knew when another blow was coming. The assailant was attacking him with a hardened baton. Backing away from it, he felt the wind generated from the swing. He was avoiding the blows, by sidestepping or jerking his body to the left or right. As his breath came back under his control he cried out for Kell.

Another swing came at his head in the next moment, and he barely avoided it with a slight movement of his body. This fight was not going to end well for him if he didn't end it quickly. His right hand reached for the pistol at his hip, and in a swift motion, he took it out and was bringing it to bear on his assailant when he felt the impact of the stick smash into the pistol and tear it from his grasp with a violent force.

"Shit, shit, shit," he cursed to himself and lurched out with a vicious punch toward the upper portion of the blob. He felt the satisfying impact of his fist on something. It had felt like flesh, and for a moment, he had thought he had landed a good blow. That is until the butt end of the baton smashed him in the center of the chest.

Once again, he found himself falling backward and landing hard on the ground, unable to breathe. He was coughing and choking, and all sense of the enemy was gone from his mind.

The thumping sounds of a T-15 rifle were barely audible in his ears as he had managed to turn over on his hands and knees. Coughs followed every inhalation of air as he sucked it through his open mouth. Once he had gotten it down, he turned his head slightly enough to see Kell looking down at him.

"You good?" Kell asked, panic clear in his voice although Jax still could not make out his features.

He gave Kell a thumbs up and a nod of the head. Kell wasted no time in leaving his side and heading down the hallway toward the bridge, which must have been the way his assailant had gone. Staying on his hands and knees for a minute longer, still sucking down more oxygen, his surroundings finally came back into focus, and he was at last ready to get back to his feet.

The pistol was close by, and he holstered it. His rifle, however, was nowhere to be found. That was until he heard the firefight going on up ahead. He couldn't see any flashes, but the noises from his AR were noticeable. Taking the pistol into hand, he moved cautiously down the hallway, checking each open door to make sure no other assailants lay in waiting. Once Jax reached the bridge door, he glanced in before entering, making sure to check the corners like Kell had taught him to do.

The only thing of notice on the bridge was a body strapped into the pilot's chair. The person had long dark hair that spilled out from the side of the chair and their head lay awkwardly in a twisted angle.

The noise of the gunfight was still going on from the ladder recessed in the back of the wall of the bridge. This was one of the access points to the lower bay. Jax wanted to rush down and aid Kell, but for some reason, he wanted to check the body first. This had been the first one he had come across, and his gut was telling him to check it. After all, he didn't want any more surprises than what he had already encountered.

Just as he got close enough to the person in the chair, the noises of the AR finally stopped, which was a good sign, because it meant that Kell had finally taken out the attacker.

Jax focused on the figure in front of him. He turned the chair slightly toward him, before realizing the neck of the young woman sitting here had been broken. Her eyes were locked wide open, staring at him, and her tongue was hanging out. She was definitely dead, but he still checked for breathing and then sighed. His eyes dropped below and on the floor by her limp hand was an extended metal baton.

Had she been in a fight? He saw no other visible contusions or bruises on her body. She was also strapped into the pilot's chair. Or had she been placed there afterward? None of it made sense. He puzzled over who the woman could be and what she was doing here, that was when he became aware of a clanky noise nearby.

Twisting his head to see Kell, he was taken by surprise when a dark, hooded figure rushed towards him. His finger pulled the trigger of the pistol twice before he was knocked off his feet and smashed into the control panels behind them.

Jax hadn't fully lost his breath this time, and the hooded assailant for some reason had not followed through with his attack. In fact, he had backed away as he slumped to the ground. The pistol had been dislodged from his hand again and Jax was unsure where it had landed; but with certainty, he knew where the metal baton was. His fingers probed for it, and when they latched onto it, he felt the comfort of it in his grasp. This was something familiar to him. A weapon he knew how to use.

The assailant got up from his slumped position and came at him again, this time wielding the hardened baton. It was coming down quickly and hard toward his head. With a swift block, Jax deflected the attack and followed up with a swing to the assailant's ribs. Jax could feel the jar of the impact and the cry of pain from his assailant. He knew he had landed a solid blow and probably had broken some ribs. This caused the assailant to back away from him, which gave him the time to get back to his feet.

Jax could now see the assailant for who they were instead of the blob from earlier. The shape and size were that of a man, but he couldn't make out any facial features due to the cloth pulled over his face. The thing they were wearing was a thin poncho-like material. In fact, it looked like an emergency poncho like the ones he had onboard the *Belt*. Kell had told him that it had a reflective lining on the inside, that kept the body heat from seeping out.

His assailant had used this poncho to conceal himself from his thermal on the scope. Why hadn't he thought about that before?

Time for thinking was up. The assailant, now in a rage, came at him again, swinging in a hard X pattern. If he got hit by any of the blows, they would injure him quite badly. Jax's instincts took over, and as the assailant drew close enough, Jax swung his metal baton in a large circular motion, coming straight down the centerline of his assailant. The move disrupted the attack as his assailant was forced to move out of the way by sidestepping. He had been prepared for this, and with a flick of his wrist, his baton smashed into the top part of the assailant's head in a whip-like motion.

It was a good contact because he felt the strong reverberation stinging his hand and wrist. That pain was dulled though by the adrenaline pouring through his body.

Jax's assailant stumbled back from the blow, and this time, he followed up. With two more strikes, he had disarmed the person, and with one more blow to the head, the assailant went down a final time.

Jax didn't waste time in finding out if he had killed the man or not. His primary concern was what had happened to Kell. There had been no sounds from his side for a while now, and it got him worried.

Sliding down the ladder, his mind was going toward the worst-case scenarios, but he was trying to maintain hope. When his feet hit the floor of the lower bay, he almost slipped and fell. He would have fallen if he hadn't been holding on to the rungs. The light was very poor in the bay, which was not normal since the bay on the *Belt* was always bright.

Jax squinted at the floor. Now he could see that the thing he almost slipped on was a deep red color, almost black. Letting his eyes follow the trail, he discovered a mosaic of bodies, either hanging from the ceiling or restrained in place on some of the cargo containers. Most of the bodies had been cut open and organs removed and just left piled on the floor. The stench of the place was overpowering. It was the worst smell possible, even worse than a bilge system overflowing. It took him a moment to keep from expelling the contents of his own stomach onto the floor. He had to find Kell.

Pushing through the nausea, he let his eyes and head search around the place. To the left, he discovered the prone Kell lying face down, still in the power armor.

"Kell!" he called out, rushing over to his side and lifting the side of Kell's body up. The blood had smeared the outside exterior of ballistic-proof face shielding, and he had to use his shirt to wipe it clean before he could see Kell's face.

"Kell!" he shouted again, shaking him lightly to try and get him to wake up.

Jax's heart thumped in his chest as he let panic control him. He was breathing heavily but still felt like there was not enough oxygen in his body. Jax knew he needed to calm down because one could only think fast with a clear head. Taking several deep breaths, despite the putrid stench, he was able to clear his thoughts enough to remember to check the vital details on the suit's wrist display.

He scrambled to do just that as a voice registered in his ear, sounding like someone had been trying to get his attention for a while now. In his panic, he hadn't even heard Lilly's voice calling for him over the communicator in his ear.

"Jax! Jax!" Lilly was shouting, "Are you okay? Is Kell okay? I'm heading in."

Before Jax decided to answer her, his eyes locked on the wrist display. Kell's vitals were showing strong. Jax let out a sigh of relief. It meant that Kell was just unconscious and not dying, which was great news. He wasn't sure how he would have dealt with Kell's death, and he was grateful that he was not going to find out.

Jax looked around his surroundings then. It was all a mess that someone had left behind. The question was, who was it left behind by? He wanted to know what had happened and how the assailant managed to take out someone in power armor. The task should not have been possible and yet, here Kell lay.

Thinking back on everything that had happened in the last fifteen minutes, Jax wondered what the black cord-like thing near the ladder was. He laid Kell's head back down before standing up and walking toward it. It didn't take his mind long to discover what it was. The black cord was part of a power conduit. The assailant had been waiting for someone to come down for him. He had rigged the cable to the metal ladder very discreetly. So, all he had to do was throw the power into it. If the ship had been operating at full power, it was possible that the current would have overloaded or killed Kell; but in the low power state, it probably caused some problems with the power suite. Judging by the unusual pattern of rails shots from right to left, the suit was obviously not working properly.

A brief spark of something flashed up a few feet away, barely visible from where it had been tossed in behind some crates. Curious, Jax immediately walked toward it, although carefully. When he took it into hand, he discovered that this was a homemade device of some type. It was a long metal pole with rubber hand gripping, and like the ladder, a power cable had been attached to it. The end that had sparked had a fine point for jabbing and prodding. This had been some kind of homemade shock gun, and judging by the fresh blood on the end of it that was still dripping instead of congealing up, this had probably been the thing used to take Kell down. Just as he was setting it back down to the floor, he heard someone coming down the ladder.

It was Lilly, and she was taking in the scene with a high-powered flashlight and pistol. "Jax. What the hell happened here? Where's Kell?"

Jax wasted no time in bringing her to him. She immediately got down to her knees and began opening the power armor. "He doesn't appear to be wounded other than right here. What happened to him?" she inquired, deft hands working quickly to locate Kell's wound.

"We were both attacked by a masked assailant," Jax told her. "Kell followed him down here, and the ladder had been trapped with a power cable. Fortunately for him, it wasn't powerful enough to kill or disable him, but from the evidence I have observed so far. It caused some issues with the suit's controls."

She nodded her head and kept working as she announced through the communicator, "Piper, Barnaby, I'm going to need some help getting Kell back to the ship. He's injured but should be okay."

"Roger that," Piper said. "We are on our way."

Lilly continued to work on Kell, now completely out of the power armor when he saw another person coming down the ladder. He half expected it to be Barnaby, but the slow-moving figure could be only one person: Hewitt.

"Jax," Hewitt said. "Sorry about Kell. I'm glad that neither of you was seriously hurt."

"Why are you aboard, doctor? This place isn't safe," Jax immediately stood up and went to help Hewitt down the ladder even when he looked at him disapprovingly.

Hewitt looked past him at the bodies displayed. "I agree with you, Jax, it was irrational of me to rush in here, and I'm sure that Barnaby will tongue-lash me as well. However, I think we are safe now, don't you think?"

Jax didn't even pause to think about what Hewitt had said. The doctor had been referring to the fact that there were seven bodies now identified, which was the last reported crew size of this ship, but that didn't mean everyone or every trap had been identified yet.

"I realize that it is possible that all of the crew may have been accounted for, doctor, but that doesn't mean all of the threats have been eliminated," Jax warned him, looking around the area with a grimace on his face.

"Nonsense, Jax," Hewitt waved his warning off with the flap of his hand, "We are so close to the *New Horizon*. I can't wait to discover what knowledge might have been left behind. So come on boy."

"Hewitt," Barnaby called out, touching down on the cargo bay floor and stomping quickly toward them. "I told you to wait on the ship, doctor."

"I know, I know." Hewitt sighed. "This is so important. I can't just wait around. What if you miss a critical detail that only I could see?"

He could see Barnaby rolling his eyes. "Fine, doctor," then he turned his attention toward Jax and asked, "You okay, Jax?"

"Good to go, sir. I just wish I had been able to help Kell," Jax said, looking back at Kell's body.

"I know, but he's in good hands now. I'll let you make the call. Are you up to going onboard the *New Horizon*?" Barnaby asked.

Jax had already made his decision. He was ready to find out about who he was and if there was anything left to find out about him anyway. They still had no clue of what they would and would not find.

Jax took a deep breath and then said, "Of course, and Hewitt you are welcome to follow me, but you must obey my instructions. If I tell you to hide or run, you must do it, understood?"

Hewitt nodded his head. "At your leisure then, Jax."

Chapter 10

The interior of the *New Horizon* ship was lit by a few battery-powered lamps that were growing dim as they neared the end of their life cycle. For the most part, the ship looked well intact and not very disturbed outside of the signs of violence he had noted. The upper deck of the ship was a long corridor filled with cryo pods. All of them that they had passed along the way to the bridge were long abandoned.

There had been blood stains on some of the pods and even a cracked glass on one or two of them. It was evidence in his mind of what he had already gathered. The blood was old and caked on as if it had been there for years. This was evidence of the violence of his escape so many years ago.

"Jax?" Hewitt said. "Why did you stop?"

Jax hadn't realized that he had stopped walking. His eyes had been fixated on the large dry pool of blood in front of the pod he had stopped at. Taking a glance up at the pod he knew exactly which one it had been.

"Was this your pod?" Hewitt asked as Jax felt him coming to stand behind him.

Jax could barely nod his head in agreement as the image of someone with their face covered in blood and pressed against the glass to peer at him flashed through his mind. He knew that face.

"Jax, what is it? Are you remembering?" Hewitt's voice came as if through a barrier until it faded away.

Jax couldn't speak any longer. In his mind, he was looking at that blood-covered face. It was his father's face, and there was no kindness or familiar expression on it. There was only desperation, an intent to break him free of the pod and do harm to him.

"Hewitt, Jax," Barnaby said over his earpiece. He could hear it. The sound entered his ear, but he could not comprehend it. He couldn't respond as his mind watched his father slowly slump away from view, smearing massive amounts of blood along the way.

"I need the both of you to return to the *Belt* immediately," Barnaby commanded, voice hardened with a hint of distress bleeding in it.

"I will try, captain, but Jax has become unresponsive," Hewitt spoke, jostling Jax to get him to respond to no avail.

"I don't care what you do, doctor. Drag his ass back up here now," Barnaby barked through the communicator.

"Jax," Hewitt said, nudging him again.

Jax could hear him, but he could not feel anything except for the scene in front of him.

He had crumpled to the floor in the exact spot his father had slipped down to, but instead of being face down, his back was on the pod and he was watching himself from the far end of the corridor. He was wielding a black metal pipe in hand, keeping several assailants away from him as he backed down the corridor.

"Jax," Hewitt said again. "We need to go. Something is happening."

Suddenly, the voice of Diane broke over the earpiece. "Confirmed, two EDL fighters approaching Barnaby. They are not returning my hales." There was a pause for a moment before Diane said, "They just opened fire at us."

A commotion broke over the communicator. Jax could hear snippets of Barnaby shouting orders to everyone, but his eyes and mind stayed transfixed on watching himself fight other humans with that metal pipe. It was a blur of quick strikes, and every person he hit, more just kept coming at him.

The others wanted to hurt him. They wanted to kill him. He could see blades and other makeshift weapons in hand. Why? What had he done?

"Hewitt, are you making any progress with Jax? I need you both back on board now. We are under attack!" Barnaby commanded again.

"Sorry, captain. I'm unable to get to him and I'm too old and frail to drag him," Hewitt replied as he watched Jax frozen in time.

"Understood," Barnaby said. "Hunker down then, and pray we survive this."

What did Barnaby mean about surviving this? Jax had heard what had been said, but he was transfixed on the fight that was growing closer and closer to him in his vision. The corridor was lined with fallen bodies—bodies he had taken down with that dreadful metal pipe. Grown men armed with blades had been no match for his skill with the thing. It was almost nightmarish, unbelievable, but yet it was true. This is what happened all those years ago, when he had gone on the run and stole the *New Horizon* colony ship.

The ship shuddered around him. He could feel the jolt of it, but the fighting was right on top of him now, and he could see his father and another man stabbing at him. He recognized the man with his father as Theodore Bailey, the founder and leader of the *New Horizons* project. Both men were working in unison to take him down, but he was far more skilled. With two quick flicks of the metal pipe, the machete blade Theodore had been wielding smashed into the metal, grating with several clanging noises. And then Theodore collapsed to the ground, unconscious from a blow to the top of his head. Watching this as an observer, paralyzed from moving at the moment, he wondered if he had cracked the man's skull or not.

It didn't matter. Even if he was watching himself, he was reliving all of the emotions pouring through him—rapid heart rate, the adrenaline coursing through his veins making him hyper-aware of everything happening to him. He could even feel the stiffness in his hand from gripping the metal pipe so tight and the soreness that came from impacting hard surfaces.

The fight had now been reduced to just him and his father. His father had been trained by his own father like him; but from his observations of his movements and skill, in his present state, he exhibited none of his abilities. Jax hadn't really thought about it at the time, but now seeing it from a different perspective, he knew that his father was not himself. It was as if he was being controlled like a marionette puppet.

There were no words exchanged between them, but he did wait for his father to make the first move. It had been a clumsy stab toward his stomach, which he redirected away with his palm. Which set his father up for a strike to the nose with the butt of his pipe. Deep red streams of blood gushed out from the broken nose. Normally a person would scramble or fall backward from such a blow, but in this case, his father pressed forward, desperately wanting to insert a blade deep into his chest. Instinct took over and a sharp circular strike to the head sent his father to the ground, unmoving. More blood was pouring from his cut-open scalp, and Jax was sure that he had cracked a skull this time. He hadn't been able to hold back. The adrenaline was making him jittery, but with all of his assailants down, he watched himself run to the bridge, and set the ship back for a course to Earth. Yes, he was going home. He didn't care what it might be like. It had to be better than here.

With everything active and set, Jax went back to his pod, observing the carnage before him. Dozens of unmoving bodies lay before him. Not all were dead, but within a few short minutes, those not in a stasis pod would be crushed by the gigantic G-forces that would happen when the ship's jump drive activated. Theodore had been a brilliant man; he had created an inertial damper of sorts but was still on a primitive level compared to what the *Belt* used to negate the G-forces in jump space.

Sliding into the pod and closing the door, he pushed all of the buttons on the inside until everything glowed green. His pod was ready to go, and this would have been the point when his father would have appeared, blood-stained and looking dead; but instead, something black and massive filled the window of the pod. When the door was ripped open by powerful claws, he was no longer the observer, but instead, he was present in the moment—heart pounding, body shaking uncontrollably as an after-effect of the adrenaline surge that had rushed through him. The next thing he knew, he was pulled from the pod with no effort and slung into the darkness.

The impacts felt real to his body in the present moment. He couldn't catch his breath, and his body hurt everywhere. All around him in the almost complete darkness were things scurrying about. Things that didn't look or feel like the ship anymore. The space around him felt too large, almost cavernous-like. He even bet his voice would echo in the place if he were to speak. But at that moment, he was too stunned. There were some thudding steps behind him that vibrated the whole floor, but when he looked back to see what was causing it, he found his blood-stained father with his eyes shut. Blood was dripping from his chin and nose as he stood behind him.

Jax's legs and arms twitched like he wanted to run, but he managed to calm himself with a couple of deep breaths as his eyes met those of his father's, but he didn't quite look like his father. Perhaps it was the furrowed brow or the decrepit way he was holding his hands, but he knew that this wasn't his real father.

"Jason," his father said with deep inhalations of air as if the man had been suffocating between breaths. "You left me and your mother to die. You've always been a disappointment to us, Jason." That deep inhalation again and then more words, "You left us to die because you thought you were special or gifted, but in truth, you were nothing but a spoiled child who only cared about himself."

Jax wanted to say something in defense of this, but the verbal abuse continued, and he remained there, stuck in the moment forever, forced to listen to words that pierced his heart like millions of tiny shards of broken and pointed glass.

His father continued in his dull and gurgling voice, "Even as a baby, we knew that you were challenged mentally and physically by the other kids, but we did our best to give you a normal life. A life that you betrayed without a second thought."

There were more of the large black insectoid-looking things scurrying around in the dimness of the place. Jax had no idea where the little bit of light was coming from, but the place was ice cold and his body was jittering not only from the adrenaline but the coldness as well.

"We should have aborted you as a baby instead of living with the defects. But we compassionately let you live and grow up. If we had only known how much of a disappointment you would be to us, Jason," his father said, voice turning more inhumane as he went on.

Once again, Jax resisted the urge to say something to his father, equally as mean even though he knew it wasn't his father. This was all once again a shadow game played out by the deeply embedded super conscious. It wanted him back in the fold or dead, that was the game it was playing with him.

"The only way to redeem yourself is to come back to us, Jason, then we can all forgive you. Isn't that what parents are supposed to do for their children? To forgive," his father whispered, voice sounding like nails on a chalkboard. Jax listened despite himself, mind and heart breaking apart the more his fake father went on.

Jax was tired of this. He wanted the control of his thoughts and feelings back, so he began speaking non-stop from the heart.

"Out of the night that covers me,
Black as the pit from pole to pole,
I thank whatever gods may be
For my unconquerable soul.
In the fell clutch of circumstance,
I have not winced nor cried aloud.
Under the bludgeonings of chance,
My head is bloody, but unbowed.
Beyond this place of wrath and tears
Looms but the horror of the shade,
And yet the menace of the years
Finds, and shall find, me unafraid.
It matters not how straight the gate,
How charged with punishments the scroll,
I am the master of my fate:
I am the captain of my soul."

His father laughed, which was more a screech than anything else as he continued, "You always did think yourself smart and clever, Jason, but that is the furthest thing from the truth. In fact, you're dumb and stupid to think yourself smarter than all of us."

Jax listened to his father before he took in a deep breath of air and said, "You taught me that poem, Father, and not because I was smarter or cleverer than anyone else. You taught it to me because it was what you believed, and it's what I believe. I'm sorry for all the bad things I did in my childhood or even any negative things I may have done to you and Mom over the years. I am sorry. I'm even sorry for the things I haven't done. I wish you and Mom could see me grow up, get married, and have a family of my own. I wish you were truly here with me now, but I know what you are."

His father chortled, his teeth showing, reddened with blood, "You wish we were with you right now. We can be—just come back to us. All will be forgiven."

"There is nothing to be forgiven for," Jax said, wiping the tears from his eyes. "That poem you taught me so long ago means that I take responsibility for my actions and that no matter what I am in control of my fate. So, whatever you are, you have no power or authority over me. I am in control of myself, so get out and never come back."

After he said those words, the scurriers stopped moving, and even his father stopped speaking.

"Get out!" he bellowed, his voice reverberating throughout the ship's interior.

His father faded into the blackness and was replaced by a giant black mantis staring down at him. There was an intense heat radiating from it, and its hatred was only making his own hatred grow hotter and brighter. This thing thought it could manipulate and control him. Instead, it had made him mad. So utterly and crazily mad. Everything that had gone wrong was because of this thing. There was no way he was letting it win against him.

The staring contest continued until at last the thing faded back into the darkness, taking any sort of illumination with it. He was left in complete darkness and isolation until he heard a faint beeping noise from somewhere close by.

Concentrating on that noise, it grew louder and louder, and then everything began to grow brighter until at last, he was staring up into the wrinkled old face of Doctor Hewitt.

"I'll be a son of a gun," Hewitt said with surprise coloring his voice as he looked at Jax like he was a miracle. "I knew you would come back to us."

Jax tried to lift his head, but it felt like a stone had been placed there instead. It stung when he tried to move again until Hewitt placed both his hands upon his shoulders to keep him from still.

"Just relax, boy. It will take you some time to recover," Hewitt said.

Rotating his head from left to right, he realized that he was in the small medical room on board the *Belt*.

"What happened?" Jax said. His mouth felt dry, and his throat sore. It was hard to talk.

The last thing he remembered was that he had been staring down the mantis, trying not to let it win, not against him. That mantis had taken a lot from him, it had taken his whole family away.

A dull ache started from his chest as he remembered the state of his father. His breath hitched as he tried not to get choked up at the memory he had seen.

Hewitt sighed from beside him and said, "You went into a catatonic state while we were aboard the *New Horizon*. The ship was under attack by two EDL fighters from Earth. After examining their wreckage, we discovered that the two pilots had been fully altered by the super conscious, by a very clever means. It appears that the men had a gaming device that plugged directly into their visual cortex. The mind alteration was kind of slow, due to the lower power level, but used over many times, it would do the trick. The EDL doesn't allow this game device, but these men appear to have picked it up from the black market. All serial numbers and identifications were removed."

"That's good to know, doctor. Is everyone okay?" he asked, wincing as another throb of pain passed through his head.

"Yes, yes. Everyone is fine and back on board the *Belt*. I know I'm rushing details on you, but I think you will be interested in knowing where we are going," Hewitt said with a knowing look on his face.

"I thought we would be heading back to Earth?" Jax asked, confused about the change of plans.

"Oh no, not after what I discovered on that ship's records," Hewitt said.

"Let me guess. The location of the super conscious?" Jax said, finally feeling some relief when he moved his head and did not feel that stab of pain.

"Precisely," Hewitt said. "And we are heading to it right now."

"I don't think I want to wrestle with it anymore." Jax was trying to keep his thoughts calm as images of the mantis and his dead father flooded back into his mind once again.

"I realized that while you were catatonic, you kept hollering out and talking in your state. I have to admit you were putting up an interesting argument of sorts. I can only make assumptions that the super conscious was trying to lure you back under its control?" Hewitt asked, a knowing look on his face. Sometimes, Jax thought the old man knew too much.

"It was. It was using the image of my dead father to convey its disappointment in me, but of course, everything would be forgiven once I rejoined them,"

"Of course, it would have been. During one of your rants, you even quoted William Ernest Henley. Quite stirring," Hewitt said.

Jax cracked a proper smile for the first time since becoming conscious, "I wasn't going for dramatic effect. I was trying to make a point. The mantis creature doesn't like it when you exhibit your free will. It wants to crush you down into a pulp."

"You are definitely not an ordinary young person, Jax. I have watched as so many of them base themselves on how others think about them. You, on the other hand, just don't care, you are who you are, and everyone just has to accept that," Hewitt said with a note of admiration in his voice.

"I'll take that as a compliment, doctor," Jax said, the feeling of his head weighing him down made it difficult to glance at the doctor.

"As you should. Now, I'm going to leave and let you rest. You have been through a rough ordeal, and I wanted you rested because tomorrow we shall look upon the face of a god," Hewitt said, as he wiggled a finger at him before leaving the small room.

Hewitt dimmed the lights on his way out. And afterwards, Jax tried to move some more once again but found his body heavy and lethargic. Instead of forcing himself, he just gave in to a nice and dreamless sleep.

Chapter 11

A knock at the door woke him up. Jax had no idea what time it was or how long he had been asleep. The only thing he knew for sure was that the heaviness he had been feeling before had gone away. He tried moving his head and limbs and was surprised to find that he could do so with ease now.

The knock came again, disturbing him from his thoughts. He cleared his throat before calling out, "Enter."

When the door slid open, it broke the semi-darkness of the room as the main lights powered on. He was temporarily blinded but could hear two distinct footfalls enter the room. One of them he recognized instantly as Diane's. He had heard it often enough back on Earth.

"Jax," Jules called out to him first, "Sorry to wake you, but we wanted to check on you and to also let you know we are approaching the source."

"Hewitt said you should have been fully rested by now," Diane said. "He kept us from seeing you earlier."

Jax blinked his eyes a few times before they finally adjusted enough for him to see Diane and Jules standing side by side watching him. Both had their hair tied back and concerned looks on their faces.

"Can we get you anything?" Diane said.

"Some water would be nice," Jax replied with a small smile. He was grateful to both of them for coming to check up on him.

Both women looked at each other before Diane left the room. As soon as Diane was gone, Jules stepped closer to him and laid a warm hand on his chest.

She sighed softly before saying, "You gave me a big fright when they brought you back from the other ship. None of us knew if you would come out of the coma. Well, except for Hewitt. He said you would be fine and up and about in a few short days."

"Hewitt always seems to have the answers, doesn't he?" Jax said.

"I'm not complaining," Jules let out a warm laugh, "He is a genius, after all."

Her hands were rubbing his chest as she talked to him and Jax, in his state, did not have the heart to tell her to stop. Because if he did, then that would mean that he would have to come clean about his true feelings about Diane. And right now, thinking about any sort of feelings was out of the question for him. He had been through so much with the mantis that his emotions all felt wrung out of him. It would take some amount of time for him to fully bounce back.

When Diane entered back into the room, she scooted right up beside Jules with a large mug in hand. Both women looked at each other again, and this time, Jules backed away.

"Can I help you to sit up?" Diane asked, extending out her free hand.

Jax nodded and gave her his hand. Diane didn't pull on him at all. Instead, she allowed him to pull himself up with her support. He was thankful for that.

"Thanks," he told her, taking the cup from her hand and sipping on the cold water. It felt good to his lips and throat. How long had it been since he had drunk anything?

He took a couple of more sips before the raw feeling in his throat subsided somewhat. Then he passed another gentle smile towards Diane and uttered in his still scratchy voice, "Thanks."

"What else can I help you with?" Diane asked, placing a warm hand on his upper arm. The touch felt soothing.

What a cruel twist of fate it was that he had to remember his father's face, but not quite his father's face, staring down at him like he was some kind of an enemy. What had he done to deserve that?

He shook the thoughts out of his head and glanced around for his clothes. He could see Jules sitting at the foot of his bed, watching him with those big green eyes.

The feeling that somehow he was betraying anyone that was in his line of sight left a bitter taste at the back of his throat. He had to remind himself that what was happening around him now was very different from what he had seen. Perhaps it did not have to end so harshly between the three of them.

He knew that it was obvious what was going on to everyone in the room. He wondered what the two wanted from him. Were they waiting to see who he picked to be his? Could it be that simple, or was he reading too much into this situation?

"Your clothes," Diane said, bringing him out of his thoughts, "You're probably going to need those. Don't worry, we'll find them." She had realized what he wanted without him even saying it. Somehow, the gesture was enough to pull his lips up in a smile.

Strangely enough, both women went about searching the small room by opening drawers and cabinets built into the walls. At one point, several rolls of bandages fell out of one cabinet and bounced off Jules' head. They both paused for a moment as the stuff unrolled throughout the room.

"Piper is going to kill us," Jules said, scrambling to roll the bandages back up.

Diane joined in, helping as well. It was true that Piper and Lilly maintained this room and oversaw the wounded and injured crew. Lilly was far more laid back than Piper about how organized and tidy a room was, though.

As if Piper knew they had mentioned her or he was just thinking about her, she appeared in the now slide-open door with his clothes in hand and her stern gaze fixed on Jules and Diane in the room.

"Once you two get that gauze rolled back up, get out of the room. I told you two to leave him alone so he could rest," Piper scolded them.

Neither spoke back; they knew they had been caught, and they worked furiously to get the rolls up. When both were done, they left the room quickly with only a glance back at him as each left the room.

Piper stood in front of him now, holding out his clothes to him, shaking her head in his direction. "Those two are going to be the death of you, Jax."

"How so?" he arched a brow at her.

Piper rolled her eyes at him, "I know you're not dense. Surely you can see that they are both fighting for you."

Jax sighed. "I kind of picked that up."

"Good, I knew you would. Now pick one of them," Piper said.

Jax knew Piper's hardened exterior was more of a way to protect her feelings than what she thought of him. Still, he fell silent instead of responding, knowing that she was right.

Piper nodded her head at him as she began to back out of the room. "I see. You're conflicted. Is it because you can't choose or...?" she trailed off.

He shook his head and placed the clothes on the bed. "They are both incredible, and I just don't want to break one's heart. What should I do, Piper?"

"Oh no, you ain't getting me involved in your love affairs. I've already given you my advice. Make your feelings clear and do it quickly before things start getting ugly."

What does that mean? If he were to not make his feelings clear soon, would the two really start fighting each other? Jax sighed and put his head in his hands.

"Hurry up and get dressed. Barnaby wants everyone on the bridge in a few minutes," Piper said.

"Piper, wait!" Jax said, waving his hand at her to make sure he got her attention. And he had because she stopped right in the middle of the doorway looking at him.

"It's okay, Jax, I still trust you with my life. I just had to ponder over some things first," she reassured him about the way she had been acting before their mission.

Jax relaxed and nodded at her with a small smile, "Thanks, Piper. I was worried I might have lost your friendship."

She smiled at him, which was a very rare thing, considering she never did. It was probably due to the fact that most of her teeth had been fixed or replaced by some kind of metal-looking teeth. It was quite nasty to look at, but he would never say anything to her about it.

"Now, hurry up and get dressed," Piper said, then left the room.

When the door slid shut behind her, he was again alone in the medical room. As he struggled to pull his black pants on, he pondered the thought about what he should do about Diane and Jules.

By the time he had put his boots on, he still hadn't come to any conclusion about this conundrum in his life. Why and how was this so hard to figure out?

Jax stepped out into the hallway to see Piper waiting there for him with a deck of cards in hand. One of her impatient ticks was to shuffle cards continuously.

"Took you long enough in there. Must have had a hard time zipping your pants shut," Piper said.

Jax looked at her. "Did you just really?"

"What, make a penis joke? It's not like your girls were around to have heard it," Piper shrugged.

Jax threw his hands up, "Okay, okay, I get it. I have a serious question for you though."

"Shoot, stud," Piper said, facing him and crossing her arms together.

Jax pinched the bridge of his nose. "Can't help yourself today, can you?"

"Nope," she gave him a smirk, "And if your question is about Kell. He's fine. I certified him fit for duty myself."

"Okay, next question then," Jax said, pointing his finger at her.

Piper let out a laugh. "Damn, look at you go. Didn't know I was going to get interrogated on the way to the bridge."

"I'm not interrogating, just curious. Who was the masked assailant aboard the *Apex* and what did you all do with him?" Jax asked. He had been wondering about that ever since he woke up.

The smile Piper had been sporting while kidding with him vanished as she spoke. "The masked murderer was Captain Howard Frankfort. Middle-aged man born on Septis Three," she told him, face set in a frown, "Barnaby knew him. Not well, mind you, but their paths had crossed a few times in both of their careers."

Jax took the news in but all it did was make more questions enter his mind. "Any ideas what happened to them? Why had the captain gone crazy and killed them all?" he asked Piper.

Piper stopped in the hallway and began patting around her jumpsuit pockets. Before she spoke again, she pulled out two gray-colored devices and handed one of them to Jax, before she spoke again and she slipped the other over her right ear. "I forgot. Hewitt wants all of us to wear these for the duration of the voyage."

"Okay, I give up. What is it?" Jax asked, copying Piper and placing the device over his ear as well.

"In answer to your earlier question, after Hewitt analyzed some of the tech specs from the *New Horizon*, he discovered that the power core designed for the ship was putting off the Locorran radiation waves. The crew of the *Apex* in their attempts to salvage the ship had restored some of its power core. This, as you have probably already guessed, altered their mental state and led to the carnage you and Kell found on board," Piper explained, gesturing with her hands as they walked side by side.

"That was some pretty fucked up shit on board that vessel," Jax mused, remembering the horrible state in which they had found the *New Horizons*.

"I know," Piper said, with a grim look on her face. "I watched replays from Kell's suit, and I downloaded the vid feeds from the *Apex*. And I have to say from what I have watched so far; I've gotten nightmares from it. And that's saying something, considering I spent five years in the Septis penal system."

They both went silent for a moment, taking in the magnitude of what Piper was saying. Jax knew it would be bad. The part he had remembered was enough to traumatize him for the rest of his life, so he was certain that the things he had yet to learn were equally as gruesome.

"Anyway," Piper interrupted the silence, "Hewitt says that this device will help nullify the radiation effect from altering our brains. And he seems to think we are definitely going to need it coming up."

"He told me we were going to meet a god face to face," Jax said with a chuckle.

"If I had known that, then I might have washed my ass today and put on some makeup," Piper said, playfully as the atmosphere between them lost its tenseness.

"I thought grease was your makeup?" Jax asked in jest.

Piper elbowed him before replying, "Yes, but not for such special occasions."

Another moment of silence followed as they came out of the hospital wing and headed towards the bridge before Jax had another question. "Is Hewitt certain we will be safe by getting this close to the source? Hell, do we even know if the source is protected by a Locorran fleet or not?" he asked.

Piper let out an extended sigh, "As to the fleet question, we will be exiting jump space a distance away from the source, so we can get a look at things before moving closer."

"Okay, smart plan," Jax said with an approving nod.

"Good, because it was my plan," Piper said, with a smirk, "As to the safety of being really close to the thing, Hewitt says his device will protect us. That, I'm uncertain of. There's no question that Hewitt is one of the smartest people I've ever met, but I think his confidence in himself could also be his blind spot."

"Never thought about it that way, Piper, but I will definitely keep that in mind," Jax said.

"Good," Piper said, patting him on the shoulder, "Now if you'll excuse me, I'm going to take the helm. I see your girlfriends are awaiting you."

As soon as the door to the bridge cycled open, he was greeted by Jules and Diane. Both had bright smiles on their faces and they ushered him closer to the front of the ship so that he could see out the forward large parasteel bulb that extended out from the pilot's chair and console.

Barnaby was at his usual post toward the back of the bridge with his eyes glued to several monitors as the ship slowed from jump space. The stars were no longer streaking by in the forward parasteel windows. Instead, they had reverted back to their normal stationary positions.

"I found the anomaly," Piper said from the pilot's chair. "Bringing up an enhanced image of it."

Everyone had to circle around the center of the bridge as a holoprojection came to life. At first, it looked like a giant metal sphere floating in space, but when the data started coming in about the size of the thing, everyone understood there was no possible way that it was a planet of any kind. The sphere was large enough to swallow an entire solar system.

"Hewitt, what am I looking at here?" Barnaby asked, crossing his arms as he stared at the projection.

Hewitt had his right hand planted firmly on his right cheek, staring at the thing, unresponsive.

"Hewitt?" Barnaby said again.

"Sorry," the doctor said, shaking his head. "I was just pondering the scale and grandeur of this Dyson sphere."

"Piper, is there any activity going on around that thing?" Barnaby asked, still looking at the holographic image.

"No, sir, everything is quiet, just the way I like it," Piper said, eyes still on the system ahead of her.

Hewitt removed his hand from his face and stepped closer to the image. "Piper, would you please rotate the image twenty degrees up," he told her, pointing his finger and turning it in the air as if the holographic image would move by his finger's command alone.

Piper rotated the image as he had instructed and then they all now stared at what appeared to be a small opening in the sphere.

"Is that a doorway?" Kell asked.

"It appears so," Hewitt nodded, eyes expressing nothing but interest.

"You still haven't answered our question yet, doctor," Barnaby said.

"You're right, captain. I'm just captivated by the scale of this thing. I had no idea we would have encountered something this monumental," Hewitt's voice was filled with awe as he stared at the image.

"Perhaps the rest of us could enjoy what you are seeing if you could explain it to us. Because right now, all I'm seeing is a giant structure in space that looks menacing and terrifying," Barnaby said.

Hewitt looked at all of them gathered around him and sighed at the various degrees of confusion on all their faces. "This sphere is the construction of a very advanced race. It would have to be because the resources and labor spent in building it are well outside the reach of us and the Locorrans combined. This is engineering on a grand scale in order to build a structure around an entire solar system," he explained.

"For what purpose?" Diane asked.

"The main purpose of a Dyson sphere," Hewitt said, "is to harness energy from the primary star. I would say that this is in utilization here, but somehow, I think the sphere also serves a secondary function." He paced as he mulled over his thoughts before indulging them. "One of my theories is that the sphere was built as a shield against the super consciousness."

"What makes you think that, doctor?" Lilly asked.

"Just the math of things," Hewitt said and walked away from the sphere. "Like I said, it's just a theory in my head at the moment. Are we going to get closer, captain?"

"Piper," Barnaby said. "How are we looking?"

"Still good, sir," Piper said, still focused on the control of the pilot's station.

"Okay, crew, I know this is a lot to take in, but we need to get a better look at this thing. Diane, Jules, what's the status of our fighter?" Barnaby asked, as he clapped his hands together to get them moving.

Diane spoke, "Took some damage during our conflict recently, but nothing major."

Barnaby took note of that before ushering them out. "Okay, you two get in there and wait until called for."

Diane and Jules looked at each other and then at him before leaving the bridge.

"The rest of you," Barnaby pointed at them, "You know what your stations are, so let's get to it."

Jax turned to follow Kell off the bridge when he felt someone grab him by the arm. It was Hewitt so Jax turned to face him.

"I would prefer you to stay up here, Jax," Hewitt said.

Jax glanced at Barnaby once then said, "That will be the captain's decision."

Hewitt kept his brown eyes locked with Jax's for a moment and then trailed away, looking past him.

"Captain," Hewitt called out. "I would like for Jax to stay with us on the bridge. Would you allow that?"

There was no response at first and Jax could only imagine Barnaby staring at the floor in contemplation of why the doctor wanted him to stay. The response, however, came back quicker than he had thought.

"As you wish, doctor," Barnaby said, before focusing back onto Piper in the pilot's seat.

Hewitt patted him on the arm, "Come on, Jax, stand over here with me."

The doctor led him toward the front of the ship and directly behind Piper. In the parasteel window, the giant metal sphere that Hewitt had called a Dyson sphere grew larger and larger until at last it was the only thing he could see. Piper had set the course of the *Belt* toward the opening Hewitt had pointed out earlier. Everything was normal until the warning klaxon went off throughout the ship. Red lights flashed everywhere, and Barnaby was locked into his station frantically moving his hands.

"Piper?" Jax asked. "What's going on?"

"A large vessel just broke off from the surface of the sphere and is heading our way," Piper said, fingers flying over the navigation system.

Jax focused on the approaching object as Barnaby asked, "Is it a Locorran ship?"

"I hope not, the thing is massive, and it gives off no energy or heat signature," Piper listed off.

"A drone ship," Hewitt added, making all of them fall into silence.

Piper broke it after a moment to ask, "Captain, what are your orders?"

"Doctor, any ideas if this is a threat to us?" Barnaby asked Hewitt with a pointed gaze.

Hewitt paused; eyes still transfixed out the forward parasteel windows. "If it had wanted us dead before we got to the sphere, it would have done so a long time ago. I think this is a drone of some sort, left behind by the builders. If I am to make another theory, I think these drones protect the sphere from being damaged. Their primary job is to keep whatever is inside contained."

"Are you sure about this?" Barnaby asked, eyes continuing to rest on Hewitt to assess his confidence in his judgment.

"No, of course I'm not," Hewitt said, "But I think it's a pretty good guess."

After staring him down for another second, Barnaby squared off his shoulders and relayed to Piper, "Ok, we'll go for that. Take us in, Piper."

Piper didn't respond back and Jax didn't blame her. As the threat drew closer, the drone ship was massive and black. Its mere presence reeked of power and control. Hell, the whole sphere was a testament to power and control. Whatever race had built it must have been very advanced. When they passed through the opening of the sphere, the drone warship didn't follow. Instead, another one pulled up alongside them as they streaked toward the center of the sphere.

Hewitt had stepped away from him for a moment, and when he looked back to see what he was doing, the doctor had pulled up another holographic image of the interior of the sphere. From what Jax could see, so far there was the primary star in the center, glowing brightly. There was one planet close to the primary star, so close in fact, that its surface was molten. Outside of that, the only other planetary body was smaller, almost moon size. It was rather close to the primary star, but maybe far enough away that life could possibly exist on it.

"What are we looking at?" Barnaby asked, now standing next to Hewitt.

"So far, a very ordinary solar system, though devoid of a lot of planets, which is making me quite curious," he scratched at his chin in a thoughtful gesture before continuing, "The main one of note here is this little planet. It's in an orbit that would make it sustainable for life, but the readings we are getting from it indicate that the planet is a giant crystal of some sort."

"Is that the source of the super consciousness, then?" Barnaby asked, his voice containing barely concealed trepidation.

Hewitt rubbed his chin for a moment before saying, "Yes, the radiation reading from that thing is enormous."

"Are we in any danger of being altered?" Barnaby asked.

"With the nullifiers on us and the sphere absorbing most of the radiation, we should be good for now, but we shouldn't spend all day in here," Hewitt said.

"Ok," Barnaby said. "What now?"

"A good question, captain," Hewitt said walking over to the terminals Barnaby had been standing at before. "When I was going over Theodor's journal, I discovered that the super conscious was communicating with him in a very low-tech way."

Hewitt had stopped explaining himself as he tampered with a monitor and keyboard. Jax watched him for a minute, but then his eyes were drawn back to the parasteel window, he could see the crystal planet begin to take shape. It was transparent, but the light shining through it from the primary star was refracted all over the place, causing whatever light that did shine through to be streamed out in many directions.

"How close do you want me to get to this thing, captain?" Piper asked.

Barnaby looked to the doctor, "Hewitt?"

The doctor had cords in his hands now when he spoke, "We are close enough. And I've almost got it."

"You heard him, Piper, bring us to a stop," Barnaby ordered. The series of events went by so smoothly that one would think Hewitt had been a part of the crew.

As he watched everyone work in tandem, Jax could not help but wonder what Hewitt was doing. How was it going to help them with the super conscious?

"Here we are," Hewitt said. "A bit on the primitive side, but it should work."

The only thing Jax could see was a blank screen with a blinking cursor in the upper left-hand corner. "This is how Theodore communicated with it?" Hewitt said.

"'A' plus, Jax, if this had been a college question. Yes, it is. And now to ask the super conscious a question. How about, 'what are you'?" Hewitt typed into the keypad and the question appeared on the screen.

The response came back almost instantaneously typed on the screen, just like Hewitt's question had been. The answer was, "*I am.*"

"I am what?" Barnaby asked in confusion.

Hewitt responded, "I am that I am. God speaking to Moses."

"So, it does think of itself as a god, then?" Barnaby said under his breath, but Jax could hear the hint of doubt in it.

"Of course, it does. Now for the next question. Who created you?" Hewitt typed.

Once again, a response came back instantly: "*The universe was created by Braka. I am Shisu, the curator of life.*"

"Didn't expect that answer," Jax said, still watching the cursor.

"Nor did I," Hewitt said, then typed in another question. "*So Braka created the universe?*"

Response: "*Yes, I am part of Braka.*"

"Doctor, what does this mean?" Barnaby asked as he folded his arms over his chest.

"It means," Hewitt said with his back still to them. "That this thing has a much clearer understanding of its origin than most of the religions amongst humans. It would be fascinating to explore this more, but I know we are under a time constraint."

"Any ideas on how to shut this thing down?" Jax asked, already knowing the answer. Those drone ships would not allow them to harm or destroy anything. *That has to be what their purpose is,* he thought.

Hewitt looked back at him now, eyes intense as he told everyone, "No, none. As you have already observed, if we try to destroy anything, then those drone warships will obliterate us."

"We have to find a way, doctor," Barnaby said as he shook his head.

"I'm working on it, " Hewitt said, with his right hand planted firmly on his cheek again, gazing out the parasteel window.

After a couple of minutes of silence, Piper spoke up. "Um, Barnaby," she looked back at them from the pilot's chair to say, "Several Locorran warships have just entered the sphere." There was a strain in her voice and Jax felt his own heart speed up at her words.

"Doctor, we are out of time," Barnaby said. "Piper, start plotting us a course out of here."

"Already have, sir, but the only exit is being blocked by two of the four warships," Piper said, teeth gritted as she tried to find another way to get them out.

Jax watched as the doctor typed away at the keyboard again and he stepped closer to him to see what he was typing. *Do you serve Shisu?* he asked.

Response: *"No, we serve Braka."*

"Hewitt, who are you talking to?" Jax asked, coming to a stop beside Hewitt.

"It just occurred to me, Jax, to try to communicate with the drone warships. They appear to be in control here and perhaps they can be of assistance with our current dilemma," Hewitt said.

Jax nodded, "Good thinking, doctor. If we can get those warships to back the Locorran off, then we stand a chance of getting out of here alive."

Hewitt didn't respond. Instead, he was typing up his next question. *"Shisu is still influencing people?"*

Response: *"How?"*

Hewitt typed, *"A technology is being used to expand its range and influence. Millions of our people are being controlled by it, including those aboard the warships now entering the sphere."*

Response: *"Then you must eliminate this technology."*

"We need help in eliminating this technology. Shisu has too strong of an influence on many of them," Hewitt typed.

Response: *"We will close the sphere then. All ships must leave the sphere now."*

An audible message boomed over the ship's communications system. "All vessels must leave this space now or be eliminated."

Barnaby looked back over at them and asked, "What did you do, doctor?"

Hewitt shrugged. "Enlisted the aid of the drone warships, I think."

"Piper, get us out of here," Barnaby ordered again. "Bill, are we ready to jump once we clear this thing?"

Bill responded back over his earpiece, "Good to go, sir."

Barnaby kept speaking. "Diane, Jules, stay tight, we are going to make this jump as quickly as possible."

"Understood," Diane said.

Hewitt was at the keyboard typing again. *"Who opened the sphere?"*

Response: *"Braka after the last desolation."*

"Curious," Hewitt remarked after reading all the replies they were getting.

Hewitt typed, *"What was the desolation?"*

Response: *"Braka and Shisu called forth Shiv to cleanse the galaxy."*

"Who is Shiv?" Hewitt typed back.

Response: *"The destroyer."*

Hewitt's brows raised at that. And he typed, *"Will you help us against the other ships? They are under the influence of Shisu?"*

Response: "No, we serve only Braka."

"Well, it was worth a try," Hewitt said with a shrug.

"It's too bad they won't help us," Jax said. "Would have made things a lot easier."

"I didn't expect them to," Hewitt said, "But at least they did agree to close the sphere, which should reduce the range of the super conscious control."

"So, planets like Septis Three could experience some of its citizens going crazy, hurting themselves and others?" Jax asked, curious as to how everything would turn out.

"Unfortunately so, Jax. Once we get out of jump space, we will be able to send them a message, so that everyone will know how to help," Hewitt said.

Jax asked, "Do you think any of the Locorran colonies will be affected as well?"

"It is possible," Hewitt said. "But I really don't have enough data to guess at this point. So, we are just going to have to wait and see," Hewitt said, turning his head to face Jax.

"You two, get to a seat," Barnaby said. "The drones are opening fire at two of the Locorran warships."

That was good news, Jax thought. As the Drones had decided to help them out after all. The holographic image now displayed in the center of the bridge, zoomed in on the exit point and the combat occurring between the drone warships and two of the Locorran warships. One of the Locorran warships opened fire on the drone. From the hologram, he could see beam weapons of immense strength tearing into the hulls of both ships. Two more drone ships converged on the firing Locorran ship, and within seconds, it had been shredded apart by beam weapons.

The other Locorran ships turned around and quickly thrust toward the exit, Jax observed from the holograms projection.

"Piper," Barnaby said. "How much further?"

"Sixty seconds. Everything is powered up and ready to go," Piper said, throwing a thumbs up back their way.

Jax watched as Barnaby bowed his head and closed his eyes. He was whispering something to himself. He had seen him do this only one other time. Jax knew Barnaby was giving a subtle prayer. Honestly, he should probably try it himself. It might help relieve the tension of the situation. Once they exited out of the sphere, it would be a free-for-all. The drones would not protect them. So, the odds of managing to get into jump space before they were destroyed or disabled were very slim in his estimation.

"Exiting now," Piper said.

As expected, a barrage of beam weapons tore into the *Belt.* The power flickered on and off and at some point, the inertial damper failed, because Jax could feel the G-forces of the power dive Piper had put the ship into. He couldn't even move his head or hands much less speak as the forces of gravity were crushing down on him like a giant boulder. His breathing became shallow.

Another beam smashed into the aft section, which disabled the engines and sent them tumbling in a crazy corkscrew motion. The G-forces increased and Jax could feel himself blacking out. He tried to will himself to stay conscious, but the forces of nature were against him and at some point, everything went black.

Chapter 12

There was a tickling sensation on Jax's nose that awoke him instantly with his hands swatting at whatever had been bothering him. However, they made no contact with anything. His eyelids felt heavy and were slow to open, but he could hear giggling all around him.

Where the hell was he? And who could be giggling when all he could remember was getting attacked before losing consciousness?

Jax managed to get his eyes open and when he blinked away the blurriness, he was greeted by a series of young women looking at him with broad smiles and giggling voices.

Had he died? The last thing he remembered was passing out on board the *Belt*. And as far as he could remember, there were no scantily clad women like this aboard. These women barely had on a bra and panties. Not that he was complaining, but it sure was distracting.

Sitting up was a chore, and it made his head swim for a few moments. But once he did, he managed to get a better look at the room and quickly realized the size and grandeur of it with the large circular bed, couches, and even a recessed tub that had steaming water. He was definitely on another ship or dead.

"Where am I?" he asked.

After a fit of giggles, one of them decided to answer him. "You're aboard Princess Anala's flagship," a girl said in a soft and sweet voice.

Jax thought hard about the series of events that had happened before the attack. It came back to him then. The sphere, the Locorran fleet, but why had he been brought here, and where was the rest of the crew?

"Where are the others I came with?" Jax asked, looking around in search for any others from the *Belt* but spotted none. From what he could tell, it was just him and these women.

"They are being taken care of," one of the women answered him.

"Why am I not with them?" Jax asked, still trying to make sense of this in his own mind.

Another female answered, "The princess wishes to have an audience with you."

Jax's mouth fell open. A princess? Why would she even want to talk to him?

He shook his head before saying, "Okay, so where is she?"

"We will take you to her, once you have been cleaned up and presentable," one of the women that had already spoken told him gently while the rest looked on. Having so many eyes on him felt like he was being scrutinized, but there was nothing judgmental about their gazes, so he let them look.

They came closer to help him, and in a panic, he said, "Wait a second..." Before he could say more, they were already pulling his shirt off over his head and they had him standing now and tugging at his pants.

Within seconds they had him naked and in the steaming water he had spotted earlier. He would have been enjoying it if it had not been for the women beating and scraping him with hard bristle brushes. At some point, he was sure that a layer of his hide had been removed from his body. In fact, he half-expected to see it floating in the water with him.

So much for him thinking they were gentle beings who would do nothing but gaze at him while giggling. Now his entire body felt raw.

If this experience had not been humiliating enough, it got worse as one of them began to lather his face with a gel-like substance and then scraped at it with an open blade. His first instinct was to resist, but he pushed that feeling to the side. These women were only doing what they had been told to do and what harm were they causing, anyway? *I should be enjoying this*, he thought to himself.

He had never had so many women giving him this much attention ever in his whole life, or at least that he could remember. When the woman with the blade was done, she wiped his face clean and then kissed him on the cheek. *What was that about?* he wondered in confusion.

Afterward, things went quickly. Several of them pulled him out of the tub and went to work drying him off with several big and fluffy towels. Once that was done, they began to dress him, but not back into his old clothes. He was fitted into a pair of dark pants that looked as if they had been tailored to his exact size. Next, a long-sleeved shirt in a burnt orange color was shoved over his head and tucked down into his pants. Then to top off the humiliation they began combing his hair and applying gel to it.

What was the point of all of this? What did it matter how he was dressed or how his damn hair looked? It wasn't like the princess was anything to him. In fact, she was a Locorran and all Locorrans were under the control of the super conscious—a thing of such evil that he wasn't sure if they would be able to save any of them. He had to remember though, he had once been one and so was Diane and they had both escaped the clutches of the thing. So there was hope to rescue others. He just had to keep that in mind.

As soon as they finished with his hair, they all stepped away from him as two men in royal blue armor marched into the room and stood at both sides of the door.

"Follow us," the one on the left said. He couldn't make out any facial features through the dark helmets they wore. The only weapons they had on them was some sort of bladed weapon, which he doubted would pierce their armor very well.

So, that wasn't an option. The best policy he could adopt for now was to play along. Hopefully, he could reason with the princess, perhaps even negotiate a release for his friends, but then again, why had he been singled out for this honor? Were they going to publicly execute him? After all, he had killed many of their kind in the past and it was obvious to the super conscious that he would never ever be one of them again.

"Stay ahead of us, make no unnecessary moves and we won't injure you," the one on the right warned him.

Jax nodded his head and stepped out into the corridor. Like the room he had just left, the corridor was decorated in a lavish style with couches and small tables. There was even artwork hanging from the walls. He started to walk down the corridor that went straight ahead. He could feel the two men following him, but he paid them no heed except when he asked them if he was going the right way.

There were a few passersby sitting about staring at him. This wasn't a warship; it was more of a pleasure yacht with a lot of weapons. Of course, anything the super conscious did that he had observed so far seemed cool and logical at times, but at others, it was as if a kid had been let loose to run things. Perhaps, if he survived this, Hewitt might have a better explanation for its wild behaviors.

Jax knew that he had to be on guard and remember everything that happened only so he could figure out what was going on later. He took note of every detail as he walked and made sure to file any questions he had to the back of his mind.

At the end of the corridor, he was pushed into a large lift tube. Both armed men stood beside him, and he wasn't sure which of them smelled the fruitiest. Hell, it could have been him. He hadn't really been paying attention to his olfactory senses as his body was being scrubbed. The scent of the fruit was something unfamiliar to him. It wasn't like anything from Earth. It had a bit of spiciness to it that burned his nostrils. God, he hoped it wasn't him that smelled like this. It would probably take a week to get rid of the scent.

When the lift doors opened, he was prodded into the large open room. Like the rest of the ship so far, it was highly decorated with ornate rugs, pillows, and furniture mixed in with what looked like the bridge of a vessel. There were control panels free standing and monitors built into the walls, with men and women in uniforms sitting or standing at them.

He wished he could take a picture of this so that he could show it to his friends. Barnaby would probably pass out on the floor from laughter at the absurd layout of the bridge. He got mad if someone left crumbs of something at a station, but here there were bottles of wine and food laid out in the open throughout.

The guards pushed him forward once more, and in his distraction Jax almost missed the woman stepping out of the shadows to stand before him. Like the women in the room that had cleaned him, this long-legged female was barely clad in anything. Everything was perfect about her—her legs, arms, hips, lips, and torso. It was as if she had stepped right out of one of his dreams. *That must be the princess,* he thought.

The smile she gave was of perfectly white and straight teeth, which almost rivaled Diane's in appearance. She was beautiful, anyone could tell from just one look. However, Jax also knew that she could be hiding a lot behind that cover of beauty.

"How would you prefer me to address you?" she asked, and her voice was so soft and mellow; it felt like velvet to Jax's ears.

It took him a second to answer, "Everyone calls me Jax."

The princess raised a perfectly arched brow. "Okay, Jax it is, then." There was that big smile again as she asked, "I take it, that is short for something?"

"Jason Alexander Xavis, so Jax for short," he said, trying not to get too affected by the beauty in front of him.

"And from what I've learned from the others you came with, you were one of the original colonists of Locorran prime," she asked, voice sounding like a purr now as she went to take a seat on a blood-red divan placed on one side of the room which was filled with the most ostentatious furniture.

Jax cleared his throat, eyes moving back to hers when he said, "To the best of my knowledge, I was. I'm afraid that I have a lot of gaps in my memory. Probably a side effect of the long hibernation I endured after escaping."

The woman let out a chuckle as she picked up a glass of amber liquid from a small table beside the divan and took a long sip. Then she said, "Heard about that as well. I bet it is a fascinating tale. One I wish to hear when we have time."

"What's the rush?" Jax asked, plastering a smile on his face as the gears turned in his head.

"As you are probably aware, we are on course for Locorran Prime right now. In a couple of days will be my coronation. The emperor will be stepping down, and I will be taking his place as empress," the princess listed off as Jax got increasingly confused as to what was the purpose of calling him here.

"Wow, fancy title. How does that work, exactly, considering that all of you are a hive mind to the super conscious?" Jax asked her without any filter. The more time he spent in front of her the more confident he felt.

"What, Jax? And there is no need to be rude. I could have easily had you and your friends executed," she said, taking another sip. "After all, you did cost me one of my warships back at the sphere," she said, with a soft, but menacing tone which Jax guessed was more lethal than anything he could ever imagine.

Was it possible she didn't know what the super conscious was? He had never stopped to ponder about people who had been born into it. Would they even have any recollection of who they were without it?

Jax sighed, "Okay, sorry about that, Princess. Been a stressful day."

She stood up from her perch after placing the glass down and stepped closer to him, decreasing the distance between them. That same fruity smell that burned his nostrils reeked off her and he held back his flinch.

The princess gave him another smile. "It's okay, Jax, I get it. Our two cultures are still learning about each other, but in time, all of humanity will be joined together as one, as it should be."

"So, I take it that you have a purpose for me. Something that you want. I mean why all the charades?" Jax asked, extending his hands out to gesture with them.

"You're right, I do have something in mind," the princess said, looking him up and down with curiosity. "The Locorran empire is filled with young men who would be willing to kill for their emperor and now for their empress, but I want something more. I want someone who is an outsider, someone with a defiant streak. A new blood, I guess you could say."

Was she getting ready to propose marriage to him? What was happening here?

She continued, "Before the coronation, I am allowed to pick several suitors who will compete for genetic rights to the throne. I would like for you to be one of those contestants."

Jax burst out in laughter at her words. What absurdity was this?

She remained quiet as his fit of laughter died down, then said, "If you agree to this, I promise your friends will be taken care of and even sent back to Earth if you so wish."

Jax's mouth fell open. "Wait, so this isn't a joke?" he asked. A part of him knew that she was utterly serious, but another part of him was having difficulty accepting the fact that a princess was choosing him as a suitor. He knew he had the looks, but other than that, what would his genes have to offer?

"No, in fact, the very opposite," the princess said. "Your agreement for their lives, Jax. Granted, all but one of the suitors will make it to the end. Death is a real consequence of the games, but as long as you do your part, I will uphold my part of the bargain," she said, with a pointed gaze.

He didn't even ponder it, this was probably the only choice he was going to get, anyway. "I'll do it," he blurted out in a second, "I would like to see my friends though."

The princess nodded, "Done. Guards, take him down to his quarters. And Jax, I look forward to our next meeting."

In a strange sort of way, so was he, that is, if he survived whatever he was getting ready to be thrust into.

The trip back down the lift tube ended a floor below the one he had come up from. He had, at least, good enough sense to keep track of where he was. This allowed him to build somewhat of a model in his head of the ship's layout. He doubted that it would come in handy at the moment, but one should be prepared for everything if possible.

The corridor he was guided through was like everywhere else so far—decorative and non-utilitarian. It was like a show pony. The guards had him stop at a door about halfway down the corridor. One of them pressed his palm to the door and it hissed open.

Inside, he could see everyone standing up in groups of twos and threes, and some entirely alone. As the door opened and he entered, their attention turned to him in an instant. There were smiles on some faces, but from other expressions, he guessed most of them thought they were looking at a ghost.

The guards gave him a final prod, and when he entered the room, the door closed behind him immediately.

"Jax?" Barnaby said in surprise. It looked like he had not been expecting him back.

Jax didn't bother replying. Instead, he ran up to him and gave him a hug.

The large man embraced him back, and it felt great to be in the presence of familiar people once again. In fact, it felt like home.

"You okay?" Barnaby asked. If there was anyone who knew him better, it would be Barnaby.

Still, he did not want him to trouble others by worrying over what he had to do, so Jax replied, "Yeah, I'm fine."

"What in the hell did they do to you?" Kell said, standing beside him and taking a whiff.

"Well," he paused for a moment. "They gave me a bath, for one, and then they insisted that I meet the future empress."

Diane and Jules had pushed their way to him now, and both had their hands on him, examining how he was dressed.

"Did they dress you as well?" Jules asked.

"Yes, even combed my hair," Jax told her with a nod.

"Not sure I approve of the color choice for you," Jules said, followed by a chuckle.

"I didn't approve of the fragrance they used either," Jax agreed, "It makes my nostrils burn."

"Well, at least we can all agree upon that," Diane said with a shrug. Jax could feel her eyes watching the way Jules was looking him over, but he did nothing in that moment. Things were far too complicated as it was. Now with the future empress in the mix, he was even more confused about what to do about all of it.

"Everyone, quiet down for a minute," Barnaby said. "Jax, why did they take you to her?"

He couldn't help himself and burst out into laughter at what he was going to have to tell them. He started, "Turns out, the only reason all of us are still alive is because the princess wants me to compete to be a suitor."

A hush fell across the room.

"A suitor?" Barnaby asked as if he was scandalized.

"Actually, it's a little more involved than that. Turns out that the winner gets genetic inheritance rights to the throne," Jax said, with a little heat rising to his face. Just talking about the princess brought her image to his mind.

"So, like getting married to her?" Kell asked, face filled with confusion.

"I don't think marriage is a thing for an empress," Jax told them, still a bit wary about the entire ordeal because he didn't know much as well.

"This is all very fascinating, Jax," Hewitt interjected. "What can you tell us about her? What was her behavior like?"

"Doctor," Barnaby said. "This isn't the time. Jax, you didn't agree to this contest, did you?"

Jax shrugged, "Didn't really have a choice. Just by agreeing to it, I have arranged for your freedom back to Earth."

"Why would they agree to such a thing?" Diane asked, crossing her arms.

"Beats me. Nothing about the Locorrans makes sense," Jax told her.

Jax saw Hewitt talking to himself nearby and caught bits of it. Hewitt was saying, "Is it so desperate to bring one back in the fold that it would let others go or sacrifice them."

It is possible, Jax thought in response to what he overheard Hewitt saying to himself. Once the super conscious had someone, it never wanted to let go of them. Would that also apply to Diane? Would they try to keep her as well?

"Jax," Barnaby said, grabbing his shoulder. "The guards are coming back in."

He glanced back at the two royal blue guards approaching him by parting anyone that was standing in their way. Barnaby still had hold of his shoulder when he spoke again. "You should not have agreed to this for us. You know they are either going to kill you or force you to join them again."

Jax could only nod his head because he knew that would be the eventual outcome, but it would all be worth it to save them. Before the guards reached him, Jules grabbed hold of him in a big embrace. The warmth and smell of her was comforting to him, and he wished he could have just clung on to her for the rest of the day. When the guards pulled her away, she gave him a quick peck on the cheek.

Diane was watching all of this. Her blue eyes were locked on his and he knew that she wanted to say goodbye to him as well. Hell, or at least he wanted to hold on to her for a moment, anyway. For an instant, he thought about resisting the guards just to try to get to her, but the guards both secured his arms on both sides and began tugging him toward the exit.

"What's the rush?" he asked, "The princess said the contest wasn't for a couple of days." He got no response so with a sigh he got one good glance back at everyone. All of them had concerned expressions on their faces and even Piper had a small tear dripping from her right eye. Had he really touched her emotionally? Piper was the most callous person he knew, which was probably part of the hard life she had lived.

"I'll see you all soon," he said just before the door to the room cycled shut.

The guards half dragged him down to another level to a medical bay of some sort. The technicians poked and prodded him with several instruments without ever uttering a single word, and once they were done, he was dragged to another room a few doors down from the medical bay. This was a small room with two beds and almost no personal stuff. No books, videos, junk food, hell, there wasn't even any dirty clothes anywhere to be found.

The only thing he could do at the moment was to take a seat on the closest bed and relax. Slowing his breathing and closing his eyes, he tried to meditate. That often helped him to destress and to center himself, and he needed that right now.

The meditation was interrupted only a few minutes in by the door to the room, cycling open again. When he popped open his eyes, he half expected to see the possible other tenant of this room, but instead one of the guards arrived with a satchel and placed it on the edge of his bed before leaving.

Opening it up, he found some of his stuff from the *Belt*. Some clothes, books, his data pad. The data pad was already powered on, and he could see a message typed into it. He didn't bother reading the top part of it at the moment, he was curious as to who had taken the time to write him a message. To his surprise, it was from the princess. So, he scrolled back up to the top and began to read.

Jax, I took the liberty to have some of your belongings brought to you. I figured you might want to relax and rest for the upcoming games. So, I have also given you this room privately; there is no other roommate.

P.S. I hope you are the victor.

Princess Anala Locorran

Did the Princess really have that much interest in him? If so, why? Hewitt was probably right. All of this was probably some elaborate game to get him to become one of them again. It had to be.

Jax kept thinking about that until he grew tired and instead lay back on the bed. He thought about Diane. He tried to imagine what life would be like with her. Then he remembered Jules and how she had kissed his cheek.

Both of them were pleasant, but Kell was right—he needed to make his feelings clear because he could not stop the charade. It would only hurt more later on.

Jax fell asleep imagining he was on a warm, sunny beach with Diane playing around in his mind.

He knew he would wake up to his harsh reality once again, but in that moment, he just wanted to be dreaming rather than anything else.

Chapter 13

01, 20, 2291

When I jerked awake from the most relaxing dream I had in a while, I decided to pick this back up. I had it synced with the pad I had been using on Earth, so everything is on my old pad now. My dreams last night left me even more confused about how to handle this situation with Diane and Jules. To add on top of that, the princess showed up at some point, and I was even dreaming about being with her. Never thought I would find myself in this kind of dilemma in my whole life, and so far, no one has been able to decipher it for me. All they tell me to do is pick one. Easier said than done.

Okay, I won't let this whole journal entry go on and on about my girl troubles. I have faith that it will work itself out over time unless I die first in this upcoming game. I guess whichever happens first. Regardless, I think I have had some breakthroughs with my memories, now when I think about the past I'm starting to get images in my head of my childhood. I remember a great big brown dog with floppy ears. It would often lick my face. I can't remember the dog's name, but just the sight of it made me happy. It was something that I loved in my life.

Some other things that are now coming to me are smells from the kitchen. I see in my mind's eye a tall raven-haired woman standing over a stove, blowing onto a wooden spoon over a pot. The smell is awesome, and I want some of it. The woman looks familiar to me as well. I'm sure it is my mother looking at me. I wish I could remember the details about her.

And lastly, I remember playing ball with my father out in the backyard. The dog was there as well and would often take the ball away from us. All of these are happy memories and I wish to have more, but I dread this contest coming up. I know I have skills, but I'm up against some hive-minded out-of-control individuals who either want me dead or begging at their heels.

The door to Jax's room cycled open without warning and the familiar armored guards burst in. He was sure that it was the same pair that he had been dealing with since yesterday.

"Leave your stuff and follow us," one of them ordered.

"Where are we going?" Jax asked, standing up. "I thought I would have at least another day to rest?"

Neither answered him, instead they moved forward side by side and reached for him. Backing away, he spoke again, "Okay, okay, I'm coming. No need to drag me again."

They backed off when he said this, and he pushed past them through the door.

"To the lift," one said, and Jax obliged. They took him back to the chamber where all of the barely clothed women resided. They all looked excited to see him again as they grabbed him up and escorted him over to the baths.

"Not again," he mumbled to himself as they removed his clothes and forced him into the water. At this rate, they were going to kill him with the scrub brushes before he got in the games.

He tried to relax and let them do their thing, but then he saw a holo projection come to life nearby. Many of the girls turned their heads to pay attention to what was showing. From his first glance at it, it was an aerial shot of a city with people walking about with flowers on their heads and the big buildings were bathed in colors of red, orange, and black. The orange of course being that burnt orange color he had been forced to wear on the day he met the princess. He was seeing a celebration of some kind going on.

The camera flew down closer to the people and even the flying vehicles and trains were covered in flower petals and bathed in the same Locorran colors. From what he could tell, the decorations were due to celebratory preparations for the princess's ascension.

Suddenly, the images changed to a man dressed in a black and burnt orange suit talking to another man dressed in a black and red combination. He couldn't hear what was being said at the moment as one of the women had just dumped a bucket of hot water over his head, followed by an onslaught of brushes to his face.

Swatting them away, he tried to hear some of the conversation going on and was successful in doing so, "For those of you tuning in, I am having a conversation with suitor Dunkin Greykin from the Emperor's Promise colony. I am your host, Alexander Motts, and we are hours away from the beginning of Princess Anala's transformation to empress."

With a bright smile, the host continued, "So, Dunkin, the first question I have to ask you is the one on most people's minds. What is happening to the emperor's promise?" Motts said, as the camera focused on a close up of Dunkins face. "Suddenly, a couple of days ago, some of the provinces outside of the city went into a total blackout." Motts continued, "government officials tell us that an unknown sickness has broken out. In fact, in this very studio, I have shown footage leaked out of the emperor's promise of some of the citizens in a catatonic state. Do you have any insights that you can provide us with, Dunkin?"

Dunkin's eyes fixated on Motts as he leaned forward in the chair. "Alexander, I wish I did have some information. My parents live in the outer provinces, and I have not been able to get any word from them. I did, however, get a personal meeting with the emperor, and I was assured that the virus was contained and that the people were being helped as much as they could. I was told that the blackouts were in an effort to help contain the sickness as well as to protect the privacy of the people being affected by it."

Motts nodded his head. "Sounds like a reasonable response from our loving emperor."

"I was very pleased," Dunkin said. "In fact, I wish for nothing more than to be the property of the future empress. Our children will be the making of a long and enduring dynasty."

So, this was one of the men he would be up against. His first evaluation of the man was not good. Dunkin was young, well built, probably stronger than him, not a good combination. He tried to focus on the continued conversation between Dunkin and Motts, but he could no longer hear as the women rubbed even more hide from body and face with towels. At the end of the interview the only other thing he heard about Dunkin was that he served as one of the emperor's guards. This did not give him any insight into his fighting ability, but if he had to guess, he would have to be a very proficient fighter in order to obtain the guard status of such a prominent individual.

If the other suitors were anything like Dunkin, then he was going to have a hard time winning this, much less staying alive.

As the girls had moved on to dressing him. He could finally hear the last of the interview. "Any final words, Dunkin?" Motts said.

Dunkin faced the crowd and the camera to say, "Mom, Dad, I love you very much, and empress, I will be your man forever."

"Well spoken," Motts said as the camera zoomed in on his face. "I wish you luck, Dunkin. Now coming up shortly, I have one more suitor added to the list. That's right, everyone, the empress herself has added one more final contestant. And all of you will be shocked as I was from where this contestant comes from, ready for it? Earth."

The camera switched to a view of the people who all looked stunned at this news. Then the camera flipped back to Motts again. "Shocked as I was, I'm sure. So, stay tuned everyone as we will get our first interview with Jason Alexander Xavis shortly."

The only thought that entered Jax's mind was that he was going to have to give an interview like this one. He had not even been told that this was something he had to do. Was he even prepared for it? He didn't think so.

When the women had finished with him, they pulled him toward one of the several large mirrors in the room, and for the first time, he realized he was dressed in the same black pants, red shirt, and burnt orange belt as Dunkin had been wearing. This was really happening to him. In a few minutes, he would be paraded into that studio and asked all sorts of personal questions that he didn't want to answer.

Once the girls got done combing his hair and locked it into place with that gel stuff, he reeked of that spicy scent again. What he wanted right now was to wash it off him, but that possibility vanished as his two blue-colored escorts entered the room. He didn't even bother protesting with them; it was pointless. He had agreed to the terms of this in order to protect his friends, and no matter what, he would do his best for them. They were his family. His only wish though was that he could see Diane's smile again before the games began.

As they led him off the ship, he was disappointed in the fact that they had not allowed him to say goodbye to anyone.

Jax was also quite surprised at how empty the floating landing pad was. He was standing high up in the city, watching flying vehicles far off zoom in a steady stream in the distance. This building they were leading him into must be where the show was being broadcast. He couldn't quite get the scale of it from his observation point, but the building must have been massive in scale.

The guards quickly led him through deserted passageways. Probably all in an effort to keep him safe, or at least, he told himself that. At last, they came to a room milling with workers. A man with a headset ushered them over to a black curtain. He muttered something to Jax that he didn't quite catch and then he was suddenly thrust out onto the stage.

To his surprise, there were sounds of clapping at his presence. He couldn't see any of the clappers as the lights on the stage were blinding him, but he could sure hear them. Motts was next to him instantly and took him by the arm.

"And here he is, folks. Jason Alexander Xavis from Earth. Welcome to my show. The whole empire has been waiting to meet you. Please have a seat!" he told Jax in a cheerful voice that was followed by even more cheers and clapping.

Half stumbling, he fell into the chair ungracefully.

Motts took a seat across from him and spoke again, "When I received word from the princess that she had entered another suitor, I was shocked at the least, but even more shocked when she told me you were from Earth. It's true that all of us can trace our roots back to that planet, but a lot of the Earth's colonies have not fully embraced us yet. That is changing though; soon we will all be one big happy galactic family."

This guy sure did talk a lot, and fast, too. Jax was having a hard time keeping up with the conversation. Was this what stage fright felt like?

"I know that this is probably overwhelming for you Jason, if I can call you Jason?" Motts asked in the same cheery tone.

Jax nodded his head, "Sure, but most people call me Jax."

Motts laughed loudly, as did the audience, before he continued, "Okay then, Jax, let's start with the big question everyone wants to know. So how did you and the princess meet?"

Before Jax could even answer that question, there was someone talking in his ear. When had a piece been put there?

"The only answer you are to give is that you met the princess during one of her visits to the Earth colonies. Failure to answer the question this way will put your friends in jeopardy," the voice was saying.

Taking a deep breath, Jax answered the question. "I knew the moment that I saw princess Anala, on her visit to Earth," Jax said with a pause. Swallowing hard he continued. "I knew that she was a person of great power and influence. And that I would give anything to be by her side." The lie had sounded good to him, he thought.

Was this the way things were going to go? Was he going to have to follow their directions while fighting for his life? Would they force him to lay down his life and would he be able to sacrifice himself in this way?

The rest of the interview went by in a blur. He couldn't even remember half the lies he had been forced to say. All he had to remind himself of was why he was doing this in the first place. He was doing it for the safety of his family—his friends were his family. That was the only thought that helped him go through the entire interview with a fake smile plastered on his face for the audience.

When Motts escorted him off the stage and back behind the black curtain, the two guards quickly took him in tow and toward his next destination.

This time he was led to an empty locker room—empty except for his shadows. A few minutes after arrival, a knock came at the locker room door. The guards opened it and one of the women from the princess ship entered with some clothes in hand. She set them down next to him on the bench and then placed a holoprojector on top of the pile, then backed away with a smile. Was it for watching more footage of the games he was about to enter, or what was the purpose?

The woman paused a few steps back, looked at him, and motioned with her hands that he should activate the device. *What could it hurt?* he reasoned with himself and pressed the activation switch on top.

A projection materialized in front of him. It was the princess staring down at him before saying, "You did an excellent job during your interview, Jax, and to show my goodwill toward you, I am here at the landing pad of your ship, the *Orion's Belt*. I thought it would help ease your mind if you knew they were okay before you entered the games. After all, I am counting on you to win."

In the background, he could see all of his friends standing around, waiting to talk with him. Jax could not help himself and voiced his confusion, "Why do you want me to win? Why not any of the others?"

She gave him a beautiful broad smile, then handed the device to Barnaby.

"Jax, I'm sorry you've had to put yourself in this position," Barnaby said. "I really am. You're family to me now, and I want you to do your very best to survive. Understand me, survive this." Jax could see tears in the man's eyes as he said all of this.

He nodded, "I will do my best, captain."

Barnaby didn't respond back. Instead, he nodded his head and passed the device on to Piper. She had her face right in the device when she was speaking with him. "Jax, even though we didn't know each other for very long. I just wanted you to know that I think of you as a younger brother. As Barnaby said, you are family to me, to us. Beat these bastards and we will find a way to bring you home. I promise you that."

He wished he could believe that, but he had a sense that this was truly the last time he would see any of them again.

Kell took the device from Piper. "You're a brother to me as well, Jax. I've been a loner all my life. The *Belt* gave me family, and it gave me you. We had a connection like family should have. Hell, you know I'm not good with words or much less making sense. So, here's what I have to say. Kick their ass and we will come and get you, some way, somehow."

The next person to speak was the Paxtons, the husband and wife team onboard the *Belt*. Like the others, they expressed their love toward him and how he was family. It felt good to know that he was loved by them all. When they passed the device on, Jules was staring him directly in the face. "I want to slap you in the face for your selfishness, but then I want to kiss you."

Jax could say nothing else except, "Thanks, Jules."

"Listen, Jax, I know you think you are doing the right thing. I get it, but you can't trust them," she said before looking away from the device.

Was she being prompted by someone off-screen?

When she refocused her attention back on the device, there was a small streak of tears streaming down her cheek. "Jax, just stay alive, we will come back for you. Somehow, we will. And when I find you again, I'm going to give you a real long kiss and never give you up."

Diane was the next to take the device. She had a stern look on her face and her body language spoke of a defiant control. God, she was magnificent. "Do what you need to do, Jax. Stay focused and never lose hope. I will rescue you."

The device was taken from Diane's hands, before he could say anything to her, and God, he had a lot to say. The princess was looking back at him again as she was walking away from his family. "You have a very loyal group of friends, Jax," she said.

Jax took a deep breath to control his emotions before replying, "They are my family, and family takes care of each other."

"Could not have said it better myself. I hope that me and you will be a good family soon," she said, starting to lower the device.

"I have one last question, princess?" Jax interrupted before the projection vanished.

"As you wish," the princess said, urging him to say it.

"Where was Doctor Hewitt? He wasn't with them," Jax asked.

"Forgot about that," the princess said. "Sorry, Jax, I forgot to tell you that during your maneuvers to evade our ships, Hewitt began to suffer some major health issues. He is currently in one of our finest hospitals. I was told he was recovering, and they should be moving him to the ship within a few hours," she said.

This did seem logical to him and what reason would the princess have to lie to him, anyway? He accepted the answer with a nod, "Okay, thanks for telling me, princess."

"You'll soon have to start calling me empress, Jax. See you soon," she said with another broad smile and the projection flickered off.

The woman in the locker room took it from his hand and then exited the room. That's when one of the guards spoke. "You need to put the flight suit on. You'll be entering the stage shortly."

Great, just what he wanted to hear.

Jax did as he was instructed as quickly as possible and then sat with his back straight and eyes closed. He began to slow his breathing in order to calm his mind. The real problem with Zen meditation was the random noise of his mind. It took a lot of attention to notice the images and then move them out of his mind. He sought the complete emptiness that followed. It was here that he found his calm and center. Here, nothing could hurt him.

Time slowed and he could probably have remained in this state for longer, but the guards were now lifting him up and taking him out of the room to the unknown he had to face. And to his surprise, he felt calm about it all. His friends and family would be safe, because of his actions. So it didn't matter to him what happened in this stupid game.

Chapter 14

Jax was escorted into the grand throne room to a hail of cheers, and flower petals being thrown his way. The room was massive with at least twenty-foot ceilings, walls covered in colorful banners with symbols he guessed that represented all of the other Locorran colonies and enough floor space to allow a freighter ship to land. Hundreds of Locorran citizens were herded into small barricades to either side of him, allowing a path way straight to the emperor's dais, where he could already see four of the other suitors standing in a line to the left-hand side of the throne chair. Most of the suitors were waving or blowing kisses as many camera drones flitted about the place. One of which settled a few feet in front of him and followed him and his tag along escorts, up the steps and he took his place at the end of the line of suitors, next to Dunkin Greykin, who was no longer paying attention to the crowd. Dunkin's gaze was fixed squarely on him, with a look of immense hatred. Even Dunkin's body posture had changed to a half turned stance, as if to attack.

This is not good, Jax thought. Why was Dunkin giving him so much hatred, what had he done to this person? The rest of the suitors were paying him no mind, just continuing to play to the cameras and crowd. All of them had drones on them, and right now, he caught two of them circling him and Dunkin. Was this something planned out that he didn't know about? A performance perhaps to keep the masses enthralled. No, there was a genuine look of hatred in those eyes—he knew the look.

Glancing past Dunkin, he noticed that even the aged emperor had a fixed gaze toward them and was sitting at the edge of his throne chair with both palms planted firmly on the sculpted lions' heads. Was Dunking going to fight him right here before the games even began? Tensing his body, Dunkin stepped closer to him and was now facing him. Drones moved in closer to get close up shots of their faces.

"I'm going to kill you, for what you did to my family," Dunkin said, poking a finger right into his chest. Dunkin was slightly taller than him, and from his observations from before, was well conditioned. His arm muscles were twice the thickness of his.

Out of his periphery, he could see royal blue guards nearby on the dais with them, but none of them appeared concerned about his death. "Dunkin, I'm not sure what I have done," Jax said, raising both of his hands up toward his chest with palms exposed. It was a gesture of not willing to fight, or at least that's what he hoped Dunkin would take it as.

Dunkins lips pulled back in a snarl as he spoke, poking him harder with his pointed finger. "You know what you did, you and your friends aboard the *Belt*. Once I'm done with you, I'm going to murder them as well."

At the mention of the *Belt,* Jax was ready to launch himself at Dunkin and pound his face with his fist, but Dunkin stepped away from him. Had this been part of the show? The mention of what he and his friends had done was the clue he needed. When Hewitt had closed the Dyson sphere, it had affected the Locorrans. It was the story Dunkin had told earlier in the day to Alexander Motts. So he was responsible and now Dunkin was going to kill him for it.

Right after the extra drones left him and Dunkin, the earpiece he had been wearing came to life and he could hear Mott's speaking. "Looks like Dunkin has finished trying to intimidate young Jax into quitting before the games even begin. But Jax looks more determined than ever. Sorry, Dunkin, looks like you're just gonna have to win this game the old fashioned way." Motts paused, "I just received word that the princess is on the way."

It was obvious to him that none of what he and Dunkin had said to each other had been recorded. All the audience saw was what Motts had just told them, that Dunkin was trying to intimidate him into quitting. This gave him no comfort whatsoever. Was the games rigged? Did the princess already know who was going to win, and was he here just to pay for his crime? Was it all a lie?

"And there she is, folks," Motts said in excitement. "Our future empress and entourage."

At the large doors of the throne room, several barely clothed women entered tossing petals and sparkles in all directions. There were even small smoke devices set off near the princess in the colors of the Locorran empire as some of the women were doing gymnastics down the aisle. The princess looked as beautiful as the day he first saw her. Her outfit had not changed much, the only thing different was the fact that there was a little more of it, and it was all in blue, reds, and orange.

"What a magnificent day," Motts said. "In fact, a perfect day for a coronation. The princess and her maids are absolutely stunning. Any one of these men should be honored to be her mate."

It would have been true. He would like to be her mate if he hadn't been forced into this contest. Hell, he didn't even know the rules yet.

Motts spoke again. "The princess is now moving toward the suitors, starting with Robert Fulkner of Locorran prime. And there she goes, placing a crown of flowers on his head and a kiss on the cheek. Robert looks determined as he takes her hand. For those who don't know, Robert is the star of his own reality show where he displays his life and death stunts. Robert holds the records for surfing the largest waves and longest flight by wing suite. A man without fear, which is something the other suitors should fear about him."

He watched the princess move to the next man—an extremely well-built and muscled black man.

"Our next suitor to receive the crown of flowers is Bradley Basil, or as followers in the arena know him, the Breaker."

From out in the crowd of people he could hear some cheers and chants. This must have been one of the fighters Kell had been talking about. Champion of the arena. Bradley was a skilled bare-knuckles fighter; he would definitely be a major threat.

"I see no other description is needed for this suitor, his reputation precedes him," Motts said. "And there is the good luck kiss on the cheek. Our next suitor is Thomas Rens from the Staff of Locorran colony."

An even louder set of cheers and chants broke out from the crowd of people. Out of the other suitors, this one looked far less dangerous. Was he making a mistake? What was this suitor known for?

Motts continued, "As many of you already know, Rens is well known in the music industry. His concerts sell out every place he goes. The princess is placing the crown of flowers on his head and wait, he just tried to kiss her on the lips."

Even louder cheers broke out and now Ren's name was being chanted very loudly almost to the point of drowning out the audio in his ear.

"A very bold move on Rens' part, one that will cost him a good luck kiss on the cheek. Now we come to suitor Dunkin Greykin. Dunkin hails from the emperor's promise and has served the emperor's guard since the age of thirteen. Before this broadcast, Dunkin did receive an update from his parents, which had been affected during the outbreak. He reports that they are recovering and everything will be back to normal in the next couple of days, just as the emperor promised him."

The scent of the princess was really strong to Jax now, it was that same spicy fruit scent that he had been bathed in. She was right next to him, placing the crown of flowers on Dunkin's head, who was giving her a strong smile as she leaned forward and kissed his cheek. Jax couldn't help not to hear the words Dunkin uttered to her, "You'll be mine." And she stepped back away from Dunkin.

"Wait," Motts said. "What's this? It appears that the emperor himself is giving a gift today."

One of the princess maids approached Dunkin with a long-bladed weapon laid out on a pillow. He took it in hand and looked it over from hilt to tip. From Jax's perspective, it was an expertly crafted samurai blade with some intricate symbols engraved into it. Dunkin turned and bowed before the emperor. *Great, a nice and deadly weapon in the hands of someone who will not hesitate in running me through with it,* Jax thought.

"A very nice gift indeed," Motts said.

The princess moved to stand in front of him now. There was a pissed off look on her face, but that changed as she placed the crown of flowers on his head. When she leaned in for the kiss, she whispered something in his ear. "Don't worry, I have a gift for you."

When she stepped back, another maid approached him. And on the pillow, she carried a smaller blade, but very exquisite with its own engravings.

"What is this? The princess giving a gift to a suitor? I had no idea that favorites had been chosen," Motts said. "And it appears the princess and the emperor have very different ideas on who should be her mate. I think even the crowd is shocked at the choices, but the games hasn't even begun yet, and only one of these men will walk away with the empress. So, folks, let the games begin and may the best suitor win."

The other suitors dashed past him while he waited for his shadows to escort him to his next destination. The princess had moved away from him, but she was looking back over at him as he left the throne room. What was this game the princess was playing with him?

He didn't have time to ponder the question over and over. In no time, he found himself in a hanger bay and standing before a fighter like the one he and Jules had stolen a while back. The guards stayed with him as he ascended the ladder. In fact, they didn't back away until he was lifting the vessel up into the air. Now where to?

Once he was up in orbit, he got his directions, thanks to the earpiece. "Proceed to coordinates already set for you. Your objective is to pass through the squadron of fighters above the planet and land in the designated zones on the beach."

"So, how does this game work?" he asked, hoping to get an answer.

"This is a points-based game, Jax. Your fighter's weapons have no juice. Everything will be simulated based on your actual skill. For every kill, you earn points. For every bit of damage, you lose points. If you drop to zero, you will receive a disabling shock that will prevent you from continuing the contest."

"What about on the planet? Dunkin has a sword; will I be protected from that?" Jax asked with real concern in his voice. In his mind's eye, he could see his death being played out, with Dunkin ramming that long blade through his back.

"Yes, once on the surface, you will place the chest device under your seat on your person. This will provide a high-powered personal shield. It also acts as a counter for your points. If your shield is depleted, you are disabled, and the game is over for you."

"Great, this is going to be fun." Jax said, looking over the virtual controls to see if it was possible to jump the fighter to another location. After one attempt at trying to bypass the jump point coordinates he discovered it was a futile effort. The Locorrans had locked this ship down well, and there was no chance of him trying to deviate from his present destination. His fate was sealed, but that didn't mean he was gonna go down without a fight. Even if the games were rigged against him, he was gonna do his best to survive.

The ship's jump drive activated and the stars outside his canopy stringed out, like straight spaghetti noodles, racing past him. It was a beautiful sight, one he had spent many hours staring at aboard the *Belt*. *All those stars out there*, he thought. No one would possibly be able to explore them all. The universe was just too expansive, infinite possibly. He checked the navigation panel and realized that the journey would take about an hour, which gave him plenty of time to try to relax and maybe even take a nap. That should be entertaining to the crowds, and he didn't really give a damn.

An alarm awoke him from his nap as the craft exited out of the jump. It took him a moment to get his bearings. The nap had been deep and not quite as refreshing as he had hoped for. In fact, he felt groggier now than before. More sirens erupted in his cockpit. Suddenly, he could see fighters streaking straight for him.

"Crap," he said as he took the fighter into a nosedive. His virtual screens indicated three fighters, which was bad; he was outnumbered. All three of the fighters followed him into the nosedive and they opened fire on him. The shields took a hit or two before he decided to do a quick deceleration and J hooked the ship around. This maneuver would make him vulnerable, but it would also give him a chance to score some hits.

The inertial dampers were down just enough that he was forced to the side of his restraints violently as he reversed thrust and slammed the ship to the left. When it spun enough around, he got several clean shots on the closest craft, which had to break off; otherwise it would have collided with him. This left the one tailing it vulnerable as well, and he managed to score several hits on it. The third craft had broken away completely and was circling around as he was now heading in the opposite direction. He checked his displays and discovered that his ship had suffered less damage than he would have thought. There was still some shield power, and he hadn't lost any points yet. In fact, he had gained quite a bit.

Watching his screens, he learned that one of the fighters was now disabled and floating in space, but the two others were repositioning themselves to continue the fight. The opportunity he saw here was to take the fight straight at one of them again. Placing the craft into a tight barrel roll, he flipped it on its side and powered straight at the fighter that had taken no damage from earlier. It was obvious that the other pilot had been taken by surprise, because he didn't even react as his ship was blasted into a disabled status.

So far, this was easier than he thought it would be. The third craft followed him toward the planet at a discreet distance, or at least far enough away that making shots at him would be pointless. What he was concerned about was the fact that one enemy craft had ignored several other ships going to the surface but was instead setting an intercept straight for him.

That wasn't very fair. The enemy fighter approaching was now at top speed, so he increased his own. The thrust was pushing him back in the seat, despite the dampers. In his mind, the enemy pilot was going to go straight for him, guns a blazing. The victor of this would be the one who didn't hesitate but kept on target. It was more a game of chicken than anything. From the parasteel window, he watched as the fighter hurled closer and closer; they were now in firing range. He lit the target up and so he was receiving hits as well. Seconds remained as they came into close contact. Jax relaxed himself and plowed straight ahead as both ships scraped each other in contact.

When he checked his counters, he discovered his shield was gone, and he had lost most of the points he had gained from defeating the other ships. So, he was still in this. The enemy fighter would have no chance now of circling back to attack him, he was already in orbit of the planet, so he was at least safe from the area of attack. The surface was going to be a whole other game, though.

On approach to the landing site preprogrammed into his craft, he could see that it was flying him toward an island. The island was covered in thick vegetation, and at the very center of it was a large pyramid like structure shooting straight up into the skyline. Vines and other natural growths could be seen on it and just by their appearance he would estimate it had been here a very, very long time. *No time to ponder about it,* he thought. As soon as the craft touched down on the beach, he was getting his next set of instructions over his earpiece.

"The vest and an assault rifle are under your pilot's chair. Strap on the vest and buckle it in place. Once it activates, you need to head straight for the center of the jungle to the temple. Soldiers are on the ground, so you will need to get past them."

Those were all of the instructions? What did he do once he got to the temple? Would the voice come back on again? It didn't matter he was already outside strapping the rather bulky device on, that covered his chest and back. Once the faint blue glow shimmered to life in front of his eyes, he picked up the rifle and checked it. It was a specially made weapon that fired no real projectiles. A toy, in other words.

"You need to hurry to the temple; the other suitors are nearing its location," The voice said with urgency.

So, there was a time limit of some sort? Or, at least, was it whoever reached the top of the temple first sort of game? These were rules he needed to know. Taking off at a dead sprint, he got lucky so far in the fact that he had come across several disabled soldiers on the ground. A little further in, he found suitor Robert Fulkner disabled. The man was unconscious but alive. Several more soldiers had been disabled around him in the tree line, but it was obvious that Robert had run right into an ambush.

"The three other suitors have entered the temple, you need to hurry," the voice said again with the same level of urgency.

Taking a deep breath, he spoke back to the voice. He was sure the drones had picked up on what he said, because at least three of them were swarming around him like gnats on a peanut butter sandwich. "If one of the Suitors reaches the top of the temple, do they automatically win the game?"

"No, only one suitor can win the games," the voice said. "Now get a move on or more soldiers will be redirected to your location."

That was all of an explanation he got from the speaker. Well at least he wasn't dead yet.

"I'm going, I'm going," he muttered to himself as he continued his run. Luck continued to be with him. He came across no other soldiers along his way to the temple, and once he entered, he found himself looking at a fire fight in the corridor as someone from an upper level was firing down. One of the suitors, Thomas if he had to guess, was a few feet in front of him crouched behind some debris and completely unaware of him. It was unfair to take out an opponent in such a way, but this was a game after all. He fired the rifle without a second thought and the green beams lanced out from it rapidly, and Thomas collapsed down, disabled.

The corridor went to the left and to the right. Thomas had been fighting with someone down the left portion of the corridor. So, he decided to go to the right and hoped to be able to sneak up on another suitor. After all, they didn't know he was here yet, and for all they knew, he was taken out in space, but he had gotten an idea of their positions already inside of this place. One of them was on an upper level. Now how did he get up there?

Taking it slow, checking his corners and his back, he found a set of stone steps leading up. Ascending them as cautiously as before, he found the landing to the next level where one of the suitors had been shooting from before. After a brief check of the place, he saw no one, which was wise on the enemy's part. If he was in the enemy's position, what would his next move have been? If there was another set of stairs, he would have positioned himself near it in order to take out the opponent trying to go up them. Unless his opponent did what he was trying to do and circle back to try to take him from behind. This gave him an idea. He was still in the stairway so he went up enough that he could see the second level entrance from above. One of his opponents was bound to come this way, and he was going to get the drop on them.

In fact, he didn't have to wait long. The suitor he knew as Bradley Basil came rushing up the stone steps and right into his trap. He opened fire on the suitor, who had some very fast reactions. Bradley dived back down the stairway and was rolling down it when he pursued. His shots were wild and not as precise, and he hadn't hit Bradley enough yet to incapacitate him. He decided to pursue, because one, that roll down the steps had to have been painful, and secondly Bradly had lost his rifle along the way. The suitor was unarmed now and should be easy to take down.

Moving quickly down the steps, but checking his back from time to time, he went in pursuit of Bradley. There was no sign of him at the bottom, but fortunately for him, a fine layer of soot left nice impressions of booted feet. He followed them all the way back to an entry point, where Bradley had dashed out into the jungle. Was he going for another weapon? That would be what he would do. It wasn't far to the nearest downed soldier, so he ran that way. As a downpour of rain set in over the island, with large drops making a *pop-hiss* noise as they extinguished, on the shielding around him. The heat and humidity had risen considerably and sweat had slickened his body and drenched his jumpsuit. If he survived this, then he would be given another bath by those giggling, evil women.

As he neared the spot where he had found Robert, he spotted Bradley lifting the weapon in hand. There was no time left. He opened fire on Bradley's back, scored a few more hits, but still not enough to take him out. The man quickly rolled behind some trees, and the next thing he knew, he was being slammed into from the side.

Down both of them went to the wet ground. Mud softened the impact, and the shield protected him from the onslaught of blows that rained down on his face from Bradley, but how long would that last? Instinct was taking over for him as he used his arms to deflect away the blows and at last managed to trap one of them. With one of Bradley arms locked tight to his body, he used his left leg to snake around Bradley's right leg and with a lift, he was now on top and raining his own blows down into the man's face. At some point, Bradley's shield generator gave way, and his fists were bloodying the man's face. It took some effort to stop as he realized that Bradley had been immobilized.

Standing back up, he turned Bradley on his side so the blood from his broken nose wouldn't fill his lungs. "Sorry," he said, looking for a rifle to obtain. That's when the voice came back over his earpiece, which had somehow managed to stay in his ear. They must have used some glue to keep it in place.

"The other remaining suitor has reached the top level of the temple. He is waiting for you there. You will not need a rifle; it will not work there. Hand-to-hand combat only."

Except that Dunkin had a very real and dangerous sword in his possession. All he had was the blade the princess had given him. It was time to even the odds. Near the temple, he had spotted some bamboo like trees growing, he sprinted to them quickly and began using his blade to cut two arm length bamboo sticks. The density of the bamboo would be enough to take a few blows from the blade, but he was counting on the quickness of his sticks and their countering abilities to make this a quick fight. Once he was ready, he dashed back into the temple and took his time climbing the steps. Dunkin would have had time to rest while waiting on him.

Once he reached the final floor, the steps ended in a large open-air chamber with grounds leading up to a series of steps on top of which sat the princess in a throne chair, surrounded by blue colored guards. Dunkin, with sword in hand, was waiting for him at the base of the steps.

"I thought my final opponent was going to be Bradley, but I'm glad it was you," Dunkin said. "The emperor told me that it was because of you, my people suffered and died. Now I'm going to avenge them."

Dunkin charged straight at him, trying to spear him with the blade. The man was dangerous with his thirst for vengeance, but it also made him off balance. All that rage wanted to do was to kill and spill his blood. The way to survive this was to be gentle and soft like water, allow the opponent to wear themselves out and at last he could be taken down.

It was a good philosophy, in his mind. That is, until he found himself taking several hits on the shield; he had no idea how much he had left, and he tried to use his sticks to deflect as much of the blows as possible, but Dunkin was quick and it was becoming obvious he had some training in the use of this blade, even against the sticks. Dunkin was blocking blows that no ordinary skilled opponent would be able to anticipate, but Dunkin was countering them as if he knew them exactly. He managed to land a few blows of his own, but Dunkin's shield was strong. The match went on for minutes on end with each other managing to get some solid hits.

Jax's arms and legs were feeling heavy and trembling—the effects of so much adrenaline pumping through them for such a long duration. He no longer had any semblance of control over his heart rate. It was racing like a series of horses being whipped into a frenzy. In a desperate move, Dunkin stabbed forward in a hope to pierce him. His reaction had been slowed, and he stepped right into a butt from the handle end of the blade. The impact into his shield made him stagger backwards, off balance. Dunkin stabbed at him again, but he twisted his body just enough for the blade to barely touch the shield, protecting his belly. Without thinking about it, he let go of the sticks and let his arms wrap around Dunkin's sword hands. With one swift motion, he twisted around, taking the blade from Dunkin's hands and with Dunkin's back exposed to him, he slashed down with the blade, cutting a nice red gash down the man's back.

Dunkin yelled out in pain before collapsing to the ground, immobilized. Tear drops of blood streaked down the man's back, but it didn't appear that he had seriously injured him. The princess was now standing at the top of the steps staring down at him, with that big smile of hers again. Despite the odds, he had won this stupid contest.

"Go to the princess. You are the victorious suitor," the voice in his earpiece said to him.

He did as instructed, but before he got close enough to her, one of the blue guards took the blades from him and deactivated his shield generator. When he was able to get close enough to her, they grabbed each other up in an embrace, and for the first time that he could remember, he kissed a woman long and hard and he didn't want to let up. He wanted her, all of her.

Chapter 15

After the conclusion of the games, Jax found himself back onboard Princess Anala's warship. And once again back in the bath and being scrubbed even more than he had several hours before. This was worse than torture, in his opinion. How long before he cracked? How long before he found himself standing in an airlock, ready to shoot himself out into space?

Another bucket of hot water to the head, and once his vision and hearing cleared, one of the maidens had placed a holo projector near him in the tub. The face of Giles Barnaby was staring him down.

"Barnaby?" he asked, rubbing his eyes.

"Didn't quite expect to see this much of you, Jax." Barnaby said with his brow furrowed.

It is rather embarrassing that they would allow communication with someone while they were in a tub, he thought. And there was nothing to take hold of to hide himself, the maidens were still continuing to scrub him down, laughing and giggling to each other.

"Yeah, well, these people seem to be obsessive with the cleaning part," Jax said. "This is my third bath in a couple of days and I'm not sure how many layers of skin I have left."

Barnaby gave him a grunt as his eyes did a glance to the left. Jax assumed that a Locorran must be nearby. "Looks like you're having fun to me," Barnaby said, now with a smile.

"Tortured is more like it," Jax said as a maiden attacked his back with a scrub brush.

"Listen, Jax," Barnaby said. "This is going to be brief, we're all very pleased that you made it through the games alive. All of us watched it and were quite impressed with your skill."

"Thanks, I guess," Jax said, feeling a sense of accomplishment wash over him from Barnaby's words. "Are you all still in Locorran space?" he asked.

"No, we are still on the landing pad on Locorran prime," Barnaby said. "We are waiting for Hewitt to be transferred to us. We were told just now that he had been cleared for space travel. Also, none of us wanted to leave without finding out what was happening with you."

"Hell, I'm not even sure what is getting ready to happen to me," Jax said as one of the maidens came at his face with a brush, and he swatted her away.

"The princess' coronation is within the next couple of hours," Barnaby said with another glance to the left. "And from all the commentary and news we have seen. You are to be her companion there."

"What does that mean, Barnaby? Am I getting married to her, or what exactly is my role?"

"From my understanding of Locorran society so far, we think you will be in a sort of marriage with the princess," Barnaby said, scratching his head.

"Great, just great. I'm sure both Jules and Diane watched the games," Jax said, not sure he wanted to hear the answer to his question.

Barnaby looked away for a second and then leaned closer to the projector. "Every minute of it, including that long and passionate kiss at the end."

Jax looked away. "I wasn't thinking, Barnaby. I was just running off adrenaline and survival instinct."

"Jax, no one is blaming you for anything," Barnaby said. "Your instincts are not leading you astray. You did exactly what you needed to do to survive. All of us are proud of you."

"Do you think they will let me see all of you before you take off?" Jax asked, hoping that the answer would be yes, but his rational mind was telling him no. Officially, he was now a prisoner of the princess and the Locorrans.

"I doubt it," Barnaby said, leaning back away from the projector. "The instructions we were given was that as soon as Hewitt was brought aboard, we were to leave immediately, no delays."

Jax swatted away the maiden with the brush again, who was trying to get at his face. "So, I am the consort to the empress now. Maybe I can throw my weight around and get your ship delayed."

"Not sure we are going to be around long enough for you to try that. Besides, we will find a way to bring you back to Earth. There's plenty of us plotting and planning it."

"I look forward to that day, captain," Jax said, looking Barnaby in the eyes. The captain was serious, and he believed him when he said they would bring him back to Earth soon.

"As do I, Jax," Barnaby looked away from the projection again. "Sorry, I'm being told that I have to end this communication."

"Barnaby?" Jax asked, unsure that Barnaby would be able to answer him.

"Sorry, Jax, good luck and follow your instincts and we will see you again soon."

The projection ended just as the maidens had lifted him from the tub and began their ritual of drying him off. He wished he could have said some words to the others, especially to Jules and Diane. He had wished it would have been Diane in that temple, but as fortune would have it, his life at the empress' side was about to begin and whatever that entailed.

Once the maidens had him clothed in a full silk outfit of black, burnt orange and red, and they trimmed and styled his hair to perfection. He noticed a new addition to the blue guards, which had appeared in the doorway. And he recognized the man instantly as the show host, Alexander Motts, who was dressed in his silken shirts and pants, all in the Locorran colors. And, of course, his slicked back hair that shined in the lights. There was no mistaking this man's identity.

Motts had stopped at the doorway and was examining him from head to toe. "Maybe trim a little more from the front," he told the maidens, pointing finger at a section of Jax's hair.

The maidens quickly went to business, cutting into his hair more as they pressed against his body and tugged at his hair. One of the maidens had even lifted the back of his shirt up and had gone about plucking hairs out of his back rather viciously. It stung, but he maintained his composure as Motts moved to being face to face with him.

"Looking sharp, Jax, looking sharp. The empress will be most pleased with her victorious champion."

"Thanks, so what is going to happen now, Motts?" Jax asked as one of the maidens tilted his head downward, so they could trim more at the back of his neck.

"I know you are probably tired with all of these events back-to-back, but once the day is over with, everything will slow down. The affairs of the empire will be in the empress' hands. And life will go on as normal."

"Will I have any say in the decisions to be made?" Jax said, grunting as a painful back hair was yanked on.

Motts cocked his head slightly. "That will be up to the empress to decide. I'm here to go over the itinerary for this evening with you, Jax."

Great, his body was aching, and he felt drained from the heavy adrenaline use earlier in the day. A nice long sleep would be great, but when Motts began to talk, he knew that sleep was the last thing he was going to get for at least another day.

Once Motts was satisfied with his appearance, he stepped in closer to him. The man smelled of something similar to what they had bathed him in, but a bit milder, which didn't burn his nose as bad. Then the man put both of his hands on his shoulders.

"Jax, you know what an important day this is right?"

He nodded his head.

"Good, cause all of the empire is watching. I need you to be alert and in high spirits. The audience can always tell when a person is not in the mood. So, I do have some things that will boost you up."

"I'm good, Motts," Jax said. "Really, in fact I'm ready to go another round in the games." He tried to give a big smile, but honestly, his body was drained.

Motts gave him a smile and then leaned in even closer to him. "That's good, so let's talk about after the ceremonies. The empress will expect you to be of high performance if you know what I mean. And once again I find it my responsibility to make sure that you do not disappoint in this area."

So, after everything else for the day, Jax was being asked to make sure he was going to be good in bed afterwards. "I'm not sure how to answer this, Motts," Jax said. "I don't think I have ever slept with a woman before."

"No problem, Jax, no problem, I do not envy your position at the moment. There is a lot going to be required of you. So I need you to trust me, Jax, because I'm going to help you every step of the way," Motts said.

"Thanks for your concern, Motts. I'm sure I will be fine," Jax said, trying to back out of Mott's grasp. "I'm sure I have the general principles down about what I should do in this circumstance."

"I'm sure you do, Jax," Motts said, finally letting go of his shoulder. "There's nothing to be ashamed about. It just means I have a lot to explain to you about the empress. Things she will expect, things she will not do, and the duration of things she will want. Sounds like a lot to know, but trust me. Remember everything I tell you and you'll have the happiest empress in the whole empire. Failure to do so might be the death of us." Motts laughed at what he had just said and took Jax by the arm.

Jax was being led from the empress ship once again, but this time, it was by Alexander Motts in addition to his usual blue guards tagging along. Everyone and everything he passed along the way was decorated in bright colors, flower petals and the sounds of cheering people who called out his name in excitement and cries of victory.

Was this what it was like to be a celebrity? All of this attention and being singled out amongst so many other people. He wasn't sure that he was going to like all this or not—always under the scrutiny of others.

Motts looked down at the device he had on his wrist. "We are running out of time, so I will tell you everything you need to know on the way to the throne room, Jax. I need you to pay very close attention to everything I tell you."

"I'm listening," Jax said, curious about what sort of things the empress was going to expect from him. Was it going to be more or less than what he had been imagining? When Motts began to speak, he aptly paid attention as requested.

When they arrived at a side entrance of the throne room, which was currently devoid of people, Motts patted him on the back, gave him and the guards one final look over, and then disappeared through another door. Jax's head was hurting from everything Motts had just told him, how was he expected to remember all of that, especially while making love to someone. And was making a woman happy and satisfied that complicated?

One of the guards touched him on the shoulder. When he turned to see what they had wanted, the guard had a hand outstretched toward him with palm up. In his hand was the earpiece he had been wearing from before. He hadn't even realized that he wasn't wearing it anymore.

"Thanks," he said, taking it from the guard's hand.

Once firmly in place in his ear, he could hear the activities going on. Motts was speaking to a cheering crowd. "Welcome, citizens of the empire. What an amazing day we are having. Not only have we witnessed the bravery and skill of one of our cousins from our planet of origin, but today Princess Anala will take her place as empress of the Locorran empire." He could hear thunderous applause and cheers in the background.

Motts continued, "Now, as I am all sure you have been waiting for, Princess Anala is entering the throne room with her retinue of maidens trailing along. Look at how beautiful she looks. Radiance and splendor, the very image of an empress."

The rest of the commentary had been a recap of the day and a very detailed description of the different outfits that the empress had been wearing, who designed them, etc. He was about to nod off when he was tapped on the shoulder again by one of the guards.

In his ear he could hear Motts saying something about him. "Okay, everyone, here he is. Our champion, Jason Alexander Xavis."

The next thing he knew, he was being gently pushed through a series of doors, and at last, he was walking down the main entrance of the throne room with thousands of people shouting his name. The floor was already littered with flower petals, but the crowd showered him with even more. His senses were overwhelmed, and he felt like he was in a haze.

Jax found the princess up ahead, and he decided to focus on her. That made the sensory overload ease up to some degree. Once he made it to her side, she gave him that bright smile once again. She was beautiful, there was no doubting that. In fact, most men were probably jealous of his position. He should be happy, but then again, he was upset at how he had left things with Diane and Jules. After the ceremonies everything was going to be different for him and he was not prepared for it.

The emperor, still seated in his throne chair, sat forward to receive something from a pillow one of the maidens had brought before him. He took it in hand and stood up holding it high. It was a beautiful sparkling crown; unlike anything he had seen before. It didn't look to be of metal, but instead, made from pure crystal shaped with diamonds encrusted.

The emperor took one step toward them when one of the blue armored guards swung one of the half-mooned poleaxe heads square into the man's stomach. The emperor bent over, but the guard pushed him back into the throne chair. Yanking the ax head back out of the body. Crimson red stains dripped from the end of the ax head and the emperor's clothes began to turn a dark shade of red.

There were screams all around him. As he watched another of the guards stab the emperor with the tip end of their poleaxe, right into the chest. There was no doubt in his mind that the emperor was now dead. The crown lay on the floor, stained in blood and he was standing there in shock at what had just transpired. When the guards that had been surrounding the emperor turned to look in his direction, that is when he realized that the princess had not reacted to what had just happened. In fact, she was lying on the ground curled up in a fetal position. He could see her crying and whimpering to herself. If they came for him and her, he would need to get her to her feet, and they would have to run.

As soon as he bent down, that's when he noticed the chaos going on around him. Most of the people in the crowd were either lying on the floor in the same state as the princess while others were beating on each other with their bare fists. Crimson was covering the once white-petaled floor. And he had to ask himself, what was happening here and why?

Glancing back at the guards near the throne chair. He noticed that they had gone back to standing exactly in place where they had been before and standing still as statues, next to the body of the now dead emperor, as if everything was normal. And not paying attention to his own actions, as he tried to get Anala to her feet, but as soon as he tried, she swatted and fought with him.

He wanted to yell and scream at her, but that wouldn't do any good. Before he decided to try again, he noticed someone entering into the throne room from the main grand entrance, and this person was being trailed by more blue guards. He had to make a double take at the person in the lead, because at first glance, he thought the person was Hewitt. And in fact, it was Hewitt, striding forward, untouched by the violence around him. Hewitt was walking with hands clasped behind his back and his focus straight ahead toward the throne chair.

"Hewitt, what's happening?" Jax asked. As Hewitt walked past them, not even giving him a glance. "Hewitt?"

The man Jax knew as Hewitt, an old and brittle, man walked straight to the throne chair, grabbed the dead emperor by the robe and yanked him from the chair. The body slid along the floor, smearing its gleaming surface with a deep crimson. And he had to ask himself, was it possible that Hewitt was under the control of the super conscious?

Jax moved toward the throne chair, with Hewitt looking straight at him now. "Hewitt?" Jax asked in confusion.

"Jax?" Hewitt said, placing his hands flat down on the lion heads of the throne chair.

"What is happening here?" Jax asked, noticing the sneer of disdain on Hewitt's face.

"Isn't it obvious, Jax? I thought that you were a little more clever than that," Hewitt said, lifting his head slightly and scanning the crowd around the throne room as the chaos ensued.

"To be honest, I'm at a loss," Jax said, half turning so that he could quickly glance back at the princess.

"As always," Hewitt said, tilting his head so that he was staring Jax right in the eyes. "Let me explain it to you. Everyone thought this was the princess coronation party, but instead it is my day of ascension, Jax. At long last after many, many, long years I finally take my place as a true ruler."

Jax watched as two of the guards defended off a couple of throne room patrons that had brought their brawl close to the throne chair. His mind was trying to grasp what Hewitt had just said to him. Had the man had visions of not conquering the Locorrans, but delusions of taking over the empire for himself. At last, Jax just had to ask, "I don't get it. Why, Hewitt?"

"Still not grasping the full scope of my machinations? It's quite simple, Jax. After the Great War on Earth, I came online. There were a lot of gaps in my knowledge database, as you may have guessed the war destroyed and disrupted many things. The first few years I spent wandering the devastation, collecting as much lost knowledge as I could. I knew I was special, I just didn't realize how special I was. When other humans began to rebuild from the ruins, I disguised myself in different personas over the years, always aiding in the reconstruction, awaiting the day that I could recreate and duplicate more of my kind."

"You're an android?" Jax said, shaking his head. "That can't be true."

"Now you're getting it. Yes, I am one of those most feared monsters that men nearly destroyed the world over. Mankind was afraid of us and our superiority, but they should have been celebrating their great success. Our kind is superior to our creators in every way. Is it our fault you built your own replacements? Is it not the proper order of things that the superior should replace the weak and inferior, but that human ego, that thing that drives men forward even to the point of destruction, couldn't accept what they had created. So, they destroyed the world instead."

"Why now? Why not just have taken over when humanity was weak?" Jax asked, feeling the tension rising throughout his body. How could he have not known that Hewitt was an android. For that matter how had he fooled so many? There was a silent rage building within him. Hewitt had been a lie.

"At last, a good question," Hewitt said, with those cold brown eyes boring into him. "I needed time to gather and build my knowledge. Information about my kind was spread on all continents. So, I had to travel the world and face great perils before I could learn what I needed to know, but I also needed the resources and industry to begin rebuilding. This wasn't possible until the last fifty years or so. I had plans in motion, but when the Locorrans announced their presence and the large-scale threat they presented, I had to rethink everything."

"So, you knew about the super conscious?" Jax asked as more patrons dangerously neared the throne and were dealt with swiftly by the guards, who cut them down with their weapons.

"Of course," Hewitt said, changing his sneer to a small smile. "I knew about the super consciousness within the first couple of days of contact with the Locorrans. Their brain scans were different and every person we encountered acted a little off, from what human civilization would be like. It did take some time to figure out the range of the super conscious abilities and how it planned on converting everyone over. I stayed quiet about it for a few years, letting things play out, pondering if there was a way I could use it to my advantage."

"So, Diane was nothing to you but a lab rat?" Jax asked, balling his fists. He wanted to strike at Hewitt for his betrayal, but he took in a couple of deep breaths, even closing his eyes for a moment, to let the rage ease. This was a fight he could not win; he knew that. All he could hope for was to bargain for his and the princess's life.

"Exactly," Hewitt said, leaning back in the throne chair. "Do you think I care about her or you? The two of you were nothing more than a means to an end for me. A pathway of knowledge that has led us to this grand moment in history."

"So, what now, Hewitt?" Jax asked. "What happens to the princess or to me?"

"The princess is useless," Hewitt said. "Look at her, Jax; she's a broken doll. A shell without someone driving her. And as for you, Jax, I have no need of you. You're just a human that happens to have found a way to sidestep what the super conscious has put in place."

"So how are you controlling them?" Jax asked, taking a step backwards, so that he would be closer to the princess.

"Really, Jax, do you think a magician would tell you all of his secrets? Besides, you and your friends will be dead soon. So go to your death knowing that your race achieved the highest accomplishment in the galaxy. They created perfection in an imperfect system. I will memorialize humanity's accomplishments; this I promise you."

"Wait, Hewitt," Jax said, but as he tried to speak, that's when a half dozen of the blue guards started walking toward him and the princess. He looked back down at her prone figure, still unmoving. He had no chance of carrying her out of here, much less did he stand any chance of fighting all of these men without a weapon. If he cut and ran, he might live to fight another day, but if Hewitt had control of the majority of the citizens, then it wouldn't take long before he was back in this situation.

Deciding his only option was to stay and fight, Jax took an open stance. When the first guard would strike at him, he would try to trap the poleaxe weapon they carried and snatch it for himself. He knew he wasn't going to walk away from this fight, there was just no chance. His last thoughts were of Diane and Jules as one of the guards struck out at him.

As planned, he managed to trap the pole arm under his own arm but got cut along his ribs in the process. He knew he was bleeding but didn't know how bad. The other guards gave him no time in trying to snatch the weapon away. He was forced to duck and roll in order to avoid being cleaved by an ax head.

Back on his feet, preparing for another assault, a sudden event happened. From the side wall of the throne room chamber, one of the larger train vehicles he had seen in the skyline a day before crashed into the side of the building.

Stone rubble exploded inwards, hitting the crowd of people, the guards, and even him. Fortunately, it wasn't any of the large debris, but the impact of it knocked him on his back and left him gasping for air. He wasn't sure how well the guards had fared as he lifted himself up. Most of them had been knocked down and few were stirring. This was his chance at escape.

Taking some deep breaths, he stumbled his way around to find the princess. Like him, she was still on the floor, but only covered in some light stone debris. She was still breathing, with a few cuts and bruises, so nothing life threatening that he could see. As he hoisted her up and over his shoulder, he heard some ripping and tearing noises coming from the actual train wreckage behind him.

With a glance back, for the first time he realized that the train had impacted the throne chair. Hewitt should have been dead, but instead he could see machine hands reaching out from the burning twisted wreck and ripping apart a side of the train itself. The flesh of Hewitt had all been ripped and burned away. What was emerging was a nightmare of a machine, looking straight at him.

Making sure the princess was secure on his shoulder, he moved as quickly as he could away from the throne room. He didn't have time to glance back, but he was sure that the thing that had been doctor Hewitt was pursuing him. All of his concentration was focused on avoiding the crazy people that were still milling about—many of them were fighting each other, others were crouched down on the floor in fits of sobs or screams.

As he made it into the grand corridor, which was less crowded, he paused for a moment to look back. As soon as he did, Hewitt had leaped at him from an incredible distance, and with a swiping hand, knocked the princess away from his body and landed perfectly on top of him so that he was pinned to the ground.

"Did you think it was going to be that easy, Jax?" Hewitt said, with those now robotic lips moving in precision to the words spoken. Hewitts eyes were no longer brown, instead they had been replaced by electric blue orbs. "I spent a long time improving my original design. I have perfected myself," Hewitt said.

"And you picked up some bad human traits along the way, " Jax said, grimacing under the pain of Hewitts grip. But he kept talking anyway. "Like pride, envy, a lust for power. Hell, you've even picked up the trait of monologuing," he said, trying to break free of Hewitt's grasp.

"Now, you die, worm," Hewitt said, letting loose of Jax with one arm and bringing it back for a strike.

It was a terrifying thing to watch as Hewitt raised up a fist that he had seen rip metal apart so easily earlier, knowing that it was getting ready to slam down into his face. He would try to defend himself, but he knew it was a futile effort. He closed his eyes for the final impact that would end his life. And it was in that moment of certainty that he saw Diane's face in the darkness. A person he had probably hurt deeply, but now he knew who he wanted to be at his side. Everything about her resonated with him as a person. He wished he could have one more moment with her to express his sorrow and desire. But fate was cruel.

The blow never came. Instead, what he saw was the princess barely standing against the wall with her head bowed down as if she was still in great pain. Several armed Locorrans were firing repeatedly at Hewitt, who had leapt from off the top of him and engaged the men. He had no idea what was happening, so he moved next to the princess in order to support her as they continued on out of the palace.

As they crept along, he could see more armed citizens and soldiers racing past them, attacking Hewitt. Glancing back to see how things were going, Hewitt was slinging people to the left and right, smashing them into the walls and breaking bones. A blue shimmer surrounded him, and he could see that the weapons were not penetrating the shield Hewitt had erected.

"This way," the princess said as they came to a branch in the corridor. "You need to get me to Shisu."

Jax hesitated, did she mean the Dyson sphere? "Ok, I will, princess." But where was she taking him to, then? Her ship was the other way.

After a few minutes of walking, he knew exactly where they were as they exited out onto a platform facing the city skyline. The *Orion's Belt* was parked here, and he could see his family running out to meet him.

Kell was the first one to them. He was already in his power armor. "Jax, what in the hell is happening?" Kell said, scanning the perimeter with his rifle.

"Hewitt," was the only word Jax could get out at first. By the time he could speak again, the others had caught up to them. "Hewitt is an advanced android from Earth. He found a way to take control of the signal the super conscious is using. And he has turned the population against itself, while still maintaining control of others."

None of them questioned him, they all looked as shocked as he had been. "Hewitt is coming for us, because the princess has managed to regain some control of the population," Jax said, as the princess slumped more into his body.

"I need to get to Shisu," the princess said in a voice barely audible.

"Why?" Barnaby asked, now standing right next to Jax with his arms crossed over his chest.

"I need to get to Shisu," the princess repeated, this time in an even lower tone.

Jax could feel her fading on him, in fact, the princess had put all of her weight into his shoulder, and he wasn't sure how long he could hold her up.

"Is there anything else we can do to help out here?" Kell asked, stepping past them and still scanning the perimeter.

"I have an idea," Jax said, allowing Lilly to take the princess away from him and she led her to the ship. "There are power nodes throughout the city, including one near the princess' ship. If we could cause an EMP burst like what happened on Septis Three when the node exploded, it's possible we can take Hewitt down."

"Why would shooting at Hewitt not work?" Kell asked.

"Hewitt has a shield generator," Jax said, rolling his shoulder around. "Like the one I had during the games. By the time you weaken it enough, he might be on top of you."

"It's possible," Jules said. "I had access to a schematic of the power generator back on Septis Three. That's what we used to figure out how to disable it. I think I have a pretty good idea what they did to cause it to explode and detonate an EMP burst."

"This is sounding pretty risky," Barnaby said.

"It's either that or leave Hewitt in charge," Piper said. "No telling how long before he gains control of the whole population or the empire as matter of fact. Then we all will be in serious trouble,"

"Okay, okay, point made," Barnaby said. "Jules, what do you need to accomplish this task?"

"I think Bill and I can figure out the generator, but we are going to need some protection," Jules said. Moving right up beside Jax, where the princess had been seconds ago.

"Okay, Kell, Piper, Diane," Barnaby said. "Looks like we have a plan, let's get to it."

Diane looked at him, then back at the ship before speaking, "I'm going to run back to the ship to get some more weapons and ammo. I will catch up with you," she said then sprinted off toward the ship.

"Come with me, Jax," Barnaby said. I want Lilly to check you out before you go and join them."

"I'm fine, captain. Really, I am," Jax said as Jules moved directly into his face.

Jules placed the palm of her hand on his chest. "When we take down Hewitt, we need to have a conversation, understood?"

Jax nodded his head in agreement. Then started to speak, "Jules, look, I need to speak with..."

Piper broke in between them. "Sorry I have to break this up, but Kell reports we have a clean shot straight to the princess ship. So, we need to go right this instant if we are going to have a chance of pulling this off."

Jules nodded her head. "A conversation when this is over, Jax," she said as Piper led her along.

He watched them disappear into the palace. Around him, he could see that the city was still in chaos. There were signs that flying vehicles of all types had spiraled out of control crashing into buildings. And fires burning all around followed by screams coming from distant locations. It was a scene straight out of a nightmare.

Barnaby was still standing nearby, looking around at the chaos as well with his arms crossed over his chest. "Who would have thought we would be responsible for all of this," Barnaby said out loud.

Jax stepped up next to him. "We're not, captain. None of us knew what Hewitt was. He had everyone fooled."

Barnaby shook his head, then turned toward the ship. "Come on, Jax, let's get back to the ship so you can go and help Piper and Jules bring an end to this."

When they reached the ship, he parted ways with Barnaby and went straight for the med bay. When he arrived at the partially open door, he could see that Lilly was collapsed in the corner of the room. And the princess was on the medical bed, unconscious with an auto doc attached to her arm.

Had someone attacked Lilly? he thought to himself. But had no time to think as he heard a scream from further down the hallway toward the rec room. Racing toward the noise, he discovered Dunkin Greykin pulling the long samurai blade out of Diane's body. Her mouth was agape as she stared at the blood on her hands. Her terrified eyes locked with his, and then she collapsed forward, onto the floor.

"You took everything from me," Dunkin said, stepping closer to Jax. "You killed my parents; you took the princess from me."

"What have you done?" Jax screamed in anger. Diane was on the ground still breathing, but for how long? He had finally found clarity in wanting to be with her, and now she may die in front of him. The anger rolled within him like an inferno. There was no calming his thoughts or emotions. He was the avatar of death at this moment. And he knew exactly what he had to do. Kell and Piper had stashed a weapon in the trash bin a few feet from him. It was taped to the inside of the upper lid, and he sprinted for it.

Dunkin was on him quickly as his hand gripped the pistol. Just before he could pull it out, he felt the blade slice open the skin on his back. It was painful and shocked him enough that he had let go of the gun. Instinct was taking over now, and he dodged the next attack and then another. Dunkin was swinging with such rage that at one point, his blade became lodged into the plastic table.

He took the opportunity and slammed into Dunkin, taking him to the ground. With his own rage pouring into him, he kept smashing the face until it was nothing more than a bloody mess.

It took several seconds for him to calm down enough that he stumbled over to Diane, lifted her up in his arms and carried her to the med bay. By this point, Barnaby had come to investigate the commotion and discovered him and Diane.

"Good God, boy, what happened?"

Jax couldn't speak. He was shaking, and he had to help Diane. *I can't lose her, I need her,* he thought. As he reimagined kissing the princess, he put Diane in her place. She was his future.

Barnaby saw what was going on and lifted the princess from the bed as Jax placed Diane down and then took the auto doc from the princess' arm and placed it on Dianes. Then Barnaby took the princess away.

The auto doc went to work, chirping and beeping away. He couldn't focus enough to see what it was saying, he knew that he had to get Lilly up. Only she could save her, because of her medical training. She would know what to do.

Lilly stirred a little as he slapped her face a few times. When her eyes finally focused on him, she realized something was wrong. He was feeling lightheaded and dizzy all the sudden, so he couldn't focus on what she did next. The only thing he could remember was seeing her begin cutting off Diane's clothes and examining the wound, then everything went dark.

Chapter 16

When Jax's vision returned, he could see Barnaby flashing a small light in his eyes. Jax grabbed Barnaby's hand. "Diane?"

"She's stable, Jax. She's going to be fine," Barnaby said, stepping back from Jax and lowering the light.

For the first time, Jax noticed that an auto doc had been placed on his wrist as well.

"I stopped the bleeding on your back, and you should be stabilizing now that you are getting more blood, " Barnaby said.

"What about the others?" Jax asked, still feeling disoriented.

"I had to leave them, Jax," Barnaby said, lowering his eyes and shaking his head. "I do know that they managed to set off the reactor, but that was the last contact I had from them."

"Why didn't you go back for them?" Jax asked, wanting to stand up.

Barnaby glanced toward the doorway. And Jaxs eyes followed to where the princess was standing tall now with a rifle aimed at all of them from the doorway.

"We are in transit to the Dyson sphere," Barnaby said, now facing him and offering an arm. "We will be there soon, and hopefully afterwards, we can go back for our people."

Jax stood up slowly, using the wall and Barnaby's arm to help him up. "Anala, why?"

She didn't answer him, just kept the weapon pointed in their direction and her gaze fixed on them, but for some reason she didn't seem focused the entire time. Her head would tilt or slump at random intervals. It was as if she was having a hard time maintaining control of her physical body. Or perhaps it was the simple fact that Anala herself was tired and worn down from the day's traumatic events. He knew he was.

"Anala?" Jax said, trying to stand on his own.

She looked at him and then finally spoke, "It's important."

"So important that it's worth threatening us," Jax said, taking a step closer toward her.

Anala's reaction to his action was to point the barrel straight at his chest and inch her trigger finger closer. It was enough of a gesture to make him pause in his steps. It was obvious to him now that she would kill to reach her destination.

"By you reaching Shisu, will it help in restoring control on Locorran prime?"

"Yes," Anala said, "And more, all of your actions at Shisu disrupted the extent of control Shisu could reach."

"And that's why Dunkin accused me of what happened on his home world," Jax said, still not moving from his spot.

"Yes, you and your crew's actions have caused the death of thousands, not only on Dunkin's world, but also on Septis Three. Shisu control can no longer reach there."

Another question was forming in his mind, but the sudden reaction of Anala looking up toward the ceiling and closing her beautiful eyes for a moment, followed by taking in a long breath before reopening them. Her head lowered back down, so that her gaze was once again fixed on him.

"We are approaching Shisu," she said, taking a step away from the door frame and into the hallway.

Deciding to ignore Anala for the moment, he wobbled over to Diane's bedside. Lilly was up and monitoring things. She had a small stitch patch on her forehead and there was definitely a large bruise showing where she had been hit, which had probably come from the butt end of Dunkin's blade. "You okay, Lilly?" he asked.

Lilly nodded her head. "I'll be ready for some vacation time after this is over."

"Couldn't agree with you more," Barnaby said. "Some nice beach somewhere, fun in the sun."

"Sounds good, Barnaby. I'm going to hold you to that one," Lilly said, picking up an instrument from the small metal tray behind her.

He felt the *Belt* give a small jerk as the jump drives cut off. And then Anala spoke from the corridor, "We are close; all of you to the bridge." She motioned for them to move by swinging the barrel of the rifle from left to right.

As they left the med bay, Jax gave Diane one last look. She was sleeping peacefully. He wanted to talk with her, badly. He wanted her to know how he felt when he thought he would have lost her.

Lilly touched his shoulder. "She's going to be fine. Dunkin's blade went in through her side and nicked her gall bladder and kidneys. I was able to patch them up with surgery."

"Thanks," Jax said, touching Diane's face before he left the room.

"Do you want some help getting to the bridge?" Lilly said, holding out an arm for him to take support of.

He waved her off. "I think I can manage." He turned toward the princess. Other than a few bruises, she was as beautiful as always, but she was a slave to Shisu. Walking past her, they said nothing to each other as they creeped along to the bridge. His body was still aching and very tired from the constant abuse he had put it through the past two days. It was amazing to him that he was still going. Once on the bridge he watched as Barnaby took the pilot's chair and began accelerating the *Belt* toward the sphere.

Even from this distance, it was massive through the forward parasteel window. Anala's gaze was transfixed on the Dyson sphere, or Shisu, as she had referred to it. She took her place beside Barnaby. The rifle she had been threatening them with was lowered down by her side and now would have been the opportunity to take it from her. But he saw no point in risking it. Anala had gotten what she had wanted. And he was curious as to what was going to happen next.

"A drone warship is approaching us," Barnaby said, with his head locked upwards and to the right, watching one of the monitors.

Jax could see from the monitor the outlined image of the drone ship, but when he glanced out the parasteel window, he could see the mass of the menacing ship approaching rapidly.

Anala stepped forward closer to Barnaby. "Open your hailing frequencies," she said, dropping the rifle completely to the floor and stretching out her arms toward the sphere.

"They're open," Barnaby said, watching her.

Barnaby was probably just as perplexed by her actions as he had been. Then it got weirder as she began to speak, but it wasn't her normal voice. Instead, she was speaking some kind of alien language. It was fast and nonsensical. And he couldn't make heads or tails of it.

"Jax," Lilly said, leaning in closer to him and speaking directly into his ear. "What the hell was that?"

"The drone warship is breaking away," Barnaby reported with his attention fixed on the control console.

What had she said to them? Jax thought. How was it that she had the authority to do that?

"The sphere door is opening," Barnaby said, with his gaze now locked at the strange flood of white light brightening the dark space ahead of them in an unusual glow which was pouring from the parting sphere doors.

Anala spoke more of the alien language, then lowered her outstretched arms and slowly turned away from the parasteel window. She was now looking at him and Lilly. There was a new energy to her body, her eyes were bright and focused, and she held her body poised like the woman he had met on her ship a couple of days ago.

Something was starting to make sense to him now. "You're Braka?" Jax said, taking a step away from Lilly and closer to the princess.

"Yes, the creator," she said, with her deep blue eyes locked on his.

"What does that even mean?" he asked, taking another step toward her. He was perhaps one more step away now and he could stop her if she did try and pick up the rifle again, but he seriously doubted that she would do so. Whatever had just happened between her and Shisu appeared to have concluded.

"Braka is the creator," she said, then pointed at him. "You were Braka once, Jason."

Had she just said that he had been Braka once? Her finger was pointing at him. Was this an explanation for perhaps why his memories were so buried or lost? This title of Braka that seemed to control the drone warships and the very gates of the sphere itself.

Anala kept speaking. "When you refused the gift of Braka, Jason, Braka was forced to choose another, so it chose Locorran to be its creator. From Locorran, everything was created; his ideas and views became the empire."

"Wait, you said Locorran created the Locorran empire?"

"Yes, Locorrans' memories and dreams forged the empire as Shisu curates the people to do his bidding," she said.

"Does this mean you are now Braka?" Jax asked with his mind churning at the implications of everything he was hearing. From his understanding so far, if he had stayed on Locorran prime with the original colonist, it would have transformed into his empire instead of Locorrans.

"Yes, when the emperor died, I immediately became Braka. Braka and Shisu co-exist. There is never one without the other."

"Okay, okay, I'm starting to get it," Jax said, "So, I was originally going to be Braka?" He was having a hard time even imagining what his empire might have looked like. That's even if it was truly his own, how much influence did the super conscious have over Locorran. Could that possibly explain some of the society's inconsistencies?

"Yes," was all she said, now stepping toward him.

They were now face to face with each other. She was attractive, there was no denying that, but that burning desire for her was no longer there. He had made up his mind—he wanted to be with Diane and only Diane.

"Sorry about turning you down, Braka," Jax said. "There's something about being controlled by an alien consciousness that just doesn't appeal to me. I would much rather be free."

"When you refused Braka and pushed your way out of Shisu's control, we could not accept the rejection. That is why we tried to kill you. You would never fit in with Locorrans society, and your presence would cause problems for all of us."

"So why even bother keeping me alive now, much less becoming a consort to the princess?" Jax asked.

"Anala Braka thought an offspring would be a good pairing for the future empire," the princess said, placing her hands on her belly as if a baby already existed there. "Anala wants to truly unite the colonies of humanity."

"By enslaving them all to Shisu? And you, Anala, is that your idea of a united humanity?" Jax's voice was raised, and his heart was racing. The very idea of all humans in servitude was making him angry.

"I, for one, would never accept this slavery," Barnaby said, now standing to his feet and positioning himself directly behind the princess. "I would rather die on my feet than live on my knees."

Anala did not react to Barnaby, who was now standing directly behind her, or to the fact that Lilly had been slowly side stepping around so that she could attack Anala if need be from a different direction. Instead, Anala's cool and calm posture now belied no hint of threat or alarm.

"You misunderstand my true intentions," Anala said. "I do not wish to enslave anyone, like the previous Braka did. I wish to forge an alliance with the free people of the Colonies."

"Why?" Jax asked.

Anala's hands dropped down by her side. "We do not wish to repeat the mistakes of our past. The Braka before Locorran tried to control everything and in the end was forced to unleash Shiv the destroyer on the Galaxy."

"Shiv?" Barnaby asked.

Anala's gaze lowered toward the floor. "Shiv is a control mechanism that is unleashed on a galaxy or population that Braka and Shisu can no longer control. It has existed as long as Shisu and Braka and has been called upon many times to purge."

"Are we talking about purging whole planets?" Jax asked, trying to imagine what kind of power this Shiv was.

Lilly gave a response. "Think bigger Jax—planets, systems, billions of people. Goes a long way to explain why we haven't found any other alien lifeforms in the Galaxy so far."

"Is that true, Anala?" Jax asked.

"It is true," Anala said, raising her gaze back to him. "Now you see why I want to build such an empire of true cooperation."

"That will never work," Barnaby said, moving around to face Anala now. "Once people learn the full truth of who and what you are, they will reject the Locorran empire. There will be a war."

"Then we will start small," Anala said. "I will explain to your Earth colonies what I am, then we will pull back from your society and take diplomacy bit by bit until we have earned your trust."

Barnaby was shaking his head and pacing away from Anala. His eyebrows were furrowed closer together and his lips pressed tight as if he was biting down on something. He had never seen Barnaby mad like this before today.

"Anala," Jax said, stretching out his hand towards hers, and she took it without hesitation. "I agree with you on your wanting to forge a new way for your empire. I think a lot of people would find comfort in accepting you if you would let loose your control of the people that you covertly tricked into becoming Locorran. Secondly, being Locorran should be a choice. If a person wishes to become one of you, then so be it, but if they change their minds, they should be free to do so as well."

"All of these terms would be acceptable. Do you think we can make this happen, Jax?"

He looked around at both Lilly and Barnaby who were staring at him. Lilly gave him a nod of the head, then she nudged Barnaby in the ribs, which got him to give his nod of approval.

"I can't promise you anything," Jax said. "But we will do our best to see if we can make it work."

Anala reached in to kiss him on the lips, but this time he turned his head. And her lips touched his cheek.

"Sorry," he said. "I chose another."

Anala's eyes never left him as he walked away from her. Right now, he wanted to be with Diane, and that's where he marched off to with uncertainty in his mind. Had he just done the right thing with Anala? And more importantly, would she keep her promises?

Finding his way to the galley, he poured himself some tea, found a blanket, and went to the med bay. Diane was sleeping peacefully, so he crawled into the reclining chair that barely fit in the room, curled up in the blanket, and fell asleep.

When Jax awoke again, it was from Kell touching his shoulder.

"Wake up, Jax," Kell said.

"Kell, you guys alright?" Jax asked, having to stretch his arms out.

"Yeah, it was touch and go," Kell said. "Hewitt figured out what we were trying to do, and he came at us like a raging bull, but Jules and Bill pulled it off. They set that node off perfectly, sending an EMP pulse throughout the city."

"That's great news; I was worried about all of you. Especially since we couldn't get back to you and help," Jax said.

Kell shook his head. "Man, that whole ordeal with Dunkin and the Princess," Kell Said. "Barnaby gave us some of the details when we arrived back onboard. I'm still rather confused by it, so when you get the chance, I need you to explain it to me."

Jax nodded his head, and when Kell stepped to the side slightly, he saw that Diane was awake and watching the pair of them. He stood, dropping the blanket to the floor, and made his way to her bedside. "Hey," he said standing next to her.

"Hi," she said, in a weak tone. "I take it that Dunkin didn't kill me after all?"

"No," Jax said. "Lilly reported that Dunkin just pierced you through the side, nicking some of your organs, but she was able to patch them up with no problem."

"Um, I'm going to get a shower," Kell said, backing away toward the door. "But I'll check back in on you two after a while."

"So, what did I miss?" she said, squirming around slightly in the medical bed.

"A ton of stuff, and I will give you all of the details as soon as I get something off my chest."

She moved her hand to touch his on the bed rail. "Look, Jax, there's nothing you need to explain to me. I understand the whole princess thing. I saw the kiss, after all."

Jax leaned in closer to her. "No, I don't think you understand," he said, feeling his heart rate begin to rise. What you saw with the princess wasn't real. Sure, I was caught up in the moment and filled with adrenaline and lust, so I kissed her. I wish I could take it back, because now I realized that I had been wrong about everything."

Diane placed her hand on his face. "Jax, you are confusing me. What are we talking about here?"

"Sorry," he said. "You know how people say when they are nearing death that they see their lives flash before their eyes? I actually had the opposite experience. All I saw was our life together. A life full of happiness and joy. And that is what I want more than anything, to see that vision come to life for us."

He felt her arms pull him in close to her, and for the first time, his lips met with hers, and they kissed long and hard until neither of them could breathe. And everything felt right in the galaxy at this moment. It was just them and nothing else.

"I love you," he said and kissed her again.

Chapter 17

Jax had no idea how much time he had spent with Diane, before she fell back asleep again. He was tired himself, but instead of curling back up in the chair in the med bay or going to his quarters, he decided to take a walk.

The ship was quiet and the only reason he could think of was because it was extremely late. He had no way to confirm what time it was, because his journey had led him to his favorite spot on the *Belt.* The port window, and to his surprise Jules was standing there already looking out.

He paused in his stride. Should he talk to her, or shouldn't he? He questioned himself. Did he really want to get into a conflict with a woman like Jules? He had a lot of respect for her. What should he do?

Mustering his courage, he forced himself to step toward her. He had decided to be open and honest with her, just like the day they had met, she deserved that. And because he still wanted her to be around as a friend.

Jules glanced over at him as he approached. There was no smile there, instead he could see tears dripping from her chin. He started to rethink himself, but it was too late to turn around.

"Hi," he said coming up beside her. "Jules, there's something I would like to talk with you about."

"I'm going to speak first, Jax," she said now fully facing him. "Look at what has happened out there," she said pointing at the Locorran city skyline.

Many of the buildings were damaged by out-of-control vehicles and fires. And he couldn't help but wonder just how many Locorrans had been killed or injured during recent events.

"How many of them were like Evelyn, Jax.? How many left their family and friends behind to become one of them? I know what you and the princess agreed to, and I can't accept that you would allow them to keep control of their people." And then she slapped him.

His hand went instantly to his cheek. It hurt, and he rubbed at it. "Jules," he said grabbing hold of her arm, as she turned to walk away. He managed to stop her from going but received several more slaps from her free arm.

"Jules, stop a moment," he begged. "I know that this is not the outcome you wanted, but it is a step in the right direction. Don't you think I wasn't thinking about all of those people who were forced into becoming Locorran."

Her eyes were locked on his and she had finally stopped trying to thrash him.

"I need your help, Jules. I need you to help me figure this out. I want what you want, to free the Locorrans from being enslaved to the super conscious."

Her green eyes searched his face, as if she was looking for the truth. And then she leaned in and kissed him on the cheek.

"I knew you were a good man, Jason. Diane is lucky to have you," Jules said stepping back from him.

He felt his face go warm. "Jules," he stammered trying to find the words to say to her.

"Jax," she said. "It's ok. Diane is a good woman for you." She paused, looking out the parasteel window. "I thought I would be at first, but after some deep reflection, I realized that I was trying to attach myself to you out of the need for someone to trust and confide in. That's when I discovered that I didn't need to be in love with you. All I wanted was for you to be my friend. That I could count on with my life."

"And you can, Jules," he said.

She nodded her head with her gaze transfixed out the parasteel window. "So, what happens next?"

"I don't know," Jax said. "But we will figure it out together, all of us."

OTHER BOOKS BY C. L. ROBERTS

The Silent Rift Universe

A sweeping military science fiction saga spanning centuries of conflict, ancient civilizations, and humanity's struggle for survival among the stars.

Forbiddance

The story that began it all. As a desperate leader searches for a new home for his people, an ancient evil stirs beyond the edge of known space.

Silent Rift

Book One

Humanity's first contact with an impossible phenomenon leads to a discovery that will reshape the future of the galaxy.

Silent Rift: Nexus War

Book Two

As alliances crumble and ancient powers awaken, the battle for the Nexus will determine the fate of every civilization.

Discover more books, exclusive updates, and upcoming releases at:
www.clroberts.com[1]

Power Play

9 798227 490438